Praise for the electrifying

SEARCH AND DESTROY

thriller series

WARNING ORDER

"Joshua Hood has a gift for keeping readers guessing and a soldier's eye for gripping action. *Warning Order* is a terrific follow-up to *Clear by Fire*."

—Kyle Mills, #1 *New York Times* bestselling coauthor of *The Survivor*

"Gripping, authentic, heart-wrenching. If you want to know what the front lines in America's war on terror are like, read this book. Thriller readers beware: you can't put *Warning Order* down."

—Ben Coes, author of *Independence Day*

CLEAR BY FIRE

"Hood has the foundation for an action-adventure series, with a shoot-first hero in the style of Child's Jack Reacher, Hunter's Bob Lee Swagger, or DeMille's John Corey."

—*Kirkus Reviews*

"*Clear by Fire* transports the reader to the front lines of the war on terror with such vivid detail that it leaves you looking for cover."

—Scott McEwen, #1 *New York Times* bestselling coauthor of *American Sniper*

Also by Joshua Hood

Clear by Fire

WARNING ORDER

-------- *A Search and Destroy Thriller* -----

JOSHUA HOOD

POCKET BOOKS

New York London Toronto Sydney New Delhi

Pocket Books
An Imprint of Simon & Schuster, Inc.
1230 Avenue of the Americas
New York, NY 10020

This book is a work of fiction. Any references to historical events, real people, or real places are used fictitiously. Other names, characters, places, and events are products of the author's imagination, and any resemblance to actual events or places or persons, living or dead, is entirely coincidental.

First Pocket Books paperback edition May 2017

POCKET and colophon are registered trademarks of Simon & Schuster, Inc.

For information about special discounts for bulk purchases, please contact Simon & Schuster Special Sales at 1-866-506-1949 or business@simonandschuster.com

The Simon & Schuster Speakers Bureau can bring authors to your live event. For more information or to book an event contact the Simon & Schuster Speakers Bureau at 1-866-248-3049 or visit our website at www.simonspeakers.com.

Interior design by Kyle Kabel

Manufactured in the United States of America

10 9 8 7 6 5 4 3 2 1

ISBN 978-1-5011-0828-0
ISBN 978-1-5011-6148-3 (pbk)
ISBN 978-1-5011-0830-3 (ebook)

The men and women of the military,
law enforcement, and emergency services
put their lives on hold every day to
protect this nation.
This book is for you.

CHAPTER 1

- - - - - - - - - - - -

Mason Kane stepped out of the shadows, which hung like skewed curtains over the tight alleyway, and moved silently toward the target house. Despite the "all clear" from the sniper providing overwatch to his rear, Mason's senses were on high alert.

His back was now exposed to the open street behind him, but Mason was trusting that Grinch had him covered. It was a hell of a thing, placing his life in the hands of another man, but Grinch was the best sniper he'd ever seen. If anyone had earned the right to cover his six, Grinch was the man.

Mason paused to wipe his face across the sleeve of his faded brown shirt, feeling the prickle of his thick salt-and-pepper stubble through the fabric.

"Fucking heat," he muttered to himself.

Despite the early hour, the alley was muggy, and the trash strewn across the jagged cobble-

stones smelled of stale urine and rotting veg-
etables. It was a smell he'd become intimately
familiar with during the years he'd spent deployed to Iraq, where he'd honed his ability to
fit in among the Arabs he was paid to hunt. His
dark eyes, olive skin, and knowledge of local
customs and languages allowed him access to a
Middle East that most Americans didn't know
existed.

Mason pushed all of that out of his mind a second before inching the barrel of his AK-47 around
the corner of the alley, and stepping out into the
open. He spotted a doorway up ahead and quickly
moved toward it, sweeping the AK back and forth
as he moved. Angling wide to ensure that it was
clear, he stepped out of the street and into cover. He
glanced behind him, just as Zeus's muzzle flashed
around the corner. Mason felt better knowing that
there was another gun in the fight, especially since
the man behind the trigger was one of the few people he trusted.

The stocky Libyan, and the rest of Mason's five-
man team, had been out for five days on a recon
mission just north of their present location when
they had gotten the call from Task Force 11's tactical operations center, or TOC. Instead of heading back to the safe house for some much-needed
downtime, the team was given another target and
ordered to move south.

Mason had pressed the battle captain for more
details, but all the man would say was that a mission
was in the works, and they needed to move. He

could tell right away that Zeus didn't like the idea of going in blind.

"What do you think?" Mason had asked him.

"It's a bad idea," the Libyan said as he pulled on his prized goatee. "Too many variables and not enough intel."

Before Zeus had a chance to say anything else, the captain called back with another bombshell.

"The DOD's source is already on the ground. The mission's a go if you're there or not."

"Shit," Mason swore. He knew there was only one man they'd use for this mission: his old friend Mick Boland.

Mason stepped back out into the street and was moving up to the target house when Grinch hissed over the radio, "Fuck, I've got a rover."

Mason froze as a man emerged on the street and bent his head to light a cigarette. Mason could smell the acrid tobacco burning as the man touched the end of the cigarette to the lighter and then blew out a jet of smoke.

"No shot," Grinch whispered across the radio.

"Time to get up close and personal," Mason murmured, easing the AK to his side. He silently slipped his custom-made JK knife from its sheath at the front of his chest rig before taking a careful step forward.

The bullet wound he had sustained to his thigh eight months ago throbbed as his right foot made contact with the ground, and he winced while pressing the AK against his body so it wouldn't bang against the concrete.

Mason was close enough to smell the sweat of the inky outline, which stood out among the heavy shadows. He knew that he was running out of time. Any second now, the *azan*, or call to prayer, would be blasted from the speakers festooning the mosques dotted around the tightly packed neighborhood. If he didn't get his men off the street before then, they were screwed.

Already the American was running down a list of contingencies in case they were compromised, but with Boland on the ground and the strike team birds coming with or without his team in position, his options were severely limited. They were going to have to suck it up and pray they could stay hidden.

Mason stepped forward, clearing his mind, and carefully set his right foot between the jagged pieces of concrete littering the tight side street. He could feel the blood pounding in his ears, amplifying every step he took. Then the target moved.

Mason froze, holding his breath while the man shifted his weight to his right leg in an effort to get comfortable.

"One more step," the American thought—at the same moment his left foot crunched down on an unseen shard of concrete.

The Arab flinched at the sound, his head turtling down to his shoulders, and he whipped around to see who was behind him.

Mason had the blade low, meaning to drive it into the base of the man's spine, but as the jihadist turned, his eyes wide with horror, he found himself out of position.

There was a flurry of movement: the fighter opening his mouth to scream and Mason driving his forehead into the crown of the boy's nose. Mason couldn't let him warn the men inside, and as the warm jet of blood sprayed across his face, he was already jamming the web of his left hand into the boy's mouth.

The youth recovered quickly, grabbing Mason's shirt and pulling him close as the knife came up. The boy was surprisingly strong, and Mason felt his ankle roll when the fighter grabbed the AK-47 hanging from his neck and tried to choke him with the sling.

Mason slammed the blade into the hollow between the fighter's neck and shoulder, so hard that he felt the hilt grind against the collarbone. Zeus appeared next to him in a flash, his hands reaching out for the boy's rifle. Mason pulled the young jihadist closer, feeling the boy's dying breath against his hand and the rough fabric of his shirt as they stumbled into the building.

Mason's momentum carried them into the corner, where he dumped the body against the wall. Bright arterial spray welled up beneath the blade's hilt, misting over the wall, as the boy's heart hammered in his chest. Mason watched his face grow pale and his chest heave as he fought against the icy grip of death, but the blade had pierced his heart, and a moment later the boy took a final, shaky breath and went still.

Zeus moved past him to pull security down the hallway, an M18 claymore mine peaking out of his assault pack.

"On me," Mason said into the radio before limping to the door.

His ankle throbbed in his boot, and he could feel it swelling as he yanked the knife out of the fighter's shoulder. The blood creeping down the boy's shirt reminded him of wine spilled on a tablecloth as Mason wiped the bloody blade on his pants and slid it back into its Kydex sheath.

"My bad, boss," Grinch said after he slipped through the door, pausing to let Mason count him in.

"And here I was thinking you were worth a shit," he said, smiling to let him know he was joking. Mason tapped the medic, Blaine, and T.J., the breacher, on their shoulders as the two men slipped into the house. Counting himself, that brought his count to five, and he knew that the team was all accounted for.

"Keep babying him, and he's never going to learn," Zeus said, yanking the claymore from his pack before kneeling to attach it to the door.

"Don't be jealous—you're still my favorite turd," Mason said, grinning at his best friend.

"I'm not jealous," Zeus replied. "I just don't think he's ready to take over, even though you're getting too old for this. Do you need an aspirin for your old-lady ankle?"

"Fuck off," he replied, his ankle still throbbing.

Mason knew that Zeus was right. He hadn't been a hundred percent for the last eight months, but he thought he'd done a better job hiding it. The fact that he was unable to keep anything from Zeus wasn't surprising, especially after all they had been through, but Mason still refused to admit what was becoming increasingly clear.

He was slipping, and he should have never agreed to this mission.

Mason's team was carrying the wrong gear for this operation. He'd wanted to go back to the safe house so they could trade out their battered AKs for the suppressed Heckler & Koch 416 assault rifles they usually carried, but the captain overruled him.

"My sniper is the only one with night vision, and it's dark as shit out here," Mason tried to explain.

"Not my problem. Just get to the grid," the faceless captain ordered.

"Fuck that. I'm not putting my team at risk for this bullshit," Mason said before hanging up on the man.

He hadn't even slipped the sat phone back into his cargo pocket before it was ringing again. This time it was Colonel Anderson, the commanding officer of Task Force 11, on the line. Mason cursed as soon as he recognized the number. He knew it was going to be a one-way conversation before he even answered.

Mason and the colonel had never gotten along.

The first time they'd met—eight months prior—
Mason and Zeus were in handcuffs after members of the task force had captured them in Libya.
Anderson had been a major then, and Mason was
charged with treason. It didn't matter that Mason
was cleared; Anderson had already made up his
mind that the olive-skinned operator was a piece
of shit, and never wasted an opportunity to let him
know it.

The colonel cut right to the point: "You can get
your ass to the objective, or you can let Boland go
in by himself. It's your choice."

Mason knew he was being played, but he didn't
have a say in the matter. Loyalty had always been
his weakness, and Anderson was taking full advantage.

"I think it's time for a vacation," Zeus announced,
bringing Mason back to the here and now.

"Not again," Mason said.

Zeus had been talking about different exotic
locations for weeks, and ignored Mason's exasperated reply, "Look, we have work to do."

"I've narrowed it down," Zeus said as he finished emplacing the mine.

Outside, the opening wail of the call to prayer
echoed over the city, coaxing it gently to life. It
was a sound Mason had come to hate because it
reminded him that no matter how many men he
killed or how much he suffered, he could never go
home again.

"Save the travel agent shit until after Boland's—"
Mason heard movement coming from the floor

above. He raised a finger to his lips as he slipped a suppressed Glock 19 from its holster.

He limped over to the stairs, the pistol pointing to the second floor while Zeus moved across to his right. The Libyan scanned the landing with his own pistol and then motioned that he was going first. Mason felt Grinch's hand on his shoulder, signaling his readiness. He checked to ensure that there were still two men pulling security on the bottom floor before the three of them slipped up the concrete steps, covering the landing as they moved.

Zeus moved to the near side of the hall, with Mason tight on his back. Grinch crossed the narrow space, pulling security on the right side of the hallway. Zeus slipped to the threshold and peeked in, his pistol at the ready. Unlike Mason, he carried a modified 1911 that the American had bought him for his birthday. Holding the .45 in front of him, he scanned the room, taking in two empty sleeping mats lying near the back wall.

Zeus was ready to move on, but waited while Mason surveyed the room. There were two mats, but Mason had killed only one of them. He didn't like the fact that there was one fighter in this building unaccounted for.

Finally he turned and squeezed Zeus, allowing the Libyan to pan across the next doorway—before his pistol snapped up in a flash and he fired. Mason had just enough time to see two men in the room before the thump of the suppressed .45 barked once.

The heavy round nailed one of the men in the

center of the forehead, blasting his lifeless body back flat on the mat. His comrade scrambled to produce a pistol from underneath the filthy covers, but Mason stepped into the room, his Glock coughing twice before the fighter could raise the pistol toward Zeus.

"Guess he wasn't asleep," Zeus shrugged as Mason checked the man's body. He discovered a stack of papers and began stuffing them into the dump pouch hanging from his waist. Every bit of intel that they found would be taken back to the task force's analysts and cross-referenced against its massive databases. The seemingly innocuous "pocket litter" had provided troves of actionable intel in the past, and it had become a standard operating procedure for them to gather as much as they could carry.

"See what happens when you try to be sneaky?" he said, throwing the blanket over the dead man's head before searching around the sleeping mat for more evidence.

Out in the hallway, two shots rang out, followed by a man's scream—then the fleshy smack of a body hitting the ground.

Mason felt a sliver of fear rush down his spine as he wondered if one of his men had been hit. That was followed by an instant burst of relief when Grinch came over the radio.

"Need one," the sniper said.

"Go," Mason told Zeus as he began checking the other man for any pocket litter.

"We have a problem," Zeus said a few moments later, forcing Mason to cut his examination of the room short.

Stepping cautiously out into the hall, he saw another sprawled jihadist, blood pooling along the chalky concrete floor. Mason stepped over the body, marked by the two bullet holes that Grinch had punched through the man's forehead. Nearby someone had scratched "Death to Infidels" into the wall.

Entering the room, he saw Grinch drag another dead fighter's body out of the doorway and begin checking his pockets. The target house was turning out to be much bigger than it had appeared from the outside, and Mason began to worry that the location was too large for his small team to secure.

"Two for two," he said to Zeus, who rolled his eyes. "I told you Grinch was shit hot." Mason groaned, enjoying his friend's annoyance.

"You're upset because he won't leave you anyone to shoot?"

"Whatever," the Libyan said wearily from his place next to a desk propped up against the wall. "Take a look at this."

Two small computer monitors flickered. On one of them, Mason saw several live feeds that he recognized immediately as the outside of the house, while the other one displayed a bird's-eye view of the entire objective.

"Is that what I think it is?" he asked, following

the thick black cable, which ran up the wall and through a hole in the roof.

"They knew we were coming," Zeus said.

Mason tore his eyes from the hacked Predator drone feed, taking in the maps and photos attached to the bare concrete wall. None of it made any sense, and alarm bells began going off in his head. The reason his team had been ordered to abandon its recon mission and to occupy the target house in the first place was to provide overwatch for a mission that hadn't even existed two hours ago.

"How in the hell is this possible?" Mason asked aloud. "I thought the whole reason Boland was on the ground was because he was making sure his source didn't leak this kind of shit."

Mason had no idea how Boland had gotten involved in the operation in the first place. Hell, he wasn't even on the task force. What he did know was that instead of controlling the source from a safe location like he was supposed to, Boland had apparently chosen to physically take him to the target location and get eyes on the high-value target himself.

It was a bad idea, and Mason couldn't help but wonder how much of a hand Colonel Anderson had in the decision. If Anderson was calling the shots, it might explain the reckless desperation Boland was showing in this operation.

His old friend knew better than to place himself in harm's way. In fact, it went against everything the two men had learned during their time in Delta Force. Calculating risk versus reward was the mantra they had learned from the moment they were selected to join the unit. It had been beat into their heads through selection phase, and right now it seemed that the risk was way too high.

"What the hell?" Mason felt like he was missing a vital piece of the puzzle.

"I think we're being played," Zeus said, ripping one of the pictures off the wall and holding it up for Mason to see.

As he stepped forward to get a better look, he felt his blood suddenly run cold.

"Oh shit," he said, instantly recognizing the dark-skinned, ragged, and bearded man smoking a cigarette outside of a café as Boland.

"If they know Boland's face, then he's been compromised."

"We need to go, right now," Zeus said.

"I have to let David know," Mason said, pulling the satellite phone out of his cargo pocket.

David Castleman was the only reason that Mason and Zeus were on the task force in the first place. Eight months ago, when Mason was labeled a traitor and placed on the kill-on-sight list, David was the only man in the CIA who thought he was innocent. The man had protected him long enough that Mason was finally able to prove the real traitor's identity.

He was just extending the stubby antenna when a burst of automatic fire erupted downstairs.

"Grinch, find out what the hell is going on down there," he ordered.

He turned to Zeus. "What the hell have we gotten ourselves into?"

"*We* didn't do anything," Zeus pointed out angrily. "What have *you* gotten us into?"

CHAPTER 2

Turkish-Syrian Border

The sun was just beginning to come up over the airfield as Renee Hart hustled across the tarmac to the waiting Mi-17s. The rotors of the Russian helicopters whined, blowing her short blond hair against her cheek as they began to spin up, and forcing her to duck before she hustled up the ramp and took her seat.

She pulled her helmet over her head, catching her reflection in the small window set in the thin skin of the helo. She was pretty in a girl-next-door type of way, but within her clear blue eyes was a hardness forged in combat.

Renee was the last member of the strike team to board the helo, and she looked out of place among the burly, bearded warriors. Despite being only five foot six, she had gone through the same training they had, and she'd earned her right to be there.

Her heart was hammering from the short sprint

across the flight line, and after tossing her assault pack onto the oil-soaked floor of the helo, she took a second to catch her breath and survey the cramped cargo compartment.

The task force borrowed a page from the CIA's playbook by buying five Russian helicopters with the hope that they wouldn't draw unnecessary attention. The agency was notorious for using a tactic until it proved ineffective, and figured since they'd successfully used it to insert the legendary Jawbreaker Team in Afghanistan, it should work in Syria, Renee saw. The only problem was that this time the team was operating without the official support of the American people.

Renee thought the birds were pieces of shit, and most of them hadn't moved from the hangar since being delivered from Iraq. The fact that two of them were running was a testament to the skill of the CIA ground crews, but she still had serious concerns about their airworthiness.

From her place near the ramp, she could smell burning oil mixing with the clean smell of the early morning as the rotors roared overhead. A crisp breeze blew in from the west, carrying with it the smell of wood smoke. Renee knew that the women of the local village were already up, preparing the traditional flat bread the men would eat before beginning the day's work.

The helicopter lurched forward as the pilots increased the throttle, and the helo began bumping down the runway, causing her assault pack to bounce on the floor. Using her feet to hold it in place, she glanced at the rest of her teammates, who were joking among themselves.

As usual they ignored her, but she knew that any moment the jokes would start. The alienation wasn't anything new; it had been going on since she became the first female operator in the all-male Special Operations program. But the chauvinism was getting old, and sometimes she questioned why she even bothered trying.

"Hey, bleeder, you sure you're ready for this?" Sergeant First Class Jake "Warchild" Carson shouted from his place near the front. Despite the fact that she had more combat experience than most people in the chopper, he never missed a chance to make her feel like an outsider. "We don't need to stop so you can grab some more pads, do we?"

Renee felt a flush of anger creeping up her neck, and she fought the desire to punch her team leader in the throat. She had no doubt that she could take him down in a second, but she was still playing nice, wanting to avoid unnecessary conflict.

"He's fucking with you. Don't take it personal," Master Sergeant Jonathon Parker yelled over the rotors.

Renee forced a smile and lifted the hand mike from the radio stuffed into her assault pack.

Like the rest of the team, Parker had been in the military for more than ten years, and he was a well-rounded operator. He was handsome in a rugged kind of way, and at six foot four, he was the tallest man on the team. He was also the only person who'd taken the time to get to know her or learn about what she had done before coming to the task force.

"Hey, Parker, you better not be moving in on Mason's girl," Warchild yelled.

Renee shook her head, knowing that Warchild was secretly threatened by Mason. The way he acted around the legendary operator was almost juvenile, and Renee knew enough about male psychology to realize that it stemmed from the fact that Mason intimidated the hell out of Warchild.

Sergeant Major Jason Mitchell leaned forward on the nylon bench, his titanic bulk squishing the operator next to him into the skin of the helo.

"Hey, shithead, why don't you do everyone a favor and shut the fuck up?" he shouted.

The man was built like a tank, and as he glared at Warchild, Renee wondered if he had to get his uniforms specially made. The M4 rifle in his massive hands looked like a toy, but there was nothing childlike about the rage etched on his face. Mitchell had fought with Mason in Iraq and had no patience for those who sought to sully the warrior's fragile reputation.

Renee knew it was all a one-way dick-measuring contest, and that Mason's expertise was a sore spot, but it was nothing compared to how threatened her team leader was by the experience that *she* brought to the team. Warchild's fragile ego couldn't stand the fact that she'd once served as team leader for one of the army's covert Terrorist Apprehension Teams, and it made him lash out whenever the opportunity arose.

Back then Renee's job had been to find, fix, and finish suspected terrorist cells before they were able to strike. Her extensive knowledge of the different terror networks had made her a valuable commodity. But everything changed the day she met Mason Kane.

Renee had uncovered a link to a Colonel Barnes, along with the Black Ops unit he was operating out of the shadows in Afghanistan. When Barnes took his men off the reservation and decided to prosecute his own war on terror, Mason had helped her hunt the colonel and his rogue team from the foothills of Pakistan to the heart of Damascus.

She'd learned up close and personal that Mason was someone you wanted on your side in a gunfight. He was a coldhearted son of a bitch, but Renee knew that he also had a soft side. He was without a doubt the most loyal person she'd ever met. As for Warchild, well, she would soon see if he had what it took to back up his big mouth.

The helicopter thundered toward the objective, and her thoughts turned to the mission briefing they'd had before jumping on the birds. The analyst had informed them, "We have been looking for Khalid al Hamas for quite some time," motioning at the Arab displayed on the monitor. "Our source on the ground has confirmed that he is in very tight with the Iranian Quds Force, and the reason he is in Syria is to meet up with *this* guy."

The slide changed to a younger man with a closely cropped beard and a slender, almost feminine nose.

"This man is Jamal Latif, the ground commander for al Nusra. He's become a serious pain in the ass after pushing the Syrian army out of Aleppo. Recently, he declared jihad on anyone refusing to adopt al Nusra's particular brand of ideologically motivated hatred. Christians, Sunni, Shia—it really doesn't seem to matter to Latif. He just likes to kill people. His handiwork is all over the internet, and he seems to be on a personal mission to bring mass crucifixion to the twenty-first century."

He displayed a low-angle shot of ten naked, bloody men hanging from a row of makeshift crosses.

"Fucking animals," Renee muttered.

"Yeah, the guy's a savage," Colonel Bat Anderson, the task force commander, said from his chair at the front of the room. "We got it. But tell me why this warrants breaking mission protocol. How do you know that either one of these guys are going to be there?"

"I'm glad you asked, sir. We have an ace in the hole on this one. Due to excellent cooperation between the DOD and the CIA, we have managed to insert a deep-cover asset within Abu Fariq's camp, and our source has verified that the target will be at the objective no later than 0800 hours."

Something told Renee that the source had to be Mick Boland. Besides Mason, he was the only person in Syria who had the skills to pull off something like this. She'd met him only a few weeks earlier after the operative had shown up mysteriously at the task force's hangar.

Mason had been surprised to see his old friend, and after a few beers, they began swapping war stories from their time in Iraq and Afghanistan. It was obvious that they'd been through some serious shit together. Yet the longer she watched Boland, the more Renee felt that something about him was off.

He appeared gaunt, filled with a nervous, almost fatalistic energy that made it impossible for him to sit still. She thought that the stress of combat might be finally getting to him, but since she knew that Boland had saved Mason's life in Iraq, she didn't want to say anything without some sort of proof.

Later that night, she hacked into the DOD database, hoping to find anything to calm her fears. Most of the files had already been redacted, and after fifteen minutes, she was about to give up. Just as she was getting ready to log out, Renee found a DOD communiqué that made the hairs on the back of her neck stand up.

The document had been marked for deletion, and was labeled "Eyes Only," which meant that it was way above her pay grade. However, Renee didn't hesitate to open it. Like most interservice memos, it was brief and extremely vague, but the tone was urgent. According to reports from the field, Boland had slipped into Syria a week before showing up in Turkey with an unnamed piece of equipment that he was supposed to emplace. Before he had the chance, though, he was briefly detained by members of the Syrian opposition and relieved of his gear. There was no mention of what happened next.

"Hey, are you good?" Parker asked, jarring her back to the task at hand.

"Yeah, I'm just surprised we launched so fast," she said.

"They must really want this guy," Parker replied. "That analyst said the order came from the top."

"Hey, bleeder," Warchild hollered at her. "Are you going to do a radio check or gossip all day?"

Warchild had designated her the RTO, or radio operator, which was not only a totally unnecessary job but also the most menial job Warchild could come up with. Nevertheless, Renee was a professional, and she handled the responsibility as if it were the most important one on the team.

"What do you think I'm doing, dick?" she mumbled before depressing the mike's talk button. With that, the small screen on the PRC-150 high-frequency radio lit up.

"Any station this net, this is Savage 7 Romeo, radio check, over," she said into the hand mike.

Renee, having already double-checked the radio before getting on the bird, knew it had the correct crypto installed—which made the frequency secure from outside listeners—but she needed to make sure it was functioning properly before they hit the objective.

"Savage 7 Romeo, this is Tomahawk 6 Romeo, we read you, Lima Charlie," a voice replied through the hand mike.

The Mi-17 shook, and cold air blasted through the cargo hold. Shivering, she flipped the radio to the air-to-ground net and tried to make radio contact with Mason.

"Ronin 6, Savage 7 Romeo, radio check," she said.

She glanced at her watch, knowing that it was time for them to check in. After a full minute of waiting, she tried again.

"Ronin 6, Savage 7, radio check, over."

She was about to flip to a different frequency when a man's voice came through the net:

"Savage 7, Ronin 6, we have a problem—" Mason said.

The transmission was cut off as gunfire erupted in the background.

Something was wrong, Renee realized. This was supposed to be a simple smash and grab. Whatever the hell was going on, they were heading right toward it.

CHAPTER 3

- - - - - - - - - - - -

It was late when President Bradley closed the black notebook containing the daily intelligence brief. He tossed it on the low mahogany table that separated the two immaculate white couches in the Oval Office. Secretary of Defense Winfield "Duke" Cage could tell his boss was tired as he rubbed his face.

Jacob Simmons, the national security advisor, looked at his watch before leaning forward in his chair. Cage knew that he was hoping to get an answer before the long day finally came to a close.

"Mr. President, the limited airstrikes are working," Simmons began. "We are hitting them where it hurts, and I say we stay the course."

"Jesus," Cage said, trying vainly to control the anger he felt boiling up inside him. He knew Jacob wasn't naïve enough to believe what he was saying, but he couldn't listen to his bullshit a second longer.

"You are out of your mind, Jacob," he said. "The airstrikes aren't doing shit, and you know it. Please excuse my French, Mr. President," he added hastily as the leader of the free world scowled at his profane outburst.

Bradley bore a striking resemblance to a young Robert Redford, and like the actor, he was usually very laid back. But one thing Cage was learning the hard way was that the president hated profanity.

"What I am trying to say is that limited strikes will not accomplish the mission."

"You have to give it time," Simmons responded.

"You've had almost a year. How much time do you need?" Bradley demanded.

"Gentlemen." The president's chief of staff, Craig O'Neil, interjected from the high-back chair to the president's right. "It's late, but let's try to keep this civil."

"There is nothing civil about this," Cage replied, unable to fathom why he was the only one grasping the significance of what was occurring in Iraq and Syria. "We have intel that al Nusra is moving into Iraq to join up with ISIS. Do you want to wait until they dismantle everything our soldiers died to achieve before you make a decision?"

"Enough," Bradley said finally, smoothing the front of his tailored jacket. "Seventy percent of the American people are glad that we are out of Iraq, and there is no way I'm upsetting my base by sending troops back to Iraq. End of story."

Cage settled his muscled bulk back into the couch, realizing that this meeting was not going the way he'd planned. He had allowed himself to believe that the president was finally going to make a decision—finally do something to combat the violence flooding into Iraq—but it was obvious that he'd been wrong.

"What do you want to do, Mr. President?" O'Neil asked.

"Keep hitting the targets outlined in the brief," he said, nodding toward the folder on the table. "Right now I think that is the safest option."

"Yes, sir," Simmons said, getting to his feet.

"Goddamn it, Jacob, you know better than that," Cage bellowed, causing everyone in the room to stare at him. "This weak-ass strategy is all wrong, and you know it."

"Mr. Secretary," Craig began, but he stopped as soon as the president raised his hand.

"Let me remind you," Bradley said, turning to Cage, "that you may be the secretary of defense, but you still work for me."

Cage's jaw muscles rippled as he absorbed the warning. Under the previous administration, he'd lost his temper in this very same room, and it had cost him his military career. He was about to make the very same mistake when the chief of staff got to his feet.

"Mr. President, I have no doubt that Secretary Cage will do as you wish. We all know how passionate he is about Iraq and know he means absolutely no disrespect."

Only by sheer force of will did Cage place a stranglehold on his emotions. He had to take the olive branch that O'Neil was offering. Still, he felt his anger burning like a white-hot poker as he got to his feet.

"My apologies, sir. I get carried away sometimes," he lied.

"No worries, Duke," the president said, pleased to see he was being reasonable. "It's one of the reasons you are so good at what you do."

Fifteen minutes later, Cage was back in his office, staring at the last sip of bourbon filling the bottom of a crystal tumbler. The glass looked fragile in his powerful hands, and as he watched the golden liquid swirling on the bottom, he wondered why he put up with this shit.

Before being sworn in as the secretary of defense, he'd been the youngest chairman of the Joint Chiefs of Staff in history. He was well versed in the art of war. The reason he'd agreed to take this damn job in the first place was because Bradley had practically begged him.

"If he's not going to listen, then why the hell does he call me to these damn meetings?" he asked, looking over at Jacob.

"Duke, you can't take it personal. You just have to realize that there are some things you can't control."

Cage drained the highball in one quick gulp, savoring the burn as the bourbon made its way down his throat.

"What time is it?" he asked, heading over to the

half-empty bottle of Knob Creek waiting on the cherry credenza.

"It's about 0400 in Syria," Jacob replied.

Cage nodded, set down his glass, and grabbed the rectangular bottle. He twisted off the cork, which squeaked against the neck before popping free, and poured a generous amount of the amber liquor in the highball glass before offering it to Simmons.

During their time in Special Forces, Cage had preferred beer, but Jacob Simmons had always been a whiskey man. The SecDef was starting to understand why the National Security Advisor preferred the fiery taste of good bourbon.

"Want another hit?"

"Why not? I'm not going anywhere," Jacob said, the leather chair creaking as he leaned forward to hold out his glass.

The two men had been friends since West Point, and had bled together in more countries than either one could remember. After Cage's legendary blowout with the previous vice president, Jacob had stood by him when he was forced to retire early.

Simmons had also been there when his son was killed in Iraq, and then a few months later when his wife finally lost her battle with cancer. There wasn't another man in the world that Cage trusted more.

"It would be so much easier if you'd stop pampering his ass," Cage said after filling Simmons's glass.

"It can't be obvious," Simmons replied.

"Fucking politics. Bradley has no idea what's

going on over there. He's as bad as the last guy, scared of his own fucking shadow."

"He's new; give him time. But you have to stop thinking that I'm on his side. I'm the one who raised the issue with the president in the first place."

"How much longer?" Cage asked, ignoring the Rolex Submariner on his wrist.

"Thirty minutes, max," Simmons said, taking another sip. "Try to relax. You've done everything you can do."

A lot was riding on the president's decision. Cage always fought his own battles, but now he was the one sending the warriors into harm's way, and it was a heavy burden. The two men stood alone in their assessment of ISIS, and Cage knew that President Bradley desperately wanted to avoid another war. In fact, the only reason he'd agreed to the operation was because he hoped that if they cut the head of the snake, the body would die.

Cage, on the other hand, knew that this was just the beginning. If the president refused to face reality, Cage was going to have to force him to make the right decision.

CHAPTER 4

- - - - - - - - - - - - -

Mason was turning toward the door when a bullet cracked past his ear—so close that he heard the 7.62 round snap as it cut through the air. He dove to the ground, searching vainly for the shooter. As he landed, he felt a sharp sting cut across the back of his arm.

He'd been hit.

The roar of the Kalashnikov echoed off the gray concrete walls, making it impossible to locate the direction of fire.

"Where is he?" Mason yelled as the rounds slammed into the wall above his head like hammer blows, sending shards of cement cutting into the back of his neck.

One of the computer monitors exploded in a shower of sparks just as Zeus dove behind the table for cover and the shooter traversed his fire across the room. Zeus cursed loudly, unable to locate the source of the gunfire.

Mason knew he had to move.

He scrambled away from the wall, leaving a smear of blood as he pushed off. Directly across from him, a piece of brown and red fabric had been nailed over what he'd thought was a window, but from his place on the floor, Mason could see the base of a concrete step behind the curtain.

He flipped off the safety, noticing the fabric snap as another burst cut through, and fired three quick shots through the center.

"The curtain. He's behind the curtain," he shouted, scrambling out of the line of fire. Mason's knees burned as he scraped the floor, tearing his pant leg.

Once out of range, he scrambled to his feet. He ignored the sharp pain from the bullet wound that refused to heal, and ripped the curtain from the nails securing it to the wall. Knowing the gunner was less than five feet away, he flipped the AK to full auto and stuck it around the corner. Yanking the trigger to the rear, he let the muzzle climb as the Kalashnikov chewed through half a magazine.

His ears were already ringing from the first salvo of fire, and Mason could feel the pressure driving back from the muzzle, slapping him in the skull like the palm of an invisible hand.

A flash of reddish mist splattered across the wall perpendicular to his line of sight, followed by the sound of a man shrieking in pain. Mason released the pressure on the trigger, and for a second, silence fell over the room. So much for the surprise element, he thought grimly. Everybody for blocks around had been alerted by now.

He reached down to rip the mag out of the rifle and was just about to slip a fresh one into the mag well when he heard a metallic *tink* above his head.

Mason rocked the magazine forward, yanking it to ensure it was secure, just as a dark green orb bounced out of the hidden stairwell. The Russian grenade seemed to hover at eye level, and before he even realized that he was moving, Mason snatched it out of the air and hurled it back up the stairs.

"Oh shit," he thought, realizing what he had just done. He turned away from the opening and screamed, "Grenade."

The concussion blew out of the stairwell like a freight train, spewing shrapnel and noxious black smoke into the room in a rush of overpressure. Mason let go of the rifle, cupping his hands over his ears. He could only pray that he hadn't blown out his eardrums.

His equilibrium off, he stumbled, retching on the smoke that burned his lungs. He had to steady himself against the wall. The thick haze obscured everything in the room, like premature twilight, and he thought he heard gunfire coming from downstairs over the ringing in his ears.

"Zeus, are you good?" he croaked, unable to make out the voices coming over the radio.

"Why did you do that?" the Libyan demanded.

Mason staggered into the stairwell, his muzzle fixed on the body lying near the top. The fighter's left leg was ripped to shreds, and beneath pinkish bits of sinewy meat, Mason saw blood squirting weakly from the femoral artery. The blood looked black as it pooled on the step, and above the corpse, dark, jagged fingers marked the spot where the frag had detonated.

The explosion had taken off the man's head, leaving him unrecognizable, but out of habit, Mason still kicked his rifle away. He continued up the stairs he hadn't known were there until he was standing on the roof.

Dawn was breaking in rosy fingers along the horizon, and Mason took a greedy gulp of fresh air while scanning the roof for any additional threats. His attention was drawn to a gray satellite TV dish, pointed skyward, and he realized that this was how the fighters had hacked into the military's UAV, or unmanned aerial vehicle, feed. Next to it, a freshly sandbagged position protecting a Soviet-made DShK .51 caliber machine gun gave him pause.

A similar position had been set up to his right, but instead of a machine gun, the fighting position had two American-made Stinger missiles stacked inside it. "Kill us with our own weapons," Mason thought. What else was new?

Realizing that he was out in the open, Mason took cover behind a low wall. With all clear for the moment, he turned his attention to the pain in his arm. He winced and gingerly probed the wound with his fingers. The pain radiated up his arm, and he craned his neck to get a better look. The bullet had left a nasty tear along his triceps muscle.

"Christ, it hurts," Mason thought.

The swelling made it difficult to bend his arm. But it was the large amount of blood soaking his assault shirt that concerned him. He dug awkwardly into his kit for a roll of gauze, knowing he needed to control the bleeding.

Mason used his teeth to rip open the sterile plastic pouch and began looping the gauze around the wound, holding the free end under his chin. He managed a loose, dangling loop, but even as he pulled it tight, he could tell it wasn't going to hold.

"Fuck this shit," he cursed, getting to his feet. "People hiding behind goddamned curtains."

One thing he knew for certain: the mission was compromised. Mason reached for the sat phone, knowing that he had to warn David, but as he did, he realized he'd dropped it when taking fire.

All he could think about was that Boland was out there by himself, with no idea that he'd been compromised. No matter how much Mason wanted to believe that everything was going to work out, he knew his friend didn't stand a chance.

The city reminded him of Ramadi and the many times he and Boland had been ambushed while operating there. Mason couldn't think of a worse place to be out by yourself. Entire buildings were missing huge sections of their roofs, while others lay in piles of rubble. From his perch on the roof, he couldn't find a single wall that wasn't pockmarked from small-arms fire. Obscene holes, blackened and charred around the edges, revealed the insides of apartments, like cutaway dollhouses, displaying the shattered lives of the innocents caught in the cross fire.

What was left of the city reminded him of a bum who'd gotten the shit kicked out of him, and the buildings that lined the streets resembled punched-out teeth in a shattered smile. Back home in East Los Angeles, it looked like a war zone sometimes, but that was paradise compared with this hellhole.

He heard Zeus talking behind him and forced his attention back to the mission at hand.

"They are calling for you on the radio," Zeus said in Arabic. "Here, let me do that shoulder right."

Mason reached across his body, mindful of avoiding pain, and depressed the hand mike while the Libyan moved to tend his bandage.

"Ronin 6," he said simply.

"Ronin 6, Striker 5, I'm ten minutes out."

It was Boland, and Mason felt relief wash over him.

"Striker, be advised you are compromised. I advise immediate abort."

"Ronin 6, say again?" Boland asked incredulously.

"Striker 5, abort," he yelled into the hand mike.

"Break, break, break. Ronin 6, Striker 5, this is Tomahawk Base," a voice said, suddenly cutting through his transmission. "The mission is a go. I repeat, the mission is a go."

"Tomahawk Base, we found intel. We found fucking pictures of Striker 5 on the objective. I say again: Striker 5 has been compromised."

"Striker 5, skip rope," the voice said.

"What the fuck?" Mason shouted, realizing that whoever was on the other end of the radio had just told Boland to switch to another frequency.

"Striker 5, this is Ronin 6, how copy?" he asked. Meanwhile, Zeus tightened the bandage with a sharp tug, causing him to flinch.

The Libyan looked at him, a frown crossing his face. "Looks like you suck at first aid, too."

Mason scowled at the man who'd saved his life more times than he could remember. They had been through so much and always managed to find a way to survive. Yet he owed Boland, too. He knew that Zeus deserved better, but there was no way he could turn his back on Mick, no matter what they had to face.

He flipped over to the air-to-ground frequency, hoping that the strike team hadn't launched already. Zeus shook his head while Mason tried to make contact, but the radio was silent. "This mission is fucked."

"If he dies, it's on me," Mason said, preparing to hit the transmit button.

"What about us?" the Libyan asked, forcing Mason to make the hardest decision of his life.

"I can't leave him out there with his ass in the wind," he said, conducting a tactical reload before turning toward the stairs. "Get the guys back to the safe house and get the hell out of here. I got him into this, and it's up to me to get him out."

"You and your misplaced loyalties," Zeus muttered, looking away. He surveyed the destroyed city before turning back to Mason. "Look, there is no way I'm letting you go out there by yourself. With your old-lady ankle and busted-up arm, you wouldn't last for three seconds without me covering your ass."

CHAPTER 5

- - - - - - - - - - - -

Mick Boland welcomed the adrenaline coursing through his body as he switched frequencies on the Thales MBITR multiband radio and waited for Tomahawk Base to key up.

He was careful to hide his addiction from men like David Castleman, but with the legendary CIA operative temporarily out of the picture, he allowed himself a moment to enjoy the buzz. Boland caught the reflection of his dilated pupils in the rearview mirror. He savored the rush of power he felt, before glancing at the man driving him to the objective.

"Is everything okay?" al Qatar asked in broken English.

"Yeah, we're good," Boland answered confidently, despite the urgency he'd heard in Mason's voice over the radio.

Boland had met Mason at Delta selection, and the two men had hit it off right away. The deployments to Afghanistan and Iraq had formed a bond that most brothers would never know. It was a bond forged in the cauldron of combat, when your life depended on your teammate, and despite the chemical euphoria building inside him, Boland felt guilty that he'd been forced to deceive his friend.

Mason had no idea what was really going on, because, honestly, Boland had been too embarrassed to tell him. The mission was entirely personal. He felt bad for drawing the task force in to clean up his mess, but Boland knew he had to recover the gear he'd lost, or his life wouldn't be worth shit when he rotated back to the States.

"Striker 5, Tomahawk Base. Are you secure?" the voice asked, pulling him out of his guilt trip.

"Striker 5, roger," Boland said.

"Disregard Ronin 6's last—the mission is still a go. I'll advise when the birds are inbound."

"Good, copy."

Mason had done the right thing calling for an abort, but what his friend didn't know was that there was no way in hell the task force was going to scrub the operation. He'd never kept anything from the man who had helped get him this job, but, unfortunately, Mason couldn't be trusted—or controlled.

Kane was the most fearless warrior that Boland had ever met, but after what had happened in Afghanistan with the Anvil Team, there was no way he'd ever be let back into the inner circle. Barnes had seen to that. If Boland had learned anything after all these years in combat, he understood what Mason still didn't get: war was all about self-preservation.

He'd done what he could to keep Mason and his men out of the fight, even going as far as telling Colonel Anderson that it was a mistake to use Mason on this mission. But both he and the colonel knew that Kane was the only one who could pull it off. All the same, he and Anderson were all too aware of what happened anytime you let Mason off the leash; there was no telling what he was going to do.

For Boland, this operation was the only way he could redeem himself for the mistake he'd made a few weeks earlier; he prayed that Mason would find the intel he'd left at the target house and decide it was too dangerous to hang around.

He stuffed the radio into the space between the seat and the door and, when he turned, noticed Abu al Qatar watching him closely. Up ahead, a checkpoint came into view. Four men stood next to a Toyota Hilux guarding the road, and one of them stepped off the concrete median as the Arab slowed the blue Toyota Cressida and rolled down the window.

The young jihadist, dressed in black jeans and a blue Captain America T-shirt, stuck his head inside the window. "Where are you going?"

"We are going to see Latif," al Qatar said simply.

"I was not told of this," the fighter replied, shaken by the mention of his commander's name.

"Of course you weren't," al Qatar sneered. "But if you value your life, I would let us through."

"This road is closed."

"Why don't you call him on the radio and tell him that you won't let us pass? I am sure he would love to hear that."

The young jihadist looked around, unsure of what to do. Finally, he nodded his head. "Very well."

As soon as the jihadist stepped off the street, al Qatar put the Toyota in gear and gently placed his foot on the accelerator. Once the car was moving, he pulled a cigarette from the center console and lit it with shaky hands.

"I didn't think they were going to let us pass," he said.

"Relax, I told you it would be okay," Boland said.

"Yes, you did, and you were right."

Al Qatar sounded too complimentary, and Boland felt a flicker of suspicion. He knew al Qatar was a liar, but right now he was the only *friend* he had.

Abu al Qatar wasn't yet thirty years old, but he had been working for the CIA since he was twenty-three. He was the agency's only asset in Syria. More to the point, he was its only link to Khalid al Hamas, and the CIA would give anything to capture the Iranian facilitator.

"How much farther?" Boland asked.

"It is not far; just at the end of the street."

"Are you sure they are both going to be there?"

"Yes, Latif is very interested in this meeting."

"Tell me what you are going to do once we are inside."

"I will give the money to al Hamas," he said, motioning to the duffel in the backseat.

"And who am I?"

"Your name is Hassan, and you speak for Emir Baghdadi in Iraq," al Qatar answered for the hundredth time.

"Why am I here?"

"You have been sent to offer Latif a chance at an alliance."

"Very good." Boland smiled. "What do you do when the shooting starts?"

Al Qatar swerved gently to avoid a hole in the asphalt, and checked the rearview mirror to make sure they weren't being followed. "When the shooting starts, I get on the ground and hope the other Americans don't kill me," he said finally.

"Listen to me: if you don't pose a threat, they won't hurt you," Boland said.

Al Qatar gave him a queer look, and again Boland felt his hackles rise. But he dismissed the spark of doubt as soon as it came. Al Qatar was a traitor, and as long as you kept that in the forefront of your mind, he'd never get the upper hand.

CHAPTER 6

Renee kept trying to get hold of Mason as the pitch of the Mi-17's rotors began to change. She'd needed a situation report but was running out of time.

Renee looked down the half-open ramp, where the caramel-colored sand was beginning to give way to the gray cityscape. She knew that Mason wasn't prone to exaggeration, and if he was calling for an abort, she couldn't fathom why they were ignoring him.

"Five minutes," the pilot said over the internal net.

"Get ready," Warchild yelled from his perch near the door gunner.

Renee knew her team leader couldn't care less what she had to say, but maybe if she could get Parker to listen, they could avoid flying into a hot LZ.

"Ground team is calling for an abort," Renee shouted at Parker.

The man frowned behind his dark sunglasses and ran his hand over his thick brown beard. He checked the GPS strapped to his wrist and said, "We are almost on target. What did Tomahawk Base say?"

"They said continue mission," Renee replied.

Parker depressed his push-to-talk button that allowed him to talk on the team's internal net. "Be advised, Ronin 6 is calling for an abort," he began.

"Too late for that," Warchild yelled back, not bothering with the radio while getting to his feet and checking his rifle. "We all know Mason Kane is chickenshit."

Renee knew there was nothing else she could do. She tried one more time to get hold of Mason before slipping her left arm through the strap of her assault pack.

"Hey, stop fucking with the radio and pay attention," Warchild yelled the moment she let go of the push-to-talk button and slung her rifle.

"Two minutes out," the pilot said calmly as he dropped the helo closer to the ground. He cut the nose north and pushed the throttle forward.

The two door gunners leaned out of the bird to get a better look at the ground. Meanwhile, the crew chief lowered the ramp before taking his seat behind the 240 Bravo machine gun mounted to the floor.

The helo came in so low that the heavy prop wash blew laid-out clothes and sleeping mats off the roofs of the houses, casting them high into the air as it passed over. Renee saw armed men running out onto the roofs, their rifles aimed up at the bird as the pilot twisted it back and forth across the sky.

The city definitely wasn't empty.

Renee looked anxiously toward the cockpit. Through the dirty windscreen, tracers flashed past the lead Mi-17.

"Put us on the ground," she begged half aloud.

The 240 Bravo chattered behind her, and she snapped her head back to the ramp in time to see tracer fire bending up toward the bird like a whip cracking toward flesh. The gunner fired another long burst, sweeping the machine gun across a rooftop just as enemy tracers curled into a half moon and cut across the bottom of the helicopter.

The rounds hitting the thin skin of the helo sounded like hail beating on a tin roof. The electric motors of the door gunners' GAU-17 miniguns spooled up with a buzz. A split second later, they came to life with a *waaaaamp* as the gunners returned fire.

Even though they held down the trigger for only a dozen seconds, Renee knew that they had fired almost a thousand rounds apiece. The ground fire stopped immediately, but the knot in her stomach did not unclench.

"One minute," the pilot said, checking his air speed.

The Mi-17 slowed, dropping the ass end toward the ground as it flared for a landing. The engine strained and the rotors angrily beat the air, washing a brown cloud of sand and dirt over the bird as it hovered.

Before she lost visibility, Renee caught a flash of light erupt from a rooftop just below the lead helo. In that instant, everything went wrong.

The unmistakable trail of the surface-to-air missile arced toward the defenseless Mi-17. It disappeared in the dust cloud, but the heat-seeking missile didn't need to *see* to find its target. It was locked onto the heat pouring from the engine, and Renee knew it would cover the hundred yards in the blink of an eye.

The dust cloud parted suddenly, giving her a clear view of the missile as it slammed into the engine cowling of the lead helo. It exploded in a ball of flame. The rotors, sheared off at the base, peeled back the top section of the Russian bird like a can opener. The tail veered violently to the right, and as the Mi-17 lost lift, it pitched forward and slammed into the ground.

Renee heard the door gunner yell, "RPG, right side." The flame spouting from the minigun reflected off his helmet as he twisted it toward where the missile had been fired.

The pilot jerked the bird to the left, throwing Renee hard against the skin of the helicopter. The copilot rushed to apply power. The bird sluggishly tried to respond, but the opened ramp caught the side of a building.

The nose of the chopper was abruptly forced down. Renee felt her feet slip out from under her, and she grabbed hold of the nylon bench as the bird began to yaw. The pilot was trying to get the nose up, and she slipped toward the open ramp, her rifle banging against her knees. With a panicked cry, the crew chief tumbled off the ramp.

He disappeared, and the safety line attached to his back jerked taut as he fell toward the ground.

She heard herself yelling over the screaming rotors, amid dinging warning bells. Then a bright ball of flame erupted near the tail rotor, spewing flame and hot gases into the troop compartment.

As the helo slipped hard to the left, the rotors clipped the side of a building. They disintegrated in a shrieking jumble of metallic shards, carving off concrete chunks. The Mi-17 hovered weightless for a split second, and then everything went black and it dropped toward the hard ground below.

CHAPTER 7

- - - - - - - - - - - - **Washington, DC**

Lieutenant General Patrick Vann had finally managed to drift off to sleep when his work phone erupted from the bedside table. Turning onto his side, he reached for the phone vibrating defiantly on the overpriced nightstand his wife had bought during one of her famous shopping sprees at Restoration Hardware.

The general had no idea why she would pay so much for a piece of furniture that had been purposely distressed, but right now his only concern was to answer the phone before it woke her up.

By the time he grabbed it, ripping the charger from the jack at the bottom, he felt her begin to stir beside him.

"Patrick, Jesus, it's two in the morning," she moaned, yanking on the covers.

"Go back to bed, baby; I'm sorry," he said as he climbed out of bed.

"This better be good," he grumbled to himself.

"Sir, it's Anderson. We have a situation."

"Goddamn it, what now?"

"It's Ronin 6. He called for an abort, and now the situation is going to hell."

General Vann fumbled in the dark, trying to get to the bathroom, when he jammed his toe against the side of the bed.

"Shit," he swore.

"Patrick." His wife's muffled voice chastised him from the depths of her pillows.

"Sorry, baby," he said, covering the phone as he stepped into the bathroom. The cold tiles at least soothed the bottom of his throbbing foot.

"Say that again."

"Sir, Ronin 6 called for an abort. Next thing we know, the strike team choppers are attacked. What do you want to do?"

"Did he say why?" the general demanded, closing the door behind him as he ran his hands up the wall in search of the light switch.

The lights came on in a blaze, burning his eyes. He caught his reflection in the mirror. He looked like a haggard and pissed-off old man.

"No sir, and we can't get him back on the net."

"Screw him. What about Boland?" he demanded, knowing that was all his boss cared about.

Mason Kane was a pain in his ass, and the only reason that he and his Libyan flunky were on the mission was because he was the only asset close enough to get there before the air assault.

"Yes sir, he and the source are en route to the objective. But the strike team took heavy fire before they landed, and one of the choppers took what we think was a surface-to-air missile."

Vann ran his hand through his thick black hair as he mentally walked through the hastily set-up operation. He had advised against launching so soon, but Simmons had said this came directly from the SecDef. There was too much risk involved, and despite his boss's promise that they could trust the source, Vann had his doubts all along.

"Do we have a Predator over the crash site?" he asked, referring to the drones.

"Roger that, sir," Anderson replied curtly.

"Is it armed?"

"Negative."

"Damn it. Okay—get a Reaper diverted with some ass. We might be able to pull this off, but I need assets overhead."

"What about Mason?"

"Keep him out of this."

"I know, sir, but it was my understanding that the boss was trying to kill two birds with one stone."

"Just keep me informed, and I'll get back to you."

Hurrying into the bedroom, the general opened the closet, where a fresh uniform was waiting. He was on the road five minutes later. Since the operation was being run through Simmons, Vann couldn't call Secretary of Defense Cage directly, and Simmons was too experienced to come out and say that he wanted an American asset terminated. Vann was good at reading between the lines, but he wanted to be sure before he killed Ronin 6.

Typing Simmons's number from memory, he ran his hand over his face and realized he'd forgotten to shave.

It wasn't even a quarter to three yet, and the day had already gone to hell. Still, with just a little bit of luck, he might just be able to pull this one off.

CHAPTER 8

- - - - - - - - - - - - -

Mason was halfway down the stairs when he heard the choppers coming in, followed by a loud explosion. He pushed past Zeus, making his way back to the roof in time to see the second Mi-17 lose lift and rotate drunkenly toward the ground. He watched the nose dip and then lost the bird as it disappeared below the cityscape.

The sound of metal slamming into brick screeched over the buildings like a passenger train derailing. A mushroom of dust rose slowly from the crash site and hovered over the shattered skyline, followed by a moment of stark silence. It was as if the city were holding its breath, waiting to see what was next.

Then a solitary gunshot broke the spell, spilling jihadists onto the street.

Mason was torn between racing to save Boland and the men he knew were trapped in the back of the crashed helo. He'd once been in a Chinook downed by ground fire in Afghanistan and knew firsthand that it took a minute before you were able to defend yourself. Mason had to do something to give them the time they needed to get into the fight, and as soon as he saw the two Technicals—Toyota pickups with crew-served weapons mounted to their beds—bouncing across the road that snaked in front of the downed helo, he knew he couldn't leave.

One of the pilots managed to drag himself out the window of the crippled Mi-17—just as the truck slammed on its brakes and the fighters jammed into the bed of the truck began leaping to the ground.

Mason could see blood staining the soldier's tan flight suit as he struggled out of the shattered cockpit and immediately came under point-blank fire. The first rounds hit him low in the back, and he tried to crawl for cover, but halfway there his head snapped forward, and he lay still.

Mason moved to the DShK mounted behind the sandbags at the edge of the roof and yanked the charging handle to the rear before shouting into his radio, "We have two birds down. Get ready to move to the crash site."

"Roger that, boss," Grinch replied a second later.

He swung the heavy gun onto the men rushing the helo and grimly depressed the butterfly trigger. The .51 caliber rounds rocked the gun on its tripod as he fired a short burst at the lead vehicle. Mason was trying to hit the gunner, who was perched precariously on the bed, but the first rounds fell short. Raising the muzzle, he felt his body shake from the recoil as he walked the armor-piercing rounds up the side of the technical, blowing the jihadist off the gun.

As Mason smoothly worked the rounds over the cab, the expended brass tinkled against the concrete roof like fat drops of rain. Suddenly the vehicle exploded, showering the ground with shards of debris, and Mason felt he'd bought the strike team enough time.

Now it was time to go after Boland.

He could hear someone yelling behind him, and let off the trigger long enough to see Zeus pointing at his radio.

Mason lowered his head to the hand mike, straining to hear what was coming over the net.

"Ronin 6, Tomahawk Base, we need you to secure the objective and stand by for follow-on troops," the voice commanded.

Mason knew there weren't any more troops coming, but if he followed orders, it meant leaving Boland to fend for himself. Remembering the photo they had found downstairs, he knew that his friend was walking into a trap.

He'd pulled some strings to get Boland a spot on the Defense Intelligence Agency's short list after Mick found out that his wife had zeroed out their bank account and skipped town. When his old friend had reached out for help, Mason thought he was doing him a favor, getting him a job with the DOD.

Stepping out into the room, Mason turned to face Zeus. "It's not open for discussion," he said tersely. "He's in this position because of me, and you know that."

"You are the patron saint of lost causes, you know that?" the Libyan yelled back, refusing to back down. "You got him a job, and that's it. He's the one who got picked up by al Nusra."

Zeus wasn't about to let Mason cloud the issue. They both knew that something had happened to Boland two weeks before the mission launched, and it was now blatantly obvious that the mission was not what it appeared to be.

"They knew we were coming, and we need to get the fuck out of here while we still can."

Grinch entered the room, cutting the conversation short.

"You guys need to check this out," the sniper said, holding up a handful of documents he'd found downstairs.

"What is it?" Mason demanded, more forcibly than he'd intended.

"First, calm the fuck down," Grinch said, holding out the pages. "It's a copy of the operation plan, in Farsi."

"I told you, we need to get out of here," Zeus said wearily, taking the pages.

There was a sudden exchange of gunfire downstairs, followed by Blaine shouting over the radio.

"You guys need to get down here. T.J.'s been hit bad."

"Fuck," Mason yelled, sprinting out of the room.

The first thing they saw when they made it to the ground floor was T.J. lying next to a window, his kit covered in blood. Empty shells littered the floor, and two dead jihadists were sprawled on the far side of the room. To Mason's left, a tattered couch sat at an odd angle near a wall that had been blown open.

"They came out of the spider hole," T.J. gasped. "I fucked up, man . . ."

"You're fine—stay with me," Blaine said, working to control the bleeding.

"Can he move?" Mason asked.

Blaine was one of the best medics he'd ever worked with, but Mason could tell immediately that even he couldn't save the man bleeding out on the floor.

"He's lost too much blood."

"T.J., we're going to get you out of here," Mason said, taking a knee next to the man.

A faint smile creased the dying man's face, and he tried to laugh.

"Yeah, okay, boss," he whispered, a second before going into convulsions.

T.J. was choking on his own blood, and the spatter that came out of his mouth dripped thickly down his cheek before pooling on the floor.

Mason had seen dying men before, but when T.J.'s eyes rolled back into his head, and his body seized one final time, a shot of pain raced straight through Mason's heart. The bonds the five men had formed in their brief time together were stronger than most people would ever know.

Just then, the claymore mine attached to the door exploded as someone tried to force his way into the building. Gunfire erupted through a window to the east, sending the squad scattering.

Blaine dove onto his fallen comrade, covering him with his body as rounds snapped through the room, filling it with smoke and cordite. Outside the building, a man screamed in pain, his legs torn completely off from the blast of the claymore.

"Mason, make a decision," Zeus yelled.

"We have to split up," Mason instructed. "Zeus, you and me will go after Boland. You two, head to the crash site. I have no idea how many are out there, but if the Reaper is armed, we might be able to buy some time."

"He's gone, bro. There's nothing you can do for him now," Grinch said, pulling the medic off T.J., whose sightless eyes stared at the ceiling.

"We have to move, now," Mason yelled.

Leaving T.J.'s body for the enemy was the hardest decision Mason Kane had ever been forced to make, and he knew that Blaine felt the same way. It went against everything they had been taught, but Grinch didn't hesitate. The sniper grabbed the medic by the arm, pulling him away from T.J.

"See you on the other side," he shouted, pushing Blaine toward the spider hole.

CHAPTER 9

- - - - - - - - - - -

Renee opened her eyes, blinking at the beam of sunlight streaming in through the shattered window of the cargo compartment. The sun was warm inside the dim confines of the smoking helo, and it felt good on her face. She felt protected—while outside everything was going to shit.

She could hear the deep snaps of the AK-47 and the lighter pops of the M4s returning fire as she stared up at the puffy white clouds drifting peacefully across the deep blue sky.

"Get the fuck up," she told herself.

It took a huge effort to get to her feet, and, for a second, she just stood there, squinting against the stark brightness pouring in from the shattered ramp. Renee checked her rifle and grabbed the assault pack that had been ripped off her back. Carefully, she made her way to where the ramp lay crumpled against the back of the bird.

She hopped down, feeling a burning pain in her

leg. Suddenly a black-clad fighter opened up on her from twenty meters away.

Her M4 snapped up, and she flipped the safety off before even realizing the rifle was moving. She fired twice, hitting the man in the chest; but instead of going down, he charged at her. Not backing off an inch, Renee settled the reticle of the EOTech holographic sight on his forehead and pulled the trigger firmly to the rear.

The round hit the man in the side of the head, blowing his brains out the back of his skull and pitching him forward onto the ground.

She scanned her sector before looking down at her leg. A twisted shard of metal, glistening with her blood, was sticking out of her thigh, and Renee winced as she grabbed hold of it. The pain came in a white-hot wave, slamming up through her stomach, forcing her to let go. Taking a deep breath, she closed her gloved fist around the metal and yanked it out.

"Fuuuck."

Blood poured from the wound, puddling near her feet, where it mixed with the dirt of the crash site. Renee grimaced, twisting her torso to gain access to the trauma kit attached to the back of her kit. Needing to control the bleeding or risk being out of the fight, she quickly pulled out a roll of gauze.

"Tomahawk Base to Savage 7, request sitrep, over," the radio squawked.

"You want a situation report now?" Renee muttered, limping to cover. With shaking hands, she ripped open the sterile package and packed the gauze into the wound. The pain was intense, but she bit down on her lip and finished the job.

Taking a cravat from her kit, Renee wrapped it as tight as she could around her leg and stoically tied a knot over the wound just as Sergeant Major Mitchell came around the corner.

"Fuck you," he yelled while firing into a jihadist who was creeping toward the downed helo.

"Are you good?"

Renee gingerly got to her feet and hobbled over to Mitchell. She could see that the rest of the team had already set up a defensive perimeter near the front of the bird, and despite some scrapes and bruises, everyone was ready to fight.

"Tomahawk Base, Savage 7 Romeo, stand by," she said into the radio as Warchild began barking orders.

"Parker, I need you and your team to set up overwatch while we hit the objective. I need you," he said, pointing at Renee, "to get CAS on station and get us a ride out of here."

The man might be an asshole, but in combat he was as cold as ice, and right now it was all that mattered.

"Tomahawk Base, Savage 7 Romeo. Be advised we are moving to target location time now. Request immediate close air support and extraction at LZ Bravo. How copy?"

"Roger that, 7 Romeo. Be advised you have multiple hostiles moving in from your northeast and west."

"Shit. Hey, they're moving on us," she said to Parker as the team moved out.

The bird had gone down less than five hundred meters from the target location, but a warren of narrow streets separated the two points and funneled the team down a natural choke point. The tight alleys, recessed doorways, and windows made it a perfect kill zone; and worst of all, it was the only way out.

Parker and his team sprinted ahead of the squad and set up security. Mitchell was just getting posted up when a burst of gunfire erupted from a building off to his right. A bullet slammed into the side of his helmet, knocking him off-balance, and when he turned to engage the shooter, a round cut through his arm. The sergeant major tumbled to the ground in a cloud of dust. Instinctively, Renee snapped her muzzle toward the threat and fired three quick shots, hitting the jihadist in the chest before rushing to Mitchell's side.

"Help me up," he bellowed.

Renee reached down and tried to lift him off the ground, but his imposing bulk was too much for her.

"Warchild," she yelled. Her team leader stepped into the street, firing as he moved. Three fighters rushed around the corner, firing on full auto, their AKs blazing as they charged him. Warchild stopped and, like a gunfighter from the wild west, calmly took aim and engaged—it was suddenly clear how he'd earned his nickname.

He was born for combat, and once his blood-lust was up, there was no stopping him. His finger danced across the trigger and cut the men down in the street.

"Warchild, fucking help me," she yelled again.

The team knew what it was doing, fighting its way to the objective without the need to communicate. While the enemy fire picked up all around them, they flowed off one another like water searching for cracks in a dam.

Her team leader forcibly removed himself from the battle, and he glared angrily at her before reaching down and grabbing Mitchell's left arm.

"What the fuck are you good for?" Warchild demanded as they struggled to get the sergeant major to his feet.

"You're such an asshole," she yelled back, bracing herself against Mitchell's weight.

"This is no place for a woman—"

"Behind you," she shouted just as two men appeared on a roof three feet over their heads and fired down on the team.

Renee stepped forward, placing herself in front of Mitchell. She felt the rounds pound into her chest, knocking the breath out of her and slamming her into the sergeant major. Her momentum knocked Mitchell out of the line of fire while her finger closed around the trigger.

The rifle bucked in her hands as one of the men pointed his AK at Warchild. Her chest was on fire, but she managed to gather up the last bit of energy and shove her team leader out of the way.

The expended brass glinted in the sun as it cart-wheeled from her rifle, and the fighter went down, a reddish mist flowering out from his leg. Renee gasped for breath, brought the rifle up to her shoulder, and put two rounds center mass of the second jihadist before dropping to one knee.

Warchild grabbed Renee by the back of her kit, pulling her to her feet while she checked herself for holes.

"Get off me," she managed, pulling herself free in order to help Mitchell.

She noticed the strange expression in her team leader's eyes as he realized she'd just saved his life.

"You're a beast," Mitchell praised, ignoring Warchild, who moved, unbidden, to her side and helped move him to cover.

CHAPTER 10

Al Qatar had been holding on to his revenge for so long that he could barely believe all his plans were finally coming to fruition. As he led Boland deeper into the building, he was hard-pressed to hide the smile that threatened to creep across his face.

Just like the men he was going to meet, the American had no idea that he was a pawn in a much larger game, one where al Qatar was finally the master. He'd grown tired of the baseless rhetoric the imams used to convince their impressionable fighters to die for their dogma. The only way he could strike a blow the Americans would never forget was to take his destiny upon himself.

"Did you hear that?" Boland asked, straining against the large duffel bag he was carrying.

Al Qatar had hoped the thick walls would muffle the sounds of the chaos unfolding outside, but that was obviously not possible any longer.

"We must hurry, Latif is waiting," al Qatar said, his heart pounding in his chest.

"Something's going on."

"The fighting never stops, you know that," the Iraqi said, coming to a set of rickety wooden stairs.

The building had been a bank before the war, but instead of a vault, what little money was stored here had been put in the reinforced basement. The stairs might have seen better days, but the subterranean chamber was modern, with a generator-powered lighting system and large metal safes lining one wall.

In the middle of the room, the two most wanted men in Syria stood side by side, watching al Qatar make his way over.

"I was beginning to think you had forgotten about me, Abu," Latif said, blowing a jet of smoke up toward the low ceiling.

"I apologize for making you wait. We were held up by one of your checkpoints," al Qatar said.

"Well, at least you brought my money. Who is this?" Latif asked.

"It is the man I told you about: Hamid. He was sent by the emir."

"It is a pleasure," the Syrian said, turning to Khalid, who eyed Boland silently.

Al Qatar knew the American had activated his GPS beacon the moment he got out of the car, but he was confident that the heavy walls would interfere with the transmission. He had no intention of falling prey to a drone strike, and if his men were doing their job—watching the feed he had spent so long setting up—it shouldn't be a problem.

"The pleasure is all mine," Boland began. "The emir Baghdadi sends his warmest regards. He prays that you will accept this humble token of his appreciation."

Latif smiled broadly, and when he took the duffel bag full of money, three other men materialized from the shadows.

One of them was carrying a black Pelican case. Right away al Qatar noticed that Boland was unable to take his eyes off it. The American moved his hand slowly to his pistol, while Latif knelt down and began digging through the pile of neatly banded stacks of cash, unaware of Boland's furtive movements.

But Khalid never took his eyes off the American, and as Boland took a step to the side, a thin smile played across his face.

The American's pistol flashed from its holster in a compact draw borne from countless repetitions. He almost had the front sight on his target when al Qatar took a sudden step forward and cracked Boland on the back of the neck with the leather sap he'd hidden in his pocket.

The American fell to his knees, the pistol clattering across the floor. Shouting in anger, Khalid's men raised their rifles. Boland's face showed a mixture of surprise and confusion; it was obvious that he hadn't planned for the betrayal.

Al Qatar scooped the pistol from the floor and

stepped out of his reach before turning his attention to Latif.

"Step away from the money, brother," he said.

"What is this?" the Syrian asked, slowly getting to his feet.

"Business," al Qatar replied before shooting the man in the face.

The shot echoed loudly in the confines of the basement, reverberating off the walls in a deafening roar. The bullet snapped the Syrian's head back and blew his brains out the back of his skull.

"He was a savage man. Very stupid," the Iranian chuckled, looking down at Boland with a savage grin.

"It seems that you have had nothing but bad luck since you lost this," Khalid said, motioning to the Pelican case, which held the equipment Boland had lost a few weeks earlier. "I would have thought you learned your lesson the last time we met, but alas, I was wrong."

"Fuck you," Boland groaned.

"Did you tell your American masters that you lost it, or did you lie to them as well?"

"Just kill me, and get it over with."

"Oh, you will die, but it will be very slow," al Qatar said, slamming the pistol across the American's face. He knelt down beside the American and grabbed his hair, forcing his head up.

"You don't remember me, do you? Well, I am not surprised; it was quite a long time ago when we first met."

Boland was bleeding from his mouth, and his

nose was broken. Al Qatar let go of his hair, and Boland rolled onto his side and spit half a tooth onto the filthy concrete floor.

"What the fuck are you talking about?" Boland panted as al Qatar stood up.

"We have plenty of time to talk. I just wanted you to know that I have been dreaming about this day since you killed my brother."

"We need to go," one of Khalid's men said, checking his watch.

"Very well. Give me the case and help me carry him to the car," al Qatar instructed.

"What about our agreement? I do not see what you promised in here," Khalid said, pointing down at the bag.

"You are going to have to trust me. I will have it for you by the week's end."

"Trust didn't work out so well for him," the Iranian said, motioning to the bleeding American.

"Give me the case."

Khalid studied the Iraqi for a long moment before nodding to his man, who handed the case off to al Qatar.

"If you prove to be untrue, things will not go well for you."

"Have I ever failed you?"

"Not yet, but there is a first time for everything," the Iranian said, smiling. "Bind him," he ordered his men.

The Iranians slipped a pair of zip ties over Boland's wrists and pulled them tight with a plastic click. After placing a black bag over his head, they lifted him to his feet. Then, without a word, they retreated to the back of the basement.

"One more thing," al Qatar said to Boland.

He took the small emergency beacon from the hidden pocket in the American's pants and tossed it to the ground. "We won't be needing this anymore."

CHAPTER 11

------------- Operations Center

It took General Vann fifteen minutes to get to the office, and that was with his driver keeping the government Chevy Tahoe at ninety. Despite the early hour, the Beltway had a sprinkling of cars taking professionals into the city, and as his driver weaved through the sparse traffic, Vann knew that every second could be the difference between life and death.

Vann's driver let off the gas long enough for the armed guard posted at the entrance of the subterranean garage to open the gate, and the tires squealed on the black pavement as he brought the Tahoe to a halt near the secure express elevator. The general hopped out of the backseat, slamming the door behind him before heading to the secure express elevator.

Placing his hand on the biometric scanner, Vann waited for the stainless steel doors to slide open and then inserted his keycard into the magnetic reader mounted to the panel. The small LED light switched from red to green, the doors closed, and the elevator shot up toward the top floor.

The car came to a silent halt, and the doors opened, revealing the general's aide standing patiently with a steaming cup of coffee in his hand.

"Here you go, boss," Captain Chad Brantley said, offering the cup to the general.

"Where are we?" Vann asked while they walked down a nondescript hallway, passing his office on the left.

Captain Brantley looked every inch the soldier, despite wearing civilian clothes. His dark beard was neatly trimmed, and his skin held the burnished bronze of a man who spent most of his time outdoors. His thick neck and broad shoulders gave him the look of a college linebacker, but he possessed a catlike grace that hinted at a deeper, predatory nature.

"It's a shit show, sir," he said, waving his identification card over the reader attached to the solid steel door.

The lock disengaged with a metallic click, and Vann took a sip of coffee before stepping into the chaos of the tactical operations center, or TOC. The general had developed a taste for strong Arabian coffee during his time in Yemen, and insisted that his staff keep a pot going at all times. He drank five or six cups a day.

As the deputy director of the DIA, Vann had the unenviable burden of keeping tabs on the jihadists who flowed into Syria like water from a broken dam, and the TOC was the nerve center of his un-enviable task.

He had made a name for himself in Iraq. As a member of Task Force 121, his crowning moment came in 2006, when his men found and killed Abu Musab al-Zarqawi—Osama bin Laden's heir apparent in Iraq in 2006. Vann was known for getting results, and he had left a trail of bodies as proof of his lethal abilities.

But this was different. Unlike his time in Iraq and Afghanistan, he didn't have the assets to get his people out of trouble. Worse than that, the general knew that there was no end in sight to the war he had been fighting since 2001. America was finally learning that there was absolutely no way it could kill its way out of this war, but that didn't mean the United States wasn't going to try.

The TOC was always a frantic place, but with an active mission under way, it bordered on chaotic. Individual monitors covered the walls, but the room was dominated by a large screen, upon which the Reaper drone beamed a clear feed back to the States. Vann's team members either sat before their monitors or moved briskly from station to station, passing pertinent intel. At the moment, everyone was focused on the two smoking birds lying stricken on the ground in Syria.

"They really fucked us on this one, sir," Captain Brantley said while Vann took his place at the center of the bustling room.

The general studied the downed helos and took

another sip of the coffee. There was way too much movement on the edges of the crash site. Jihadists flooded the area, but it was the lack of movement from any friendlies *around* the birds that made his stomach sink.

"What happened?"

"We think they used a MANPAD on the first bird."

"Where the hell are they getting surface-to-air missiles?"

"No idea, sir. We assume they must have limited numbers because they used an RPG to knock out the second bird. I have no idea how the pilot managed to get it on the ground," he said, pointing to the second craft, which was lodged between two buildings fifty feet from the first.

As Vann stared at the mangled tail section of the Mi-17, a figure slowly emerged from the cargo compartment. Instead of elation, the general felt a weight slowly begin pressing down on his shoulders, because he knew that now he had to find a way to get them out.

"Well, shit," he said grimly. "Someone get Anderson on the phone. Tell him I need an extraction team in the air in ten minutes, and get a fucking satellite diverted."

"Already done, sir. It should be coming online right about now," a man said, pointing up to the screen just as another feed appeared.

The general put the empty styrofoam cup on the edge of the table and reached into his pocket for an unopened can of dip. He used his thumbnail to pierce the thin paper that separated the lid from the can and said, "Find Boland."

The Reaper Brantley had "borrowed" from the CIA banked to the left, and the operator panned out with the powerful camera.

"Got him," an NCO—or noncommissioned officer—said, pointing out the light-blue Toyota Corolla that was pulling up to the objective.

Vann lifted the gold lid off the can of Copenhagen Long Cut, and used his fingers to pinch the dark tobacco together. It burned against his lip, and the nicotine coursing through his body was tinged with guilt.

"What do you think?" he asked Brantley, never taking his eyes off the two men who got out of the car and jogged toward the building.

"Depends on what you want, sir."

Besides Vann and Captain Brantley, the only other people who knew the real reason they had launched the mission were SecDef Cage and National Security Advisor Simmons. Like many others who'd served with Cage, Vann considered him the only man still dedicated to purifying America's honor after the shame of Iraq, and he would do whatever was necessary to ensure that he carried out his boss's mandates.

"I want to clean up Boland's mess and get on with the plan," he said honestly.

"Well, then, I think you know what to do."

"Striker has activated his beacon," one of the

men said as Boland disappeared into the building.

"How could Boland have been so reckless?" Vann asked, knowing the answer already.

"Everyone has a breaking point, sir."

The easiest thing for the general to do was call in a flight of F-18 Super Hornet combat jets and level the building. If Khalid al Hamas was really in there, he could end half of his problems with one strike—but there was just no way of knowing until Boland did his part.

Vann had a special hatred for the Iranian operative, and for spies in general. The fact that Khalid had strong ties to al Nusra and al Qaeda made him a very attractive notch for his war belt. He itched to give the word to fire. And if the American died, well, so be it.

CHAPTER 12

Operation Save Boland was under way as Mason stepped cautiously out into the street. He was hurrying to cover when a yell drew his attention to the end of the block. A group of fighters emerged from the shattered doorway of a building, firing as they caught sight of the American. Mason ducked below the rounds that splintered into the wall and brought the Kalashnikov up to his shoulders and fired.

The Russian assault rifle wasn't as accurate as the HK he liked to carry, but at close range, it was much more effective. The heavy 7.62 round smacked his target with enough force to knock him off his feet, and Mason smoothly transitioned over to a fighter lining up on him with his RPG.

The jihadist managed to squeeze the trigger a split second before Mason fired, and the rocket-propelled grenade screamed over Mason's head before detonating in a cloud of black smoke.

The heavily damaged buildings and rubble-strewn streets were a nightmare of tight spaces and improvised cover, and the enemy knew how to use it to its advantage. Mason knew that if he and Zeus were pinned down, they would die in the street. He ducked under the flying debris and shouted, "Zeus, we gotta move."

Bent double, the Libyan ran to an adjacent position as the American lay down suppressive fire. The jihadists were swarming through the area, on their way to the crash site, and some of them stopped to engage Mason's team before they ran past.

Acrid black smoke and the stench of cordite hung over the area as Blaine and Grinch squeezed out of the jagged spider hole to Mason's rear and headed immediately for the downed aircraft. Mason paused to watch them slip onto the street, hoping this wasn't the last time he'd see them.

They counted on him to keep them safe, but he was sending them into harm's way, which made him feel like shit. Like him, they knew what they had signed on for, but sending them out into the chaos that was unfolding on the next street over was well above the call of duty.

Mason had wasted valuable time covering Renee, and as a result he and Zeus had lost what little advantage they had. Mason's battered body already taken a beating, and he wondered if he still had enough left in the tank to make it out alive.

"Focus," he told himself, turning his attention back to the street.

The two men bounded up the street, one firing

while the other moved, stopping only to strip magazines off the dead. Reaching the end of the street, they finally caught a glimpse of the objective.

But they still had a long way to go.

Mason heard the sounds of a heavy gun firing just around the corner, and when he poked his head out to get a better look, he saw that it was coming from a Russian ZPU-1 antiaircraft gun mounted to the back of a Toyota Hilux. A fighter standing to the right of the truck was providing rear security, and when he spotted Mason peeking around the corner, he ripped off a long burst from the PKM he held low on his hip. The machine gun was nothing more than a robust AK-47, and as it bucked in the man's skinny arms, the rounds sailed harmlessly past Mason's head.

"Give me a break," he said to himself.

The firing died suddenly as the ZPU jammed. The gunner began cursing and hammered his fist on the feed tray in an attempt to clear a jam.

Mason wasn't too worried about the PKM, but he needed to move before the fighters got the ZPU back into action. Taking a deep breath, he shot out from cover, racing toward the blackened, burned-out vehicle. As he passed, he caught sight of a charred teddy bear lying forlorn in the middle of the street, a silent memento of the war's destruction.

"*Allahu Akbar . . . Allahu Akbar,*" the man wielding the PKM bellowed at the top of his lungs, chasing Mason across the open space with a wild burst from his machine gun. Behind him, Zeus calmly braced his rifle on the side of the building and put a bullet in the fighter's head.

Mason was almost to cover when rounds began pinging off the hulk he was hoping to hide behind. Zigzagging desperately, he could hear the rounds buzzing past his head like hornets as he dove behind the car.

"They're behind us," Zeus yelled while firing. Now he was the exposed one, and Mason hugged the scorched bumper of the car, trying to cover his friend.

Mason counted five men, and he expected them to rush Zeus, but instead they set up a base of fire and began maneuvering down the street, hoping to pin down the Libyan until they got close enough to deliver the kill shot.

Another RPG shrieked down the street. "Zeus," Mason yelled. "Take cover."

The rocket impacted short of its intended target, and the Libyan ducked behind a slab of concrete. The explosion blew up a cloud of smoke, which provided enough concealment for Zeus to link up with Mason.

Mason saw a figure rushing through the haze and took him down with a single shot from the AK, while one of his comrades filled the gap instantly and laid suppressive fire on the two men hiding behind the car.

The ZPU gunner finally cleared the jam and began blasting away, mercifully oblivious to the firefight unfolding behind him. Zeus stripped a smoke grenade from his kit and pulled the pin a moment before tossing it into the middle of the street. Mason hammered through the remainder of his mag, trying desperately to keep from getting overrun.

"Reloading." he yelled, snatching a fresh one from his kit. In tandem, Zeus picked up his rate of fire. The Libyan was on his knee, firing at the advancing jihadists, but still they managed to get within ten feet of their position. Mason got his rifle back up, slapped his friend on the shoulder, and pointed out the only cover left on the street, an ancient wagon filled with firewood.

"Moving," Zeus yelled, as Mason flipped the rifle to full auto, ripping a long burst through the white smoke billowing up from the canister. He fired waist high, forcing the enemy to dive to the ground while Zeus bounded toward the wagon.

The gunner of the ZPU caught sight of the Libyan out of his peripheral and frantically traversed the gun in hopes of nailing him. A line of tracers zipped across the street, and Mason flipped the AK back to semi, braced the smoking-hot barrel against the hood of the car, and pulled the trigger gently. The first round was high, and the American cursed the Kalashnikov as the ZPU cut into the wagon.

"Piece of shit," he yelled, pulling the AK tight against his shoulder. The rounds hammered the wagon, sending shards of splintered wood over the top of Zeus's head, forcing him to the ground behind it. Zeus knew he couldn't stay behind the wagon, and before Mason could reengage, he got to his feet and darted out into the open.

Mason saw a tracer round snap dangerously

close to his friend's head before closing his left eye and gently pulling the trigger to the rear. The shot broke, snapping the muzzle of his AK up as it went off. The round caught the jihadist at the base of the neck, bowling him onto the cab of the pickup.

Mason let out a low whistle and gave the notoriously inaccurate rifle a kiss just as Zeus finally ensconced himself in a recessed door frame on the north side of the target building.

The American could see his chest heaving from the sprint and waited for him to start firing before running across to join him. Together they popped the door to the objective and slipped silently into the dimly lit interior.

Mason's radio squawked as they came to an open door leading down to the basement. "All elements, be advised, the Reaper is cleared hot on the objective."

"Tomahawk Base, Ronin 6, be advised we are inside the objective," he whispered into the radio, turning down the volume as they moved down the steps.

"Ronin . . . say . . . again . . ." the radio squelched as they descended underground.

"Tomahawk Base, I say again, we are inside the target building."

Static hissed through the hand mike, and Mason knew that his transmission hadn't gone through.

"Comms are down," he whispered as they moved to the base of the rickety stairs.

"That is a clear sign that we need to get the hell out of here," Zeus replied.

"You're not telling me anything new."

Mason swept left digging his hard corner, while Zeus took the right. He kept his finger outside the trigger guard, scanning slowly across the room for any imminent threats.

"Moving," he whispered.

"Move," Zeus answered.

He stepped deeper into the basement, trying to cover the angles while his teammate covered him. Then he saw a body.

"Shit," he said, rushing over to see if it was Boland, but as he drew near, it was immediately obvious that this was not his friend. Next to the dead man, he noticed an object lying on the ground, framed by a collection of sharp boot prints that were cut into the dusty floor. He recognized it as a military-grade emergency beacon, and assumed at once that it belonged to Boland.

"They were just here," he said, squatting down to grab the beacon off the floor.

"We don't have time for this," the Libyan replied.

Ignoring him, Mason held the beacon in front of his face, taking in the tiny LED light that blinked red to show that it was not tracking. Whoever had led Boland into the basement knew enough about military hardware to realize that the satellite would be unable to track the beacon this far underground. It was becoming increasingly more obvious that there was something much bigger at play than grabbing a high-value target.

After stuffing the beacon into his pocket, he examined the prints, looking for anything that would tell of their owners. Besides their sharp, well-defined edges, Mason could tell that they were fresh by the lack of any dust in the center of the print.

Mason studied the trail, watching it disappear into the depths of the basement, and moved to follow the tracks despite Zeus's warning, "Come on, we don't have time." If Boland went this way, Mason was going to find him.

Near the far wall, a solitary bulb cast a sallow glow over a jagged hole that had been cut into the building. He panned to the far right of the opening, the AK pressed against his shoulder. Mason tried to get a look inside without silhouetting himself. Someone had gone to a lot of trouble to tunnel through the floor of the basement.

Mason was just about to step through when Zeus grabbed him by the shoulder and pointed to his ears.

Mason's ears felt like they were full of cotton after the gunfight in the street, and the only thing he heard was the hammering of his own heart. He shook his head to indicate he hadn't heard anything—when suddenly a faint voice drifted up from the tunnel.

It was all he needed.

"They are going to drop a bomb on this place," Zeus whispered. "We have to get the fuck out of here."

"You know another way out? 'Cause I'm not going back out there," Mason replied, jerking his thumb toward the direction they had come.

"Shit," Zeus hissed. The Libyan was torn, but after a second of contemplation, he nodded his assent. "What a way to go."

Mason had serious doubts himself as he stepped down into the underground passage. The sound of his boots crunching on the gravel that lined the floor made him wince. He took a few more steps before grabbing a handful of soil from the piles that lined both sides of the tunnel. Instead of crumbling, the dirt compacted when he crushed it between his fingers.

It was fresh—most likely not even two days old.

"Someone just dug this," he whispered to Zeus.

"I told you this was a bad idea," his partner said, "but you wouldn't listen. Nooooo, you must always endanger your friend's life."

Mason rolled his eyes, knowing that Zeus had to be curious about what was at the end of the tunnel.

He tossed the dirt on the ground and brushed his hands against his pants before following the tunnel, which sloped down for ten more feet.

Mason knew that any second the Hellfire missile could slam into the building, burying them alive.

Finally, the ground beneath his feet began to level off, and up ahead he could see a halo of light peeking out of the darkness. He slowed, straining to cushion his footfalls on the gravel as they approached the light. Sweat was beginning to pour down his back, and he wiped his forehead on his sleeve before sliding ever so slowly out into a small open area that had been constructed in the middle of the underground passage.

He glanced up at the wooden braces supporting the ceiling before taking in the excavation equipment nearby. Mason slipped over to a large drilling machine and brushed the dirt of a decal that read Sahid Industrial Group.

He didn't recognize the company name, but before he could take a closer look a shout echoed down the tunnel. Both men froze, their rifles pointed at the opening, their ears straining as they waited.

"Just kill him," a voice yelled in Arabic, followed by a meaty slap and a grunt of pain.

Mason flashed forward, the machines forgotten as he trotted up the gentle incline in search of the struggle. Ahead of him, the opening appeared dimly at first, and he froze—just as a shadow flittered across it and a man appeared. Luckily, the large Arab had his back to him.

He could see Boland, struggling, and another man raising the butt of his rifle before slamming it down onto Boland's neck. The captured American dropped to his knees, his face bathed in blood, a moment before one of the men kicked him hard in the stomach.

"Do not kill him," a man ordered as Mason flipped the rifle on to fire.

His finger found the trigger and he began pulling the slack out, when the radio suddenly blared to life.

"All elements, missile away," the voice said.

Why did he have to get reception back now? Mason's left hand shot to the hand mike, but it was too late.

The Arab who had just slammed his Kalashnikov into the back of Boland's head didn't bother to aim. He simply turned and sent a long burst of 7.62s into the tunnel, forcing Mason to dive flat and Zeus to pin himself against the wall.

"The Americans are coming," one of the men yelled.

"Hurry. Hurry," a voice commanded while the shooter hammered through his magazine.

Mason blindly returned fire, but was unable to get a clear shot as his target backed away. Not wanting to lose Boland, he pulled himself over the gravel, low crawling toward the end of the tunnel.

"Seal it."

Mason somehow managed to yank his last frag from his kit as a bullet pinged off the ground, showering his face with dirt and chips of stone. He prayed that Boland was out of the way while ripping the pin of the grenade. He knew that there was a very real chance that he could bring the tunnel crashing down on himself, but he had no intention of letting them seal the exit. With the Hellfire on the way and no other way out, it was the only play he had left.

"Frag out," Mason shouted before tossing it as hard as he could down the tight passage.

The grenade bounced once outside of the exit, and one of the Arabs screamed a short warning as

Mason leapt to his feet. He grabbed Zeus by the arm, yanking him toward the impending explosion. "Don't take Boland yet," he prayed.

He was almost out when the Hellfire slammed into the building.

CHAPTER 13

General Vann watched the hundred-pound missile tear through the roof of the target before detonating inside. The explosion sent a geyser of black smoke and dirt cascading into the sky, totally obscuring the feed.

It took a good ten seconds for the dust to clear, and when it did, he could see flames licking the edge of the massive crater where the roof had just been.

He had witnessed the destructive power of the missile before, but it never got old. The general wished they had something more powerful, but he was limited by the president's unwillingness to bring the full force of America's military might to bear.

"Do you see anything?" he asked Captain Brantley, who scanned the building stoically.

"Hit it again," he said.

Vann didn't hesitate. He ordered the Reaper to reengage.

"Stand by for Hellfire."

The UAV's video feed shook as the second missile shot from the wing-mounted pylon. It took less than five seconds for it to streak across the sky and slam into the target. Once again Vann was left waiting for the smoke to clear.

"Sir, the strike team is about to be overrun," the NCO monitoring the firefight exclaimed.

Vann and Brantley ignored the man, never taking their eyes off the building, which was now three walls and a pile of rubble.

"General Vann?" the man said urgently.

"I heard you," he barked back.

"There is no way to know without someone checking for bodies," Brantley commented, answering his boss's unasked question.

"Are your bags still packed?"

"They stay packed."

"Go," he said simply.

Captain Brantley nodded, before turning to leave the TOC.

"And Chad, I want a clean operation, zero blowback. Call me when you land."

"Roger that, sir."

The general turned his attention to the satellite feed, his mind quickly changing gears.

"How much time do we have left?"

"Not long, sir. The satellite is moving out of range. We are going to lose the feed soon."

"Shift the Reaper over and find me some fast movers," he ordered.

The jihadists had set up a wide perimeter to

keep the strike team from spreading too far from the crash site, and he could already see some of the fighters picking over the first helo.

They were dragging bodies out of the back of the bird, while two blocks to the east, their technicals were laying down a base of fire on Warchild's team, allowing the dismounted soldiers to maneuver on the Americans.

"Put it right in the middle of that formation," Vann said, pointing at a mass of men flooding in from the north.

"Yes sir, stand by for shot."

As he waited for the impact, he was left with the stark reality that he only had one missile left. It wasn't going to be enough to get his men out.

The screen blossomed as the missile slammed into the cab of one of the technicals, tossing what was left high in the air. The overpressure from the explosion ripped into the jihadists gathered around the vehicle, knocking them off their feet. Shards of metal began raining down on them from the sky.

He took his encrypted cell phone from his pocket, knowing that sooner or later he was going to have to brief his boss. Pushing the redial button, he brought the phone to his ear, wondering if he should tell National Security Advisor Jacob Simmons that he was sending Brantley over to monitor the situation.

The general was confident that the young captain would ensure that any loose ends were tied up neatly, but that was small comfort. The plan had spun so far out of control already, what was there to salvage?

He had advised against sending Boland back out after al Nusra had burned him, but the problem with working for Cage was the fact that the defense secretary always kept his cards tight to his chest. Vann knew something much bigger was in play than just trying to recover some stolen equipment, but for the life of him, he couldn't figure out what the bigger objective was.

"It's Vann," he said as soon as Simmons answered the phone.

"What's the status?"

"We hit the building, but we don't have a body count."

"What about Ronin 6?"

Vann could feel a wave of anger rising up inside him. He couldn't care less about Mason Kane right now. He wanted to tell his boss that they had bigger fish to fry.

"He was inside the building during the strike, but like I said, we have no idea of the effects."

"Patrick," Simmons growled. "You're doing a hell of a job, but I need to know if the targets are down."

"I'll handle it, sir. One other thing, though: I'm going to need more assets to get the strike team out."

The phone fell silent, and Vann knew that Simmons was weighing his options. The wrong decision could pull the United States into another war. "Sir, what does it matter?" he asked. "As far as I can tell, whether we fight a war in Syria, or we fight in—"

Simmons cut him off. "Be careful, Patrick," he warned. "You do what you have to do to get them out, but nothing more. It's not time yet."

"I'm going to need the F-18s."

"The president's not going to like that, but I'll see what I can do."

"Yes sir."

"And Patrick, I want Mason's body," he said before hanging up.

Vann slipped the phone back into his pocket. He had no idea why Simmons was so obsessed with making sure that Mason was dead, but he took a deep breath, figuring it was well beyond his pay grade.

"Get those F-18s on station and tell Savage 6 that help is on the way. Someone get Anderson on the phone. I need an extraction team in the air right now."

As his men jumped into action, General Vann felt his stomach churn. He was just as culpable as the man who'd put this fucked-up plan into action. He was too far invested to pull out now. That meant if things went sideways, he was going to burn.

CHAPTER 14

The gunfire had decreased after the Hellfire eased the pressure they were getting from the north, but Renee was running low on ammo. Fifteen feet to her right, Parker kicked in the front door of a building. She could hear a woman scream as he made entry.

They needed badly to get out of the open, and as soon as he yelled, "Clear," the rest of the team began falling back.

Renee was moving to cover when the firing kicked up again. A round ricocheted off the ground near her feet, and she turned to see a fighter spraying blindly down the street.

She was exposed to so many angles that it was impossible to move without getting shot at. Only by sheer luck did she avoid being hit again. As the perimeter collapsed, more jihadists rushed closer to the beleaguered strike team, eager to press their advantage.

Renee heard Warchild yelling from inside the building—he was directing men up onto the roof—leaving her to engage the latest threat. The sun that had been so pleasant earlier beat down on her exposed flesh, making her feel like an ant under a magnifying glass. She had been aware for some time that she was desperate for a sip of water and was beginning to feel the effects of dehydration.

Renee fired from the hip and felt the bolt slam to the rear as the rounds chewed across the fighter's chest.

She scrambled for a fresh mag, tossing the empty in the dirt. The lack of water was taking its toll on her dexterity. Renee tried to seat the magazine, but it bounced off the mag well. She stopped in the middle of the street, forcing herself to focus, and she'd almost gotten the rifle back into action when a round pounded her in the chest, knocking her to the ground.

It felt like she'd been hit with a sledgehammer. She tumbled backward, the magazine flying out of her hand. A wave of panic rushed up out of her subconscious, causing her to freeze up.

"Not now," she spat, fighting off the fear creeping up her spine as she scrambled to grab the magazine, which lay just out of reach.

She hadn't told anyone about the panic attacks she had been suffering for the past five months, but they were obviously getting worse, and now was definitely not the time to have one.

Warchild appeared at the door of the building. A frown filled his face as he saw her sprawled on her back. Instantly he dove out into the street, oblivious to the rounds zipping over his head and shielded her with his body.

He snapped the rifle from left to right, his finger dancing on the trigger like he was shooting a drill on the range. One of the first two rounds mushroomed inside the forehead of a fighter and the man's legs buckled beneath him. Warchild's muzzle snapped to the next target and he stacked two more rounds dead center of the jihadist's chest. Then he flipped the selector to full auto and hammered a long burst toward the men gathering at the end of the block.

"Come on," he yelled at the fighters before lowering the rifle and yanking Renee off the ground just as her hand was closing around the magazine. She had just landed on her feet when an RPG screamed from up the street. With a violent lunge, she pushed Warchild out of the way.

The warhead slammed into the side of the building, and the explosion knocked her over again. Debris slapped her across the face, acrid smoke burned her lungs, and dust stung her eyes. Yet she couldn't be a victim, she told herself. She slammed the mag into the rifle and hit the bolt release. She was looking for Warchild when a jihadist came running out of the smoke.

Renee watched in slow detachment as the fighter settled his muzzle on her and prepared to fire.

Every detail was clearly defined: from the man's dark-brown eyes to the stubble on his chin. The world had slowed, and she just stood there as his finger closed around the trigger.

She could feel the blood dripping from her face, and the chill that came from mild dehydration. Renee was vaguely aware of the goose bumps on her arms as she stood staring at the man about to kill her.

A shadow streaked from her right, and as she waited for the rifle to go off, she heard Sergeant Major Mitchell bellowing a war cry. The fighter hesitated, a look of fear crossing his face before he turned to engage the man charging him.

Mitchell launched himself into the air at the same moment the man fired, but his aim was high and Renee heard his bones crack when Mitchell's shoulder slammed into his side. Despite the fact that one of his arms hung uselessly at his side, Mitchell speared the man into the ground and drove his helmet into the fighter's face.

He wrapped his massive hand around the fighter's neck, squeezing while the man's legs kicked helplessly beneath him. A moment later the jihadist was still, and Mitchell staggered to his feet, smiling through the mask of blood that covered his face.

"Looks like we're even," he said before helping her to cover.

CHAPTER 15

- - - - - - - - - - - - - -

Mason Kane lay on his stomach, unable to see because of the thick brown haze enveloping him. He heard a muffled yell behind him, but the total darkness shrouded where it was coming from.

"Zeus," he croaked, forcing himself out of the dirt and rising to his knees.

He remembered coming to the end of the tunnel at the same moment the grenade went off, and the overpressure slapped him in the face, knocking him back. Mason had felt the ground rumble beneath him and thought he'd heard a second explosion before being knocked unconscious.

Dirt clogged his airways, and he gagged before vomiting a mass of mud and dirt onto the ground. The explosion had bent the barrel of his AK-47, and he used the butt stock to dig into the dirt around him.

He had to find Zeus.

"Fuck, where are you, buddy?" he yelled, flinging dirt behind him.

A faint yell came from his left, and he coughed, spitting a mixture of mud and bile before tossing the rifle to the side. Mason clawed at the dirt with his bare hands, scrabbling like a dog in search of a bone. Finally, his fingers brushed against something hard.

Scooping the dirt away in huge handfuls, he found the toe of Zeus's boot. Spurred on by the fear that his friend was dying beneath him, he tried to yank him out. Zeus was buried too deep to muscle out, so Mason went back to digging. As the pit grew wider, the earth began relinquishing its hold on the Libyan.

Sweat was pouring down Mason's face, and his bandage was filthy by the time he pulled his unconscious friend out of the makeshift grave. Mason checked his pulse, and he was leaning forward to begin CPR when the Libyan's filthy hand reached up and pushed his face away.

"Get off me," Zeus commanded weakly.

"Holy shit," Mason panted, falling back onto his ass to watch his partner sit up. As he did, an avalanche of black earth fell away from his body.

"What were you trying to do, kiss me?" Zeus asked, spitting out a clod of dirt.

"I was trying to save you," Mason said.

"It was your fault this shit happened," Zeus replied, tossing a handful of dirt at his best friend.

"Yeah, that was a terrible idea."

Overwhelmed by how close they had come

to death, Mason lay flat on his back, allowing his eyes to adjust to his surroundings. Zeus got to his feet and shook himself like an animal coming out of water. Dirt flew in every direction, pelting the American, who was still trying to catch his breath.

As he lay on the ground, his hand reached down to ensure that the Glock was still secure in its holster. He heard Zeus say, "Looks like we got one."

Mason stood, feeling dirt slide down his pants, and moved out of the tunnel. He inspected the man lying on the ground. "Hey, are you okay?" he asked sarcastically in Arabic, kicking the man in the side.

"Ahhhhh, damn you," the jihadist screamed.

The man's shirt was covered in blood from the shrapnel that had pelted his body, and his pants leg was burned and tattered from the blast. A jagged wound had been opened in his abdomen, and Mason could see that he was losing a lot of blood. He tried to roll onto his stomach, but the American grabbed him by the shoulders, forcing him to lie flat.

Mason knew the man was his only link to Boland, and without a moment's hesitation he brought his knee down on the jihadist's wound.

As expected, the man shrieked in pain. "What, does that hurt?" Mason asked, slapping the man's hands away as he reached up. "Who are you?"

"Fuck you," his attacker gurgled in Arabic.

"Hey, buddy," Mason said, smacking him across the face, "you don't have much time left, so let's cut the shit. Tell me who you are, or I'm going to cut your eyelids off."

Mason slipped his knife from its sheath attached to his chest rig and held it up so the man could see it. The blade had been handmade in Illinois by master bladesmith John Kiedaisch—and Mason liked to joke that it never failed to leave an impression.

"You are too late." The man smiled, dazed in his agony.

"Really? Well, guess what, I'm not going anywhere," he said, driving his knee deeper into the man's wound. "What's your name?"

The Arab twisted in pain, trying to alleviate the pressure being forced on his wound. Mason brought the knife closer to the man's face, hovering the razor-sharp point over one eyeball.

"If you keep squirming, you're going to bleed faster, so sit still," he commanded, backhanding him across the mouth.

"Listen to me," Zeus said, settling onto his haunches next to the Arab. "I know you are from Iran. Please tell my friend what he wants to know. I promise you that he will cut your face to ribbons if you don't talk. And then he will leave your body to be eaten by the dogs. Just tell him your name," he begged.

"My name is Esmail."

That was progress, Mason thought. "Where did they take the American?"

Esmail smiled sardonically, and Mason grabbed the man's face with one hand. With the other, he pushed the tip of the blade down into his eyeball.

"I told you," Zeus said, looking away in disgust as their prisoner screamed in agony.

"I asked you, where did they take the American?" Mason demanded again.

"They are taking him to the border," he cried, blood pouring from his eye.

"Who took him?"

"I do not know."

Mason stuck the blade deep into the man's nose before pulling up on the handle. The honed edge cut through his nostril, and he screamed, "Al Qatar took him. It was al Qatar."

Mason's face was set in a savage mask of fury, and Zeus could tell the jihadist would get no mercy. The Libyan shook his head while Mason continued his impromptu interrogation. "If you tell me where to find him, I will kill you quickly, but otherwise I must make you suffer."

"A village—there is a place the American used near al Hasakah, but I promise you, it is too late. Your friend is already dead."

Mason had a suspicion he was right about that. "Why did they take him?"

"You will find out soon enough," the Iranian whispered before finally succumbing to his wounds.

"Esmail, hey, are you with me?" Mason yelled, slapping him across the face.

Zeus grabbed his hand. "He is dead, my friend. Maybe next time don't stab him in the eye."

Mason looked over at Zeus, taking in the disgust written across his friend's face, before looking down at the dead Iranian. "What was I supposed to do?" Mason asked, struggling to his feet.

Zeus's eyes narrowed and anger washed over his face. "The longer you stay here, the more savage you become," he accused.

Mason slipped his knife back into its scabbard and got to his feet. He felt the dead man's blood warm on his pants leg. He knew that Zeus was right. The worst part was that he had seen with his own eyes what happened to men who ventured too far from their humanity.

He didn't get off on inflicting pain, and he knew that sometimes the difference between good and evil was a very thin line. The problem was, once you crossed over, it was so very easy to stay on the other side.

Mason had no idea how far the tunnel had taken them from the bank, but as he scanned the interior of the new building, he saw a door on the far wall. Sunlight trickled in through a hole where the knob should have been. It reminded him that they were far from finished.

Distant gunfire told him that Renee was still under fire and he needed to find his team before they could go after al Qatar.

"What do you want to do?" Zeus asked as they cautiously approached the door.

"We have to get to the helos."

Mason drew his pistol, opened the door, and scanned the street before stepping outside. He had no idea who al Qatar was or why he had gone to such great lengths to snatch Mick Boland, but he owed it to his friend to find out.

The sun blinded him as he cleared the next corner, moving south toward the sound of the gunfire. Behind him Zeus muttered curses to himself while shaking a layer of fresh earth from his AK-47.

"Why am I up here with a pistol when you have a rifle?" Mason demanded, motioning for the Libyan to take point.

Zeus flipped him the finger before stepping past him. Mason tried to keep from laughing at the man's filthy face and grime-encrusted clothing.

"You owe me a new pair of clothes," Zeus snapped, as if he knew what Mason was thinking.

The Libyan set near side security, allowing Mason to hobble across the street, where he posted up next to a bombed-out shop. Once he was set, Zeus jogged across and kept moving south.

A man dressed in filthy gray pants and a brown T-shirt came running around the corner, surprising Zeus—who fired when he saw the rifle cradled in the man's arms. The round blew through the man's throat, ripping a gouging hole below his chin. He dropped the rifle and tried desperately to plug the wound with his shaking hands. Mason could see him choking on his own blood as Zeus pushed past him, advancing to the corner.

Mason scooped the fighter's rifle off the ground, ignoring the jihadist, who slumped against the wall and slid slowly to the ground. He was about to check the magazine when Zeus yanked a grenade off his filthy kit and bounced it around the corner.

"Can't go that way," he said, sprinting past Mason.

Mason stopped a second before a hail of bullets slammed into the corner. "No kidding," he thought before running after Zeus. The grenade exploded behind them, and Zeus ducked off into a ruined shop with Mason fast on his heels.

Inside, the ceiling had collapsed, and the debris left behind formed a ramp leading up to the adjacent building. Zeus closed the door behind Mason, who, ignoring the pain in his ankle, thundered up to the top.

He reached the top and searched for a way forward. Most of the floor was gone, but a metal beam provided a narrow crossing to the other side. "Come on, Zeus."

He could feel the floor creaking under his weight as he crossed, and on the other side Mason saw a stairwell partially blocked by wooden beams and concrete blocks. They were able to squeeze through a tiny, jagged opening, and made their way back down to the ground floor.

The distant gunfire rose and fell in sporadic pops and cracks followed by moments of ear-shattering silence. Mason knew that the fighters were probing the strike team's perimeter and prayed Renee could hold on.

A firefight reminded him of a conversation between strangers. It started and stopped awkwardly until both sides felt comfortable and then it picked up in urgency.

Mason pushed down the hallway, heading toward the back of the building. where part of the wall was missing. Hugging the shadows, he had a clear view of the street and the thick column of smoke drifting over the buildings.

"What do you think?" he whispered as Zeus moved behind him.

"Going out there is suicide, so I'm sure you're going to want to do it," he replied.

Mason gave him a slight push, a grin slipping across both their faces.

Zeus was right: the street was swarming with jihadists, the majority of whom were spraying the sides of a building twenty feet away. A man knelt down with an RPG and prepared to fire. Just before he pulled the trigger, his head snapped back, and Mason noticed a helmet disappear below the edge of the rooftop.

"Looks like we found them," he muttered.

"So what do you want to do?"

The two men didn't have many options, and Mason had no intention of leaving cover without a plan. He was still trying to devise one when a technical screeched to a halt outside their position and began unloading fighters. A gunner stood behind the DShK mounted in the back, scanning for targets. Mason noted him carefully, intent on taking advantage of the opportunity before it passed. It was obvious that the men deploying in the street received some form of training. They ensured that they had interlocking fields of fire, but none of them bothered to check the building behind them, allowing Mason to choose when to strike.

He waited until five men had their backs to the gunner before panning to the opposite side of the hole. A tall Arab stood talking on a tiny cell phone, a cigarillo clutched in his hand. Unlike the rest of the men, he was armed with only a pistol, and his camo uniform was relatively clean.

"Yes, yes, we are about to attack," he said into the phone, kicking at a piece of expended brass with the toe of his boot. "What do you mean, more helicopters are coming? This is not what I was told."

The man looked up just as Mason punched his muzzle through the hole and fired. He didn't wait to watch the man fall; he simply pivoted toward the gunner and fired two rounds into the man's back.

"Grab that phone, Zeus," he yelled, jumping out into the street and clambering into the back of the Toyota Hilux.

The driver turned to see what was going on behind him, and the truck lurched forward as Zeus fired through the back window. The jihadist's brains spattered across the windshield and Mason manhandled the DShK onto target.

"Holy shit, dude," he yelled at Zeus, "Can't you wait until I'm out of the way?"

Zeus shrugged, moving to cover while Mason opened fire.

The recoil from the heavy machine gun jarred Mason's forearms as he swept the barrel down the street, cutting the high-explosive rounds across the backs of the men shooting at the building. He worked methodically, pausing to engage a man firing wildly at him from the hip.

A bullet whined past his head, forcing him to duck. Yet Mason never took his finger off the trigger. The expended brass pinged off the metal bed and an RPG screamed overhead, exploding behind him. "Get this thing moving," Mason yelled.

The Libyan threw open the door, yanking the corpse from behind the wheel, and dumped him unceremoniously onto the ground.

More rounds cracked past Mason's head, thumping into the cab of the truck. His brain yelled for him to get down, but he wasn't going to allow Zeus to get hit.

Zeus grinded the truck into gear and slammed on the gas. Mason lost control of the DShK and tumbled backward, barely managing to grab onto the mount that had been welded crudely to the floor. Mason reached up for the DShK and pulled himself to his feet, firing at the fighters caught in the open.

"Friendlies," he screamed as they sped toward the building he hoped Renee was using for cover, careful to keep the barrel pointed down the street.

The front left tire blew, sending shards of rubber thumping into the wheel well and the rim cutting into the road. Zeus fought for control, trying desperately to veer away from an imminent collision with the building. He locked up the brakes, spinning the wheel hard to the right, and once again Mason's grip slipped off the gun.

He was already off-balance when the Hilux

finally skidded to a halt, and unable to check his forward momentum Mason went tumbling out of the bed and onto the ground.

"Blue, blue, blue," Zeus yelled, using the US military's code for friendly forces.

He threw the door open, his AK chattering in his hand as Mason lay awkwardly on the ground, the breath knocked out of him.

"Get up," Zeus shouted, grabbing Mason by his wounded arm and dragging him around the corner toward the door, which suddenly swung open.

Mason worked to catch his breath, seemingly content to let his friend drag him to safety once inside. Zeus dumped him in a corner just as a soldier slammed the door shut behind him. The soldier turned, and Mason smiled at the mixture of surprise and relief covering her face.

"What's up?" he coughed.

CHAPTER 16

SecDef Cage knew that President John Bradley was pissed. What had started out as a simple smash and grab had turned into a shit sandwich, and since it was technically his operation, he knew he had to take a big ol' bite.

He'd done his best to give the president plausible deniability, but he couldn't keep a lid on the fact that the situation in Syria had gone sideways. There was a thin line between strategy and stupidity, and according to President Bradley he'd taken up permanent residence in the latter.

"How could you be so . . . *fucking stupid*?" Bradley shouted.

The president hated profanity, and Cage knew that on the rare occasions when his boss cursed, it was because he was furious. Not that the SecDef blamed him, especially after the briefing he'd just finished giving.

The SecDef hated the White House Situation

Room. It was too small and way too clean. He was used to making decisions on the battlefield, in the dirt with his men, but, unfortunately, that time had passed. He waited for Bradley to calm down, hoping he still had enough stroke to calm the leader of the free world.

The burnished mahogany table and light-blue walls made him feel like he was in the conference room of a hotel, as opposed to the bowels of the White House. At the far end of the table, General Madewell, the chairman of the Joint Chiefs of Staff, sat stoically in his Marine Corps uniform, his medals glinting from the overhead lights.

It seemed a lifetime ago that Cage had that very same job, and he could almost guarantee he knew what was going through the man's mind.

"Answer me," Bradley yelled, forcing Cage to return his attention to the president.

"Sir, it was a routine operation; it just went bad," National Security Advisor Simmons said from his spot to the right of the president.

"When this appears on CNN in the morning, do you think it's going to look 'routine'?"

What no one else in the room realized was that Simmons and Cage had prepared for this meeting four months ago, and now all they needed was a moment of calm so they could redirect the conversation.

"Mr. President, if I may." Craig O'Neil, Bradley's chief of staff, interjected, placing his hand on his boss's shoulder. The president looked up at his most trusted advisor, his face red with anger. "Mr.

Secretary," he went on, "can you please explain why you thought it was a good idea to launch a military operation inside a sovereign nation without bothering to inform the president?"

Cage cleared his throat and prepared to deliver the lines he'd been rehearsing in his head.

Bradley had originally brought Cage on as his national security advisor in hopes that the ex-chairman of the Joint Chiefs could help him deal with the Middle East without being pulled into another war. Eight months ago, the administration found itself in the exact situation Bradley desperately wished to avoid when Colonel Barnes—the commander of an off-the-books black-ops team—went off the reservation and tried to drive the US into a war with Syria.

Unbeknown to the president, Cage had been neck deep in Colonel Barnes's plan but, at the last moment, Mason Kane managed to thwart the unsanctioned operation. Cage had barely managed to shift the blame onto the acting secretary of defense, and when Bradley asked him to take the now vacant position, the president unknowingly played right into his hands. Ever since, Cage had been biding his time, waiting for another opportunity to avenge the failures of Iraq and Afghanistan and keep the promise he'd made to his dying wife.

"Well, the operation was time sensitive, and since it fell under joint DOD and CIA control, I had to make a decision or risk losing our window."

The president held up his hand. "Stop right

there," he said sharply. Then, turning to Simmons: "Jacob, did he confer with you on any of this?"

"Yes sir, and I backed it a hundred percent. I completely understand your anger, but you have to realize that there is a very good chance that we just killed one of al Nusra's top commanders, along with a high-level Iranian operative."

"This is total bullshit," Craig exploded.

Cage had been waiting for the outburst, and, like a lion pouncing on a gazelle, he attacked. "Your job is to advise the president, mine is to keep this country safe," he began. "You can say what you want about the operation, but not only did my decision save American lives, but it also provided the president with the plausible deniability that he needs."

Bradley liked the sound of that better. "Duke, you know how I feel about us all working together on these tough issues, but you have to understand my point of view. I mean, how the hell does it look to have my secretary of defense running operations without my approval?"

"I totally understand that, sir," Cage replied, pretending to be contrite. "This one is on me, sir."

Bradley was appeased, and the SecDef could see that the president was ready to welcome him back into the fold. It was time to capitalize and maybe gain a few much-needed approval points.

"How sure are you that we got the two targets?"

"Sir, we need to clear the objective before we get any hard evidence, but I feel really good about it. It was a clean strike," he lied.

"Tell me about this Khalid fellow."

Simmons, also sensing the shift in momentum, motioned grandly to the packet in front of President Bradley. It was a seamless transition, and the others in the room never realized they were being played.

"Khalid al Hamas's primary job is to enable state actors to prosecute actions against the US and Israel," Simmons began. "He has been actively arming rebels in Syria, Iraq, and Lebanon for the last five years."

Cage allowed Simmons to lay out Khalid's bona fides, and almost felt bad that he was keeping one piece of information to himself. He hadn't told his friend that the Iranian had managed to capture Boland a few weeks before the operation kicked off, and he sure as hell didn't tell him about the equipment he'd taken off their operative.

It wasn't that he didn't trust Simmons, but Cage had learned long ago that successful operations needed to stay compartmentalized.

"So he was in Syria on a visit?" Bradley asked.

"Well, actually, he was there on behalf of Abu Bakr al Baghdadi, the leader of ISIS in Iraq."

"Whoa, hold on. There is a connection between them as well?"

"Yes sir. Baghdadi needs al Nusra's fighters to back his power play in Iraq."

"Craig, I thought you said he wasn't going to be a problem," the president said pointedly to his cowed chief of staff.

"Mr. President, this is all speculation—" O'Neil began.

"That is not entirely accurate," General Madewell suddenly added. "As much as I hate telling two army boys that they are right," he said with a barely perceptible smile, "I believe that they are dead-on with their assessment."

The president shot an angry glance at O'Neil. Cage knew this was not what Bradley wanted to hear, especially given that he'd already dodged one bullet in Syria. Bradley had no interest in tempting fate, but the facts they were presenting didn't give him many options.

"How long before the media finds out that we have two helos down?"

Cage seized control of the discussion. "Sir, there isn't any media in the area, and even if there was, who cares? The media isn't the problem here; the problem is the fact that unless you authorize us to put more assets in the area, we aren't going to be able to ascertain if the two targets are down or get our men out."

"The last thing I want to do is send troops back to the Middle East," the president warned.

"No one is asking for more troops," Cage said. "We know they are heading to Iraq. If we can slip the reins off the task force and get a few eyeballs across the border, we have a good chance of nipping this thing in the bud."

"Damn it, Duke, you're asking for a lot."

No matter what the president decided, Cage was done watching politicians tiptoe around the fact that there was still a war going on. He believed firmly that a storm was building on the horizon, and in the end, the president was going to be seen as either a coward or a hero. It really didn't matter to him which one.

"General Madewell, do you agree?" Bradley asked, turning his gaze to the JCS chairman.

"The Joint Special Operations Command was built for this type of thing, sir. If you want to smash it before it gets out of hand, all you have to do is give the word," Madewell replied.

Bradley was wilting under the triple attack. "So are we talking about limited strikes, or what?"

"I think we let the commanders see what they can do with a limited footprint; maybe put a handful of advisors on the ground, and then we just pound the shit out of them," the general said, not wanting to limit his options.

"What about our guys on the ground?"

"Well, hell, sir, that's not a problem at all." General Madewell smiled, his famous Texas drawl on bold display. "You give me the word, and I'll have a couple of F-18s bomb those assholes back into the Stone Age. Then we'll walk on in and get our people back."

Bradley looked like he was in pain. This was exactly the course of action he didn't want to take, as Cage knew very well.

"Damn it, okay, go get our people back. But I want your word that this is going to stay contained."

"Mr. President, please," O'Neil begged.

The president held up his hand again to forestall any further argument. To Cage he said, "Get it done."

"Yes sir," the SecDef replied, fighting the impulse to pump his fist in victory.

CHAPTER 17

- - - - - - - - - - - - - -

"Savage 6, this is Edge 2. We are coming in hot from the northeast. How copy?" The pilot's voice sounded calm as Renee studied the map spread out in front of her.

"Edge 2, Savage 6 Romeo, you are cleared hot."

The strike team was running low on ammo, and by now the men at the other crash site were most likely dead. It was a somber, frustrating feeling, but with the F-18 Hornets on station, Renee felt a glimmer of hope.

She had passed the pilot their grid, and now they were hunkering down, waiting for the Super Hornets to clear the street.

The 20 mm cannons made a tearing sound as the first F-18 came in low. The men on the roof yelled, "Hell, yeah," as the Hornet's pilot strafed the jihadists before pushing the throttle forward and kicking in his afterburners.

While Renee waited for the second aircraft to

roll in, she could tell that the rest of her team obviously didn't approve of Mason's and Zeus's arrival. They looked mistrustfully at the two men talking in the far corner, but no one had the balls to say anything.

Warchild in particular stared hatefully at Mason. He had told Renee in no uncertain terms that he considered Kane a traitor, and he made no effort to hide his contempt for the man, despite the fact that Mason had saved their lives a half hour before.

The pilot came back on the net, forcing her to focus. "Y'all might want to keep your heads down on this next pass. We're gonna drop some JDAMs to your east to clean up some of the mess."

"Roger that," she replied. The Joint Direct Attack Munition, or JDAM, was a satellite-guided bomb, and even though Renee knew it was extremely accurate, she still put a warning out over the net.

"Tell the guys on the roof to keep their heads down," she relayed.

"Yeah, we got it," Warchild said with a sneer. "You just listen to your radio, okay?"

Renee rolled her eyes. Nothing she did would ever be good enough for Warchild.

She carried the radio over to where Mason was seated and immediately noticed that he'd been hit. Both men looked like hammered shit, and she knew they had to be operating on fumes.

"Are you okay?" she asked quietly.

Mason took a cigarette from Zeus, and after sticking it in his mouth, lit it from a battered

Zippo. He blew a cloud of smoke toward the low ceiling.

"Latif is dead," he told Renee. "Well, I'm pretty sure it was him. Someone shot him in the face. But they took Boland."

"Wait, what?"

"Boland's gone," he repeated. "They knew we were coming."

"How is that possible?"

"I don't know. How about you tell me?" he asked, giving her a hard look.

Renee never liked this side of him, and she wasn't going to put up with it. "What are you trying to say?"

"The source—who was it?"

"No idea. Anderson said he was going to check him out."

"Anderson, huh?"

It was no secret that the task force commander didn't like Mason, but Renee didn't think that he would send his own men into a trap, no matter how much he hated Kane.

She said evenly, "You know what they call you back at the task force?"

"What's that?" he demanded

"They call you Conspiracy Kane," she informed him. "Maybe it was just a bad op. Did you consider that?"

"I don't think so. I think someone is playing us." Mason bent closer and whispered into her ear, "Be careful who you trust when you get back. I don't know where this thing is going, but the last time we got involved in something like this—"

"Wait, you're not going with us?"

"I hate to break up your little chat, but the birds are inbound," Warchild bellowed from his place near the wall.

Mason ignored him. "I still have guys out there. I need you to find David. Ask him if he knows anyone named al Qatar," Mason said, getting painfully to his feet.

The sound of the approaching helos could be heard in the distance as Mason and Zeus headed for the door. As the Libyan peered out into the street, Mason turned to Warchild and said to him roughly, "You think you can manage getting them to the birds, or do you need me to hold your hand again?"

Warchild glared at him, pantomiming a pistol with one hand and turning it over before extending it toward Mason. It was the sign for "enemy front," and Mason looked the man square in his eyes before flipping him the bird.

"See you soon," he said before stepping into the street.

CHAPTER 18

- - - - - - - - - - - - - -

Abu al Qatar was tired of waiting. He rechecked his watch impatiently and then decided to head outside for some air. The satellite phone he clutched in his hand was supposed to have rung ten minutes ago. It was obvious that the Americans still didn't take him seriously.

"Where are you going?" his lieutenant Ali asked from the other room, where he was setting up a video camera.

"Outside," he answered curtly.

"Emir, is that wise?"

"What do you mean?"

"The Americans have eyes everywhere, and they are probably looking for the commando," he said, pointing at Boland, whose eye had swollen shut.

"He is not a commando, he is a man who fights for money. Besides, they have no idea that we have even taken him yet."

"Yes, but is it wise?"

"Ali, you set up the camera, and let me do the thinking, okay?"

"As you wish, Emir," the man said, turning back to his work.

Al Qatar headed out into the sunlight, slipping gold-rimmed sunglasses over his eyes. He knew that by the time the Americans learned he had taken one of their men, he would already be over the border, and Boland would be dead.

Crossing into Iraq didn't bother him, but what weighed heavily on his mind was the fact that most of his men were still in northern Syria, trying to take the border town of Kobani. That meant he had to make the trip with only a handful of his fighters.

He took a cigarette from a pack of Marlboro Reds, which he had gotten hooked on while in American captivity, and after lighting it, he greedily sucked in a lungful of smoke. The safe house was less than a day's drive from the Iraqi border, and al Qatar knew that his men would be waiting for him at the crossing. Everything was going according to plan, and as soon as his American contact called, he could move on to phase two.

Not that the mission had been easy so far. Despite all the careful planning, he was lucky to have made it out of the city alive, especially after being chased through that tunnel by someone he could only assume was another American. Al Qatar had been shocked to see the frag come bouncing out of the tunnel, and only by the grace of Allah had he avoided being hit. That stroke of luck just showed that he had been chosen to strike the fatal blow that he knew would shock the Americans into finally leaving his country.

The satellite phone chirped in his hands, and he quickly brought it to his ear. Unable to hide the exasperation in his voice, he said, "You are late."

"I had a meeting with the president. Are you at the safe house?"

"Yes," al Qatar lied.

He was at a safe house, just not the one the American spy was referring to.

"When are you leaving?"

"In a few hours," he lied again.

He might be working with the American, but he didn't trust him, and he had learned long ago not to reveal more than he needed.

Al Qatar had learned that lesson the hard way during the five years he spent in the American prison the CIA had set up outside Baghdad. The time there allowed him to learn much about his captors, including their language, but it had been the worst experience of his life. At times he wasn't sure if he was going to survive to exact vengeance on the man who had killed his brother.

"The next part of the plan is the most important. I need to know that you understand what is expected of you."

"We have gone over this already. I will use the coordinates you have given me to attack the ship as it comes into the Persian Gulf. My men are already there."

The man on the other end coughed nervously. "What about Tal Afar?"

"It will take place in the morning. We have already paid the general, and he has promised that his men will not put up a fight."

"Good, everything is going according to plan."

"Very well," al Qatar said before hanging up.

He couldn't figure out if it was the Americans' arrogance that led them to believe they could control him, or if he was being lured into a trap. He knew he would feel much better once he reunited with Jabar, his lieutenant in Iraq.

Al Qatar's preternatural ability to show people what they wanted to see had saved his life when the Americans stuck him in their dank Iraqi prison. The interrogations had been worse than he could have ever imagined, but once he learned how to tell them what they wanted to hear, he became useful.

He hadn't known anything about the weapons site where they had found him in 2003. The only reason he had gone there at all was because his brother had told him to, but the CIA refused to believe the truth. The bearded officers had tried to beat the answers out of him, but he never told them about the memory stick his brother had given him before Boland shot him in the face. Even if he wanted to tell them which files were on the stick, he couldn't, because he'd never had a chance to open it.

The water had been the worst, and he still woke

up in the middle of the night with the panic of drowning pulling at his heart. Not until he realized that he needed useful information to give the Americans did the torture stop. Al Qatar learned how to gain the trust of the newer detainees, and they began telling him all about the insurgents operating outside the walls. Whenever the Americans took him to the interrogation booths—where they kept their dogs, and the chairs they hooked to the car batteries—he would use the information to make the pain stop.

The Americans thought they had turned him, and after they assigned him a CIA contact, the fools let him leave prison.

"Emir, it is time," Ali said, pulling him out of his reverie.

The Iraqi tossed the cigarette out into the desert and came into the isolated shack, where Boland sat strapped to a wooden chair.

"I promised myself long ago that I would kill you," he said, sliding his sunglasses to the top of his closely cropped hair.

The American said nothing, refusing to look at the camera standing before him.

"You are what they call the strong, silent type. Well, that is fine; I do not need you to speak. But I would like to tell you a story."

He grabbed a fistful of the man's hair, jerking his head back.

"The day before your president sent his army into Iraq, my brother was sent to a little place outside of Samarra. He was a member of the Special Republican Guard, and God sent me to accompany him that night."

Al Qatar pushed Boland's head forward and moved over to the table where Ali had placed a long, curved dagger. He picked up the knife by its gold inlaid hilt and waved it near the man's face.

"You Americans thought that Saddam had hidden his chemical weapons in the middle of the desert, even though everyone told you that he had already moved them. How easy it is to make you believe a lie."

"Just do what you're going to do," Boland said gruffly.

Al Qatar's eyes flashed with anger, and he laid the blade on the man's exposed neck and savagely slashed upward onto his face.

"Do not be rude. I am telling you a story," he hissed.

Blood flashed from the wound and began pouring down Boland's cheek and over his beard.

"As I was saying, we managed to get there before you and your commandos came in, but while you were looking for the gas, my brother gave me the weapon that I will use to kill more than any weapon of mass destruction. You killed him for nothing," he yelled, slamming the blade into Boland's thigh. "You stopped nothing, and now you will die, for nothing."

He left the dagger quivering in the man's leg and stepped away from the camera, taking a mask from Ali. Slipping it over his head, it revealed a white skull painted on the black fabric.

"I took this off one of your men in Ramadi. He was a commando like you," he said, pointing up to the blood stains near the neck. "But unlike you, he died quickly," he said, stepping back into the frame as Ali turned on the camera.

"This video is for the infidels fighting their illegal war in Syria, and this man stands as proof of what I say. Look at his face and tell me that I lie," he began, pulling Boland's head back and letting Ali focus on him. "I stand in judgment of this man and of the invaders of the Fertile Crescent, and swear that you will drown in the blood of your oppression. Allah be merciful, for I will not."

The Iraqi forced Boland's head all the way back, exposing his neck, and yanked the blade out of his leg. The American cried out in pain as al Qatar slid the blade slowly into the man's neck, careful not to cut to deep.

He wanted him to suffer, and he slowly cut around the back of his neck, feeling Boland squirming beneath the blade. He took his time, twisting the blade and then began sawing back toward his Adam's apple. Looking at the camera, he pierced the man's jugular, allowing the bright red blood to spurt free. He looked at the camera and smiled behind the mask before viciously stabbing the blade through the side of his neck and leaving it there.

"This man's death will look like mercy in the days to come," al Qatar proclaimed icily. Then he let go of Boland's hair, and his head lolled grotesquely to the side.

CHAPTER 19

- - - - - - - - - - - - - -

From the cockpit of the Beechcraft King Air 350, David Castleman watched the sun receding slowly below the horizon in brilliant hues of red and purple. From his perch, thirty thousand feet above Mosul, he had a front row seat to the brilliant sunset being unveiled across the Iraqi city. He allowed himself a few moments to savor it before turning his attention back to the task at hand.

The Beechcraft was the latest ISR, or intelligence, surveillance and reconnaissance, platform in the CIA's clandestine arsenal. Its sophisticated bank of instruments allowed the skilled intercept officers to monitor all radio and cell traffic in the region.

"Sir, are we running an op in Syria?" one of the signal officers asked over the gentle hum of the Pratt & Whitney turboprops.

"No," David said, squinting against the rays of light that flashed over the patchwork of green fields and khaki sand spread out like a quilt below them.

"I'm picking up some chatter."

"What's the frequency?" the spy asked before entering it into one of the radio displays.

Most of his subordinates called him Mr. David, and with good reason. The spy had been at the forefront of the war on terror since 2001, and he had no equal when it came to tracking the enemy, many of whom had become expert at hiding in plain sight.

His expertise was in finding patterns hidden among the innocuous data he received from informants and other assets he had set up around the Middle East, and his many successes were the reason he was the CIA's number one man in the task force. But that had begun to change lately, starting the moment Colonel Anderson took over tactical command of the task force.

The relationship between the military and the CIA had gone through its share of growing pains. Neither side fully trusted the other, but they had always made the relationship work. However, Colonel Anderson wanted only one thing from Mr. David: the agency's ability to operate outside the letter of the law.

"Tomahawk Base, Sickle 1, LZ is clear," the radio said.

"Roger that, Sickle 1. Do we have accountability of all personnel?"

"All personnel are accounted for. You are cleared hot on crash site."

Mr. David's frown reflected on the glass of the cockpit. He realized that Colonel Anderson had played him.

What he couldn't understand was why. He'd always supported the colonel, and even if he didn't agree, he made sure that his assets provided whatever intel they needed. So for the colonel to cut him completely out of an operation seriously pissed him off.

The Iridium sat phone vibrated in his pocket, yanking him from his ruminations. As David Castleman lifted it to his ear, he motioned for the pilot to take him back to Erbīl.

"It's me," Mason Kane said. "I don't have a lot of time."

"Are you secure?"

"No."

"What's your count?"

"Four, minus one package."

"Who are you missing?" David asked, his blood running cold.

"Striker 5 has been taken, and we are compromised."

"Christ, what the hell happened?" the spy asked, breaking protocol.

"Latif is dead," Mason replied calmly. "You need to talk to Renee; I gave her a name."

"What about you? Can I bring you in?"

The phone was silent as Mason considered something. "I need access to Safehaven," he replied finally, referring to the spy's master list of safe houses in the region.

"Mason, what the fuck is going on?" David demanded. He wasn't used to being kept in the dark, and no matter how much he trusted Mason, he didn't feel comfortable giving him that type of access without knowing why.

"Look, I already have your pass code; I was just trying to do the right thing. The task force has been compromised, and until you figure this shit out, I'm going dark."

"Mason, I need you to—" David began, but the line had already gone dead.

He knew that Mason Kane didn't rattle easily, but for him to deny a pickup and to break off any further communication, things must have really gone south. Whatever had happened, Anderson had made sure that David wasn't around to play any part in the operation. Now there was nothing left for him to do but go back to Turkey and try to figure out what the hell was going on.

Someone was going to pay.

CHAPTER 20

W hat's the plan, boss?" Grinch asked as Mason slipped the battery out of the sat phone. The team had reunited and stationed themselves in a bombed-out house near the first downed helicopter.

"We get T.J.'s body," he said simply.

"And then what?"

"Then we are on our own."

At first glance, Dean "Grinch" Fitzgerald came off as a country bumpkin, but beneath his deep southern drawl was one of the sharpest men Mason had ever met. Born in western Tennessee, he'd been raised by his grandfather, a Cherokee who'd married a white woman after coming home from the war in Europe. The man had sought out the tranquility of the forest as a means to quiet the demons he had brought home, and it was in that needed sanctuary that he taught his grandson everything he knew.

Dean had joined the army as soon as he was old enough, and, like Mason, he had volunteered for the Ranger Battalion. Mason had worried that the man would have a hard time adapting to the "black" side of the house, but he'd done nothing but surprise him. He was a valuable asset, and Mason knew that Grinch hadn't even begun to realize his deadly potential.

Mason had already filled them in on what he and Zeus had learned from the man they had interrogated in the tunnel, and as they waited for darkness to fall, they were trying to come up with a plan of action.

"So we're going back into Iraq?" Blaine asked finally.

"Looks that way. If anyone has a problem, now's the time to say your piece."

"I never thought I'd have to see that place again," Grinch said honestly.

Mason knew exactly what he was feeling. All three men had spent a considerable amount of time in Iraq and lost more friends than any of them would ever admit. Mason felt like he was being forced to revisit the scene of a crime, and they all felt the fear of uncertainty.

"I don't like it any more than you do, but we owe it to Boland."

"You think he's still alive?" Grinch asked.

Mason had been trying to answer the question since leaving the strike team to its helicopters. He knew deep down that the chances were pretty slim.

"I don't know," he admitted.

"I'm with you no matter what," Blaine said, and Grinch nodded his approval.

Mason was proud of them. He'd definitely picked the right guys. "Zeus, fire up the Toughbook and see if David was tracking any safe houses near al Hasakah."

"I'm on it," the Libyan said. "Do you want to call Ahmed?"

Before the fall of Libyan president Mu'ammar Gadhafi in 2011, Ahmed had been in charge of the Libyan Intelligence Service, but when the dictator lost power, the master spy barely escaped with his life. Now he used his vast contacts to run an illegal empire that spanned much of the Middle East. Best of all, he loved Mason like the son the CIA had taken from him.

Mason hated asking Ahmed for help, but not much occurred in the region that the man didn't know something about.

"See what he can find out about Khalid, since he was supposed to be the target of this cluster fuck. The way I figure it, if those scumbags are going to cross into Iraq, they have to do it at Al Qaim or Tal Afar."

"Has to be Tal Afar, doesn't it?" Grinch said.

"Well, on the bright side, it's not Christmas, so you don't have to worry about living up to your nickname," Blaine said with a laugh.

"Real funny," the man replied, not happy with his call sign.

"I had forgotten about that," Mason said.

During his third deployment, Grinch was sent

to northern Iraq with nothing more than a photo of a bomb maker the Joint Special Operations Command called the Rocketman. He spent a week observing patterns of life around known areas of interest, and the day before Christmas, he managed to get a positive identification.

He spent the rest of the day calling in close air support and engaging targets from eight hundred meters away. By the time they made it back to the rear, they were already calling him the Grinch of Tal Afar.

"We need to get out of here as low-key as possible, so no shooting unless you have to. Let's get some rest before moving out. I'll take the first shift."

The rest of the team settled down to get a few hours of sleep, leaving Mason alone to pull guard. As he stared out the window at the fighters scouring the remains of the downed helo, his mind drifted to the man who had helped get his life back.

Mr. David had gone way out on a limb when he recruited Mason to join the task force, and he had promised that if Mason did what was asked, the spy would do everything in his power to clear his name.

Mason had originally thought he would be able to return to the States, but after a while, it became perfectly clear that this wasn't going to happen. He might not be on the terrorist watch list anymore, but there were men with power who were going to make sure he paid for going after Colonel Barnes.

The only family Mason could count on was Zeus, and as he sat peering out into the falling darkness, he knew that eventually his friend was going to tire of fighting a war that had nothing to do with him.

It was taking a toll on both of them, and days like this made him wonder how much he had left. At this rate, the only way he was going home was in a box.

CHAPTER 21

- - - - - - - - - - - - - -

Five hours after talking to Mason, David Castleman was standing on the tarmac in Turkey, his dusty leather duffel slung over his shoulder. He'd gotten the pilot to land without alerting the tower, and as he made his way to the familiar hangar, he saw a ground crewman standing near the task force's last operational Mi-17.

David walked over to the man, whose small headlamp cast shadows over the tarmac, in the hopes of getting some information before sneaking inside. He'd been mulling over the conversation with Mason during the flight from northern Iraq, and he'd hoped to have a plan of attack once he hit the ground. But as he trudged across the flight line, he was just as lost as before.

David knew that whatever was going on in Syria was tied to the upheaval starting to show up around the border. Yet this operation's roots went deeper than that. More than anyone he knew how much credibility Bradley had lost after Barnes killed President Hamid Karzai in Afghanistan, but David was still no closer to learning who had been pulling the strings in Washington. He had a strong suspicion that something terrible was waiting just over the horizon, but he was powerless to do anything about it.

"Did they recover everything?" David asked once he got within earshot.

"They got all the bodies, sir, if that's what you mean," the crewman replied, lifting a water hose off the ground. "You might want to step back, sir."

The man sent a jet of water splashing onto the metal floor, and the smell of iron wafted up to David's nose. The wave surged toward the cockpit, before lapping against the bulkhead, and receded down the ramp in a torrent of rosy, diluted blood. It sizzled on the hot asphalt before licking over David's dusty boots. Angry about the blood spilled that day, before walking off he offered up a silent prayer for those who'd given their lives.

Instead of going through the main entrance, David slipped around the side and entered through a door that was supposed to have been secured a week ago. Just as he thought, it was still unguarded, and the spy was able to walk into the hangar unchallenged.

He didn't want Anderson to know that he was back. He stayed stealthily in the shadows as he made his back to the warren of plywood-lined rooms where the operators had their bunks.

He was about to knock on Renee's door when

he saw her emerging from the shower area, dressed in shorts and a T-shirt.

"I didn't know you were back," Renee said, frowning. She unlocked her door with a key hanging from her neck.

"I just got in," he replied quietly. Stepping into the room behind her, he closed the door with a tiny click. "Okay, what happened out there?"

She was pissed. "We got our asses shot off. How could you send us in there like that?"

"I just found out about this disaster. I assure you, I had no hand in this whatsoever."

"I don't buy that. They used your assets. Want to try that again?" she demanded, cocking her hip to the side.

"You're going to have to trust me," he said, regretting the words as soon as they left his tongue.

"I did trust you, and I almost died out there."

He was starting to realize how bad the operation was. "Look, I know that you're upset, but I'm in the dark. Tell me what happened."

Renee stared at him, trying to detect his usual double speak. Then she softened and filled him in on what had gone down.

"So Anderson launched a raid in broad daylight?" David said, outraged. "Who gave him authorization?"

"How the fuck should I know? Isn't that your job?"

Someone had deliberately cut him out, David thought, taking a seat on her bed.

"They knew we were coming," she said, cold

steel in her voice. "Tell me how something like that happens?"

"Renee, I don't know. Look, I don't have a lot of time, and I have no idea what's going to happen when Anderson learns that I'm here. Mason said they took Boland, and he said you have some intel."

Renee looked like she wasn't going to tell him. He had seen that look before, the first time he'd ever met her.

About the time that Colonel Barnes stepped off the reservation, David had lost two of his assets in Morocco. The spy called in a handful of favors and finally got the name of the assassin: Mason Kane. Up until that point he'd only heard rumors about the disgraced soldier, but once he was sure Mason was responsible, David made it his business to track him down.

It took him less than a week to find the man the rest of the world had spent months searching for, and he sent a team to grab him and his partner Zeus in Libya. David was just getting into his interrogation when Renee appeared out of nowhere and tried to break Mason out. David had been immediately impressed by her doggedness. He realized that she and Mason had presented him with an opportunity to stop Colonel Barnes's illegal operation in Syria. After they pulled it off, he cashed in some favors to get her reassigned to the task force.

"Tell me what happened to Boland," he asked again.

"Mason gave me a name," she said reluctantly.

"What is it?"

"How do I know you're not going to cut me out again?"

"You know how this works—"

"That's bullshit. Here's the deal: I'll tell you what I know if you get me the fuck off of Warchild's team," Renee said defiantly.

"That isn't our agreement."

"Well, I'm making a new one. You want my help, that's how you get it."

"If you had done what I asked and kept me apprised of what Anderson was doing, none of this would have happened."

"How the hell am I supposed to help you when I have Warchild on my ass every second of the day? Do you know that he has me working as his RTO?"

David was surprised she was complaining. "I put you on the team for a reason. Don't tell me that you can't handle that tattooed animal, because I know you can."

"Don't you dare turn this around on me. This one is on you," she hissed.

He had counted on Renee to watch his back while he tried to figure out how far those who had supported the Anvil Program were willing to go, but as he looked into her hardened gaze, David knew he'd made a miscalculation.

"There is no new deal," he spat. "You either do your job, or I'll have you sent to Germany for a psych eval so fast your head will spin."

Renee staggered back like he'd struck her, her eyes blazing at his betrayal. "Fuck you."

"The name."

"Al Qatar," she said at last.

It hit David like a shotgun blast to the chest. He was unable to hide the shock that came with the mention of the Iraqi's name.

"How do you know him?" Renee asked.

"Al Qatar was a mistake," he said slowly. He tried to gather himself despite the dark memories emerging from the past. "There was a time when the agency believed that it could flip some of the detainees that were being processed in some of the camps. A directive was issued involving new interrogation techniques that attempted to rehabilitate insurgents who showed certain traits that the psychologists thought we could use to our advantage. Al Qatar was one of the first to go through the program, but he was a lot smarter than we realized—"

A knock on the door ended the conversation, and Renee cursed softly before opening it.

"Hey, I was just checking to see how you were doing," Parker said. "Oh, sorry, I didn't know you had company." The smile on his face crumbled.

"I have to be going," David said, getting up.

"Wait, what—"

David brushed past her, giving Parker a curt nod as he stepped out of her room and disappeared from view.

"What a cluster fuck," he thought. Whoever was using al Qatar had no idea that the man was a total psychopath. David had always compared him to a pet rattlesnake. Sure, it was safe as long as it stayed in the cage, but once you let it out, it was only a matter of time before it bit you.

David knew that the men who had died today were just the first of many, and as he walked down the hall, he renewed his promise to find out who was responsible.

CHAPTER 22

- - - - - - - - - - - - - - -

The moon was just beginning to rise when Mason and his team slipped out into the streets, intending to recover T.J.'s body. However, they soon learned that the house they had occupied that very morning was now crawling with fighters, making it impossible for them to get closer. Just as Mason was about to call it, Zeus handed him the night-vision scope he'd taken from Grinch's rifle and pointed at an old light post.

"What is it?" Mason demanded.

"Just look."

Mason brought the optic up to his eyes and slowly refined the focus knob. Hanging from the spot where the light had once been, he saw T.J.'s body swinging gently in the wind.

"Those motherfuckers," he cursed.

Mason had to fight back the anger growing inside of him. If he was alone on this mission, he would risk his life to reclaim the body, but he knew that Blaine and Grinch were counting on him to get them out of the city.

He handed the scope back to Zeus, harder than he meant to, and before he let it go, he pulled the Libyan in close. Looking over the man's shoulder to ensure that Grinch and Blaine were still pulling security, he said, "We don't say a word about this."

Zeus nodded, and the two men slipped back into the shadows.

It took fifteen minutes to make it back to the SUV they had left hidden on the outskirts of the city. Mason headed to the back of the truck to grab the night vision from the safe they had built in the back, before taking his spot behind the wheel. Once the men had loaded up, he set off on the drive east toward the border—keeping the headlights off to avoid detection.

In the seat next to him, Zeus draped a tan *she-magh* over his head before opening the Toughbook on his lap. The scarf blocked out most of the light, allowing Mason to focus on driving as the Libyan pecked away at the keys.

Mason leaned forward, adjusting his NODs, or night observation device, as he drove. The moonlight gave him excellent illumination, but he still had to pay special attention to the dips and potholes as the vehicle bumped across the open ground, heading for the highway.

"I think I have it," Zeus announced.

"Are you sure?"

"I'm as sure as I can be, considering I'm illegally accessing a CIA database with a stolen password," Zeus said lightly, pulling his GPS from his kit.

Once they were clear of any outlying buildings, Mason yanked the NODs from his head. He turned on the headlights, blinking rapidly against the sudden illumination. The road appeared ahead like a gray snake in the silver light of the moon, and he hit the gas to get the truck over the ditch that separated the desert floor from the highway.

Taking a cigarette from the pack on the dash, he lit it with his Zippo, and cracked the window before blowing out a plume of smoke. "Guess it's all we have."

"You know he's probably dead. Why would they risk taking him into Iraq?"

Mason knew that Zeus wasn't trying to save his own skin. They had been together so long, they could be totally honest with each other.

Zeus was the kind of friend Mason hadn't realized he needed but had unconsciously spent his entire childhood searching for. His mother was an alcoholic, his father was a no-show from day zero, and Mason had never fit in anywhere. By all rights, the differences between him and Zeus should have made them enemies, but somehow it drew them closer together. They were men without a country, and in the fire of combat, the two had become their own strange kind of family.

Sure, Mason had made sure that the task force paid Zeus more than he'd ever make in Libya, but their bond had nothing to do with money and everything to do with a loyalty most people in the world would never know.

"You may be right, but you know I have to find out." Mason spoke finally.

Three hours later, they reached Zeus's coordinates, and Mason once again shut off the lights, looking for a spot to hide the truck. He found a wadi four hundred meters from the target house. He cut the engine, and they scanned the area as they got out.

The car door creaked on its rusty hinges as Mason eased it open. The dogs barking in the distance told him that the village was definitely populated.

Moving into the unknown was not the way he liked to operate, but he knew their only chance was to hit the target as fast and quiet as possible.

He followed his team to the back of the vehicle. Grinch pulled a dusty blanket off the floor of the SUV and unlocked the hidden compartment where they stowed their extra kit. The team switched out its AKs for the more versatile HK 416, which were equipped with PEQ-15 IR lasers and the suppressors they would need to maintain noise discipline.

"Grinch, once you're in position, give us a call," Mason said.

The sniper attached his night-vision optic to the rail of his Remington Modular Sniper Rifle and unfolded the stock before nodding his assent and then disappearing into the darkness.

"Let's take this nice and easy," Mason said to Zeus.

The moon was low enough not to cast long shadows as Mason moved out, using the wadi to skirt around the village. Through his NODs, he could see lights flickering inside some of the houses and a few stray dogs sniffing at the air as they milled around in the dusty streets.

The floor of the wadi was covered in a thin layer of shale, left over from a stream that had cut the shallow depression through the desert floor long ago. Thousands of years ago, the terrain had been much more lush. Fed by thousands of similar streams, the land had provided plenty of pastures for the herders who called this place home.

Mason scanned the ground carefully as his boots crunched on the sand. He was looking for any trip hazards or antipersonnel devices that might have been placed against an enemy intrusion. Mason knew that the men they were tracking were obsessed with security, and if it had been him, he would have left a few surprises for anyone trying to sneak up on his position.

The wadi continued straight for another fifteen feet before making a dogleg to the left. Mason called a halt so he could check out the area before committing his men.

A light desert breeze carried the smell of wood smoke and animal dung from the village. Wiping the back of his glove across his face, Mason realized how tired he was. He carefully slipped out into the open, maintaining a low profile to avoid being silhouetted by the moon.

Mason settled into a crouch and scanned the area around him. He wanted nothing more than to close his eyes for a few seconds when he sensed movement ten feet to his front.

Mason adjusted his NODs, his heart thumping in his chest, as he focused on what looked like a mound of dirt. He knew that fatigue sometimes played tricks on the senses, but still nothing moved. Mason was just about to take a step closer when the pile of dirt stirred, and he realized that what he was looking at was actually a blanket.

Forcing himself to breathe, Mason prepared to slip back to his men, when a shadow loomed over the edge of the wadi. It began to elongate as the man standing above him drew closer, and then stopped, right above him.

His breath caught in his throat, and he froze, fighting the urge to look up. He heard the guard spit into the darkness, followed a second later by the sound of liquid splashing on the ground.

The smell of urine was almost overpowering as the man began pissing. Mason waited for him to finish, but the guard seemed to have the largest bladder on record. While the situation would have been hilarious at any other time, all Mason could think about was the fact that at any moment the man might look down and see him crouched in the shadows.

The ground overhead declined slightly toward his position, and as the man relieved himself, a steady stream of urine began dripping down the wall of the wadi and collecting near Mason's boot.

Finally, the man let out a long fart and began walking to where Zeus and Blaine were hiding.

"Grinch, where are you, buddy?" Mason implored silently, wondering how in the hell the guard had gotten so close without being taken out. He was afraid to use his radio, but as the seconds ticked by, he realized he was going to have to do something.

Suddenly he heard a gentle *snap* followed by a heavy thud, and then the sound of metal bouncing off the ground.

"Tango down," Grinch whispered over the radio.

"About fucking time," Mason muttered, moving his boot away from the piss puddle, then, without making a sound, he crept toward the two sleeping men.

Holding the rifle across his body with his left hand, he slipped his knife from its Kydex sheath. Mason slammed the blade into the first man's eyeball, twisting it deep before pulling it out. Turning instantly to the second guard, he placed his hand over the man's mouth and dropped his knee into his sternum.

The man's eyes shot open, and he tried to squirm free but Mason placed the blade on his throat and whispered in Arabic, "If you move, I will kill you."

He waited for the man to nod his understanding before using his left hand to hit the talk button on his radio. "Okay, come on up."

A few moments later, Blaine filed by, moving

to a position where he could cover the front of the wadi. Zeus took a knee next to Mason, covering their prisoner with his rifle.

"Did you piss on yourself?" the Libyan asked, sniffing the air.

"Shut the fuck up. You got him?"

"Yeah, I got him," Zeus said, jamming the suppressor into the man's ear.

"Do not move, my friend, or I will put a large hole in your head," he said in Arabic.

Mason put away the knife and got on his radio once again.

"Are you asleep up there? I thought he was going to piss on my head."

"Sorry, boss," Grinch said. "I had to take care of a dog, and by the time I was on target, he was right on ya."

"Where the hell did he come from?"

"There has to be a fighting position somewhere near you. The fucker just appeared out of nowhere."

"Well, keep your eyes open; we need a second."

"Roger that."

"Find out who he is," Mason said to Zeus before climbing over the edge and pulling the dead body into the wadi.

Mason stayed up top and could hear his friend begin interrogating the man as he scanned the area for the fighting position. The rocks and gravel dug into his hands and knees as he crawled a few feet forward, almost falling into a small hole that had been expertly concealed.

"Sneaky fucks," he said, regaining his balance. After ensuring that there were no more surprises waiting in the desert, he returned to Zeus.

"He says a man paid them to take him across the border just after nightfall, and then told them to come back here and guard the house," the Libyan explained.

"Was there an American with the man?" Mason asked the terrified guard.

"H-he is in the house," he stuttered in Arabic.

"How many men are guarding him?"

"There is no one. He is alone."

Mason placed his palm on the man's forehead and pushed down hard. "Don't lie to me."

"I would not, I swear it. He is alone."

"Where did they cross into Iraq?"

"Near Rabia. He had men waiting for him at the crossing."

Mason wondered if the man was telling the truth, but there was only one way to find out. He produced a set of zip ties and quickly pulled them tight around the man's arms and legs. Tearing off a section from the dead man's tunic, he used it to cover the guard's eyes and mouth.

He didn't have the men to post a guard, but left the man with a warning: "If you move from here, my men will kill you. If you make any noise, they will kill you. Do you understand?"

The hostage nodded, and Mason got to his feet, motioning for them to advance to the target.

They were twenty feet away from the target house when they noticed the wadi was filled with trash and odds and ends thrown out by the villagers. Mason quickly climbed out, sprinting to a roughly made barn so he could pull security. Inside, the animals began to move restlessly around the enclosed pen as Blaine hurried past him and took up a position ten feet away.

Zeus was the next to pass, slapping Mason on the shoulder as he crept by. Once he was set, Mason got to his feet. He gently slapped Blaine on the back as he passed, letting him know that he was the last man. Within moments, he found a spot where he could observe the target house.

The structure looked exactly like it did on the imagery they had pulled up on the laptop, and Mason scanned the open area as he waited for his men to link up with him. He tried to cover all the angles that presented themselves while checking the roofs of the adjoining buildings for any guards. By the time Blaine got set beside him, he was pretty sure they were alone.

Mason felt Zeus move up behind him, and forced himself to wait for him to squeeze the back of his arm—signaling that he was ready to move—and together they moved to the front door.

Zeus reached out for the latch, making eye contact with Mason before tossing it open. The American caught the door with his left hand, wincing as it creaked on ancient hinges. He pinned it behind his back leg and scouted out the interior with his IR floodlight. It was so dark inside that all he could see was a wall to his right, and he lifted his muzzle, signaling Zeus to enter the house.

The Libyan stepped into the room, his laser blinking as he scanned for targets. Mason hooked right, checking the hard corners and Blaine stepped in behind Zeus. The door creaked closed behind them, cutting down the amount of ambient light in the room

Mason depressed the pressure pad that activated his IR flashlight, holding on to the area while Zeus and Blaine moved deeper into the structure. The infrared flood cut through the dark interior, casting shadows that were invisible to the naked eye. Once he was sure that his sector was clear, he moved to link up with Zeus.

He came around the corner just as Blaine disappeared into the adjacent room. Then Zeus's somber voice came across the net:

"You need to see this."

CHAPTER 23

- - - - - - - - - - - - - -

David took the long way to get to his room, and let his mind mull over what Renee had just told him. He'd wanted to finish the conversation but didn't trust Parker's sudden arrival. What little advantage he had would be gone by the time Parker left her room.

Before he unlocked the door, he knelt to check the piece of tape he'd stuck to the frame. After ensuring that the makeshift seal hadn't been broken, he unlocked the door and stepped inside.

His room was void of any creature comforts, and besides the neatly made bed, nothing suggested that anyone actually lived there. Unlike the rest of the rooms, the walls were free of pictures, and the only object on display was a towel hanging from the front of his wall locker. That, and a roll of clear tape on his desk.

David spun the combination of the lock hanging from the handle and snapped it open when he felt the dial begin to tighten. The door swung noiselessly outward, revealing a neat row of hanging clothes and toiletries arranged on top of a chest of drawers. He pulled a small flashlight from his pocket and placed it in his mouth. That was followed by his small switchblade, which he stuck into a small notch he'd cut in the floor of the locker.

David pried open a section of the floor, revealing a small duffel bag. It contained a stack of passports bound together by an old rubber band and a dusty computer that had seen better days. He slipped the computer and the passports into his leather bag, closed the lid of the trapdoor, and locked the wall locker before getting to his feet.

The computer had belonged to General Nantz, Colonel Barnes's direct superior. Mason had discovered it in Bagram before killing the traitorous general in a room very similar to the one David was standing in now. He should have turned it in or destroyed it, since it connected him directly to the murder, but David was never one to follow the rules.

After slinging his leather bag over his shoulder, he ripped a piece of tape from the roll on his desk and stepped out into the hall. The spy made sure the hallway was clear before kneeling down to affix the fresh piece of tape to the door frame. Then he headed back out to the tarmac.

The hunt was on.

CHAPTER 24

- - - - - - - - - - - - - - -

What was he doing here?" Master Sergeant Parker asked as soon as he was sure Mr. David was out of earshot.

"He wanted to know about the operation," Renee answered honestly.

"I didn't know you guys were close like that."

Renee suddenly realized that Parker was jealous, which she found strange since David was old enough to be her father. She had to admit that she'd thought about what a relationship with Parker might look like, but every time the notion came up, she pushed it out of her mind.

Men like Parker didn't go for girls with baggage, and that's exactly what she had. Renee had tried having a relationship with a fellow soldier once before—in fact, it was one of the reasons she had joined the military in the first place—but it hadn't lasted, and she'd promised herself that it was the last time she mixed business and pleasure.

Looking at Parker, it was easy to see why she'd considered breaking that rule. Not only was the man extremely handsome and self-assured, but there was a gentleness about him that calmed her rough edges. He was the only man on the team who'd accepted her, and something about him felt very safe.

"You know he got me on the task force," she said.

"Is that all there is?"

That edge hadn't left his voice. "Why do you care?" she teased.

"Who says I do?" he asked with a grin.

"Oh God," she said, realizing that she was flirting, and suddenly feeling very self-conscious about it. "Did you come over here to interrogate me—or did you want something?" Renee demanded, desperate to redirect the conversation.

"You impressed the hell out of Warchild today, you know that?"

She was back on the offensive. "You act like you're surprised."

"No, it's not that, I just—"

"You what? Thought that I'd fight like a girl? I don't know what you heard, but I didn't get here on my knees."

She could see even before she finished talking that she had taken it too far. He turned toward the door. "Forget it, I just wanted to come by and check on you. That's all."

Renee realized that she didn't want him to leave, and to stall him, she began talking about David.

"He wanted to know who the target was, but he seemed more interested in the source than anything else," she said ominously.

"Who?" Parker asked, thrown by the sudden change in direction.

"David. Mason was there when Boland was taken. He managed to get hold of one of the bad guys."

"One of the guys who took Boland? Did he say anything?"

"Yeah, he said he was working for a guy named al Qatar."

She was looking for any tells, giving him away, but instead Parker seemed pleased. "Have you told the colonel? Maybe we can find him."

"No, and I hope you don't tell him either."

Parker frowned at her, not understanding, as he moved over to the bed and took a seat on the wrinkles left by Mr. David.

Renee cursed herself for saying anything. She could tell that Parker was puzzling over her hasty remarks. He'd never had to work both sides of an operation before and usually didn't trouble himself with anything that didn't concern the mission at hand. Men like him followed orders without ever asking why, and she could tell that he didn't like the idea of keeping information from the boss.

"Don't you think it's something he needs to know?" he asked finally.

"Look, I'm sorry I said anything, but we need to keep this between us. If David thinks it's important, he'll pass it up the chain."

"So you want me to keep the team in the dark about one of our own guys? That doesn't seem right."

"You have to trust me on this. Please don't say anything."

Renee could tell by Parker's expression that he wasn't okay with what she was asking. She had made a mistake, said too much, and now he had leverage over her.

"I need you to promise me," she insisted.

"Okay . . ." he said, but she wasn't sure if he meant it.

Parker left Renee's room in search of Warchild. He checked his team leader's room and, when he didn't find him, headed to the gym.

"Give me a spot," Warchild said as Parker walked into the gym.

"You want a lift-off?"

"Nah, I'm good. Just don't let me drop it on my face."

Warchild grabbed the bar, his veins popping out as he lifted it off the rack and slowly brought it down to his chest. Parker quickly counted the plates on either end of the bar and realized that Warchild was lifting 325 pounds.

"So, what happened with Renee?" he grunted, pushing the weight back up to the starting position.

"The dude from the CIA, David Castleman, was in her room. I guess he slipped in without anyone seeing him. He said that Mason knows about al Qatar."

Warchild's eyes flashed with alarm. "How is that possible?"

"Fuck if I know."

"Well, you need to find out." Warchild panted.

"Dude, how am I going to do that?"

"You're a smart guy. I'm sure you can figure it out."

"This mission was totally fucked," Parker said, voicing aloud what he'd been thinking on the way over. "We lost Sanchez and Starks, and the new guy, the SEAL—"

"Bonds—his name was Bonds," Warchild groaned, forcing out five more reps before racking the weight and jumping to his feet.

"It's fucking combat. Don't tell me you're losing your nerve already."

"You know that's not it. I just don't like putting my ass on the line without knowing what's going on."

Warchild remained hard as nails. "No one asked you to join the Anvil Program; you volunteered, remember?"

"Yeah, but with Barnes dead—"

"You believe that shit? You really think that Kane took the boss down?" Warchild asked, taking a menacing step closer to Parker.

"Shit, man, I don't know."

"All you got to do is what I tell you. You see what happened to Boland when he stepped out of bounds. Is that what you want?"

"Boland deserved better."

"Boland was a piece of shit who got sloppy. The only reason he was out there was because he was trying to fix his own fuckup."

"What do you mean?"

"Guys like him—and fucking Mason—they think they're so smart. Always running around acting like James Bond and shit. Let me tell you something about Boland. All that dude had to do was take a box from point A to B, and he got jacked by a bunch of ragheads riding around in Toyota pickups."

Parker knew his team leader hated both Boland and Mason, and he was beginning to see how personal this operation was to him.

"You're a sled dog, and your job is to pull the sled. Me, I'm a team leader. My job is to know what's going on. Do yourself a favor and get that through your head before you end up like Mason."

Parker was starting to get fed up with the hardguy act.

"You know they cleared him, right?"

"Who, Mason? Please, that dude is a terrorist and a traitor. If he and that bitch Renee knew you were with the program, they wouldn't hesitate to put a bullet in your skull."

Parker was confused. "It's not like that."

"Believe me when I tell you it's exactly like that."

CHAPTER 25

- - - - - - - - - - - - - -

The blood covering the passenger side of the Ford F-250 glistened in the early morning sunshine. Al Qatar's first thought was to have his men clean it, but after a few moments of staring at the garish vehicle, he thought it looked better this way.

Moving to the tailgate, he took a seat. Before him, a plume of thick, black smoke rose above Rabia.

Jabar, al Qatar's most trusted lieutenant, had selected a handful of his best men and overran the border crossing easily. The Iraqi police who hadn't run had set up strongpoints within the government buildings, but Jabar had burned them out, and now the city was bathed in smoke.

"Emir," Jabar said, drawing the jihadist's attention to the man kneeling before him.

Al Qatar looked scornfully at the wretched captain. The man's neat uniform was covered in the blood that had poured out of his broken nose, and both of his eyes were already beginning to swell.

"I thought we had reached an agreement," al Qatar said, blowing a cloud of smoke into his eyes.

"Emir, I only did what I was ordered," the man babbled, garnering a savage kick from one of al Qatar's men.

"And who ordered you to resist me?"

"General Husam, Emir."

"And where is he now?"

"Tal Afar."

"That is a shame, and you should have known better. Trust is what separates us from the beasts of the world. Did you know that, Captain?"

"Yes, Emir."

"Look over there and tell me what you see," he commanded, pointing to the edge of the city, where his men were hanging the survivors from the power lines that led to the train station.

"You are hanging my men, Emir."

"That's right, and all of that could have been avoided if you had just kept your word. It really is a shame."

While his men finished gathering up the border guard's equipment, vehicles, and weapons, another group was boring holes in the massive fuel tanks situated near the tracks. One of the fighters had a small video camera, and he was documenting everything in hopes of dissuading any further resistance.

Al Qatar was most annoyed that instead of heading to Mosul, he now had to go out of his way to deal with General Husam. He had a very tight timetable, and the detour could prove costly.

"Burn everything, and hang him next to the rest of the traitors," he ordered, casually tossing the cigarette to the ground.

"Emir, please," the man begged, but al Qatar turned to the doughy commander anxiously awaiting his instructions.

The commander's thin mustache glistened as sweat poured down his face. The neck of his desert uniform was soaked through, giving him an unhealthy appearance.

"Are we ready to go?" Al Qatar asked.

"Yes, Emir. I have just been told that your artillery will reach the city within the hour."

"Good. Jabar, let us be on our way," al Qatar ordered as he opened the bloodstained door and took a seat in the stolen pickup.

It took more than an hour to get his men gathered up and on the road, and by the time al Qatar could see the outskirts of Tal Afar, he was in a foul mood. The only saving grace was the black Pelican case that sat on the seat next to him. He hoped the Americans thought they had destroyed it back in Syria, but if not, he was sure they wouldn't admit it had fallen into enemy hands.

He had heard the imams preach about the "sword of Allah," but he'd never truly believed such a thing was real until Khalid told him the capabilities of the equipment in the case. The thought of knocking out American air power filled him with a wave of joy that almost made everything else he was doing seem trivial.

Still, al Qatar knew that for him to use the weapon successfully, he had to make it impossible for the United States to ignore him.

The first boom from the stolen howitzer echoed across the desert, rattling the truck as it crested a small hill. Tal Afar appeared before him: a tranquil, gray smudge on the horizon.

A flash of light erupted as the shell erupted in a shower of golden sparks and black earth, followed a few seconds later by the guttural echo of the explosion. Small-arms fire chattered sporadically in the distance, announcing the first thrusts into the city. Ali gently pulled the truck to the side of the road in order to let the rest of the fighters join the assault.

"Keep going," al Qatar commanded.

"Are you sure, Emir?"

"Don't worry, I'll be fine. But if I am not close, the men might run."

Ali waited for three up-armored Humvees to pass before sliding in behind them. The fighters that Jabar had brought with him had already spray painted over the Iraqi markings that adorned the American vehicles. "You did a good job," he said.

"I thoroughly enjoyed myself," the Arab replied. "It is a shame we wasted so much money bribing the general, however."

"Never fear, Jabar. He will pay for every cent he took."

Al Qatar had met his second-in-command at a

CIA-run training camp in Jordan, where a proxy army was being trained to fight against President Bashar al-Assad's government troops in Syria. The agency wanted al Qatar to lead the men across the border, since he'd already been vetted by headquarters in Langley, Virginia, but, as usual, the jihadist had plans of his own, and the day he met Jabar, he knew he had a man he could count on.

Jabar's father had been hopeful when the Americans toppled Saddam in 2003, and despite the lawlessness emanating from Baghdad, he told his son to be patient. Everything changed on a warm summer day in 2005 when a Shiite car bomb killed his family while they were on their way to the market.

There wasn't enough of his family left for a proper burial, and the rage growing within him demanded blood. Jabar joined a group of fighters loyal to Abu Musab al-Zarqawi, but was forced to flee to Syria after Task Force 145 killed the terrorist leader north of the Iraqi city of Baqubah.

In Jordan, al Qatar worked feverishly to fan the hatred smoldering inside Jabar, and by the time they crossed the border, the jihadist led his very own militia. Instead of fighting the government troops besieging Aleppo, his men quickly set upon the loose confederation of rebels hunkered inside the city, and in less than a month, al Qatar had more than five hundred hardened fighters under his command.

As they approached the front lines, al Qatar turned his attention to the light-artillery pieces Jabar had taken from the Syrian army. They were firing at concrete positions that had been set up along the road. Toyota Hiluxes with hastily mounted DShK and PKMs raced back and forth across the open plain, spraying harassing fire into small clusters of Iraqi infantry.

The radio on the dashboard crackled to life, and one of his men yelled for more RPGs near the south side of the city. "They have tanks, we need the rockets now."

"We must pull back; there are too many," another voice ordered.

Al Qatar snatched the radio from its mount and ordered, "You will not pull back. Tell me where you are."

The net went silent once the men recognized their commander's voice. Finally, someone spoke up.

"We . . . we are near the south wall," the man mumbled.

"Take me there before they break through," he commanded.

His knew a core group of his men were battle hardened from their time fighting the Syrian army, but the majority of the fighters at his disposal were used to slaughtering civilians. The Americans had trained the Iraqis defending the city, and some of his fighters sounded like they were on the verge of running away.

Ali punched the accelerator, while the men in the back of the Ford hammered the roof of the truck with the flats of their hands, jeering at the men cowering near the rear.

Al Qatar wished he'd brought more men from

Kobani, but he'd already lost too much fighting for the city. He'd worked hard to gather fighters who'd stood toe to toe with the Americans in places such as Fallujah and Ramadi, and they had become the backbone of his ruthless shock troops. Like him, most were Sunni, and ever since Saddam had been driven from power, they had been waiting for their chance to strike back at the Shia minority.

Once American troops left Iraq in 2011, Prime Minister Nouri al-Maliki had made the situation worse by cracking down on the Sunnis in the north, and al Qatar knew the country was ripe for regime change.

Ali stopped the truck a hundred meters short of the southern gate, and as Jabar got out of the backseat, al Qatar could see that some of the men had already begun to fall back in the face of the Iraqi armor. Jumping out of the cab, he slipped the dead captain's bulletproof vest over his head and grabbed his M4 off the seat.

In Syria, they had been forced to fight with whatever they could get their hands on, which was usually older Soviet-era weapons, but America had left behind an arsenal when it withdrew, and al Qatar was hungry to get his hands on the NATO weapons.

A few feet ahead, three of his men climbed onto an armored Humvee, its front end twisted and burned from an RPG. Dead soldiers lay facedown in the rocky soil. One of his fighters ducked into the turret and expertly charged the Browning .50 caliber mounted to the truck.

The heavy machine gun boomed as the gunner fired over the heads of the retreating fighters, causing al Qatar to plug his ears against the concussions. He ducked away from the gun, pausing to take aim at an Iraqi soldier who was trying to lead a squad of soldiers into the fray. Al Qatar lined up the iron sights on the man's back and gently pulled the trigger.

The round hit the man just below the back of his head, knocking him face-first into the ground. The soldiers who'd been following him scattered or began looking around to see who else was in charge. Given the golden opportunity, al Qatar's gunner traversed the .50 cal in their direction, cutting the massive rounds across their backs.

Off to his left, a gun crew rammed a shell into the breach of a Russian 122 mm D-30 howitzer, while one of his lieutenants formed more fighters into a chain near the back of an old Opel truck. As they began to unload more of the shells, the gunner yanked the lanyard and the howitzer roared, sending a high-explosive shell toward the city.

The retort of the huge gun sent a wave of dust billowing over the area. Like clockwork, the gunner yanked the breach open and yelled for another round.

Al Qatar, waving the dust out of his face, made a beeline for an 82 mm mortar crew, with Jabar right on his heels. The men were just getting the tube settled into the baseplate when one of them recognized their commander and slapped his teammate on the back to get his attention.

"Yes, Emir?" the man asked.

"Fire at those tanks, right now."

"Yes, yes, of course."

The man grabbed a round off the ground and hoisted it up to the tube while his comrade stood on the baseplate. As soon as he was set, he dropped the round down the tube, and the mortar bucked, slamming the baseplate into the ground.

Without a sight, they were aiming down the tube at their target, and the first round sailed harmlessly overhead.

"Keep firing," he commanded.

Meanwhile, he yelled at the fleeing fighters to "Turn and fight!" Most of them ignored him, deciding that the tank was a bigger threat, forcing him to raise his rifle as another knot of deserters tried to dart past.

"I said stand and fight!" he yelled before firing a burst into two of the men. The fighters saw the men hit the ground and quickly decided they would take their chances with the tank.

Al Qatar knew that he had to press the attack home or risk losing everything he had worked so hard to build. He hated to admit that his men might not be able to stand up to a disciplined American force when it came, but that was a problem for a later date.

"You there! Why are you hiding? Go fight them!" he berated the men hiding behind a stalled-out truck.

"But, Emir, they have—"

Al Qatar shot the man through the chest. Turning the rifle to the next man, he lined up the sights.

"Fight them, or I will kill you."

The men nodded and filed out toward the tanks.

"Jabar, I will take out the tanks," he said, catching sight of an approaching RPG team. "Tell the men to use the mortars on the infantry once they get out into the open."

Rounds cracked and hummed past al Qatar as he weaved across the battlefield, grabbing as many men as he could along the way.

One of the Russian-built T-72s stopped in the middle of the field, shielding a mass of infantry. The main gun barked as it fired at one of his technicals, and a split second later, the round smashed into the hood of the unarmored truck, tossing it into the air like a toy.

Al Qatar dove to the ground, covering his head against the burning debris that slammed into the dirt around him. He got quickly to his feet, sprinting past the burning vehicle, and slid down the embankment at the edge of the road.

Five of his men were hiding behind the embankment, watching the T-72 traverse on the artillery piece. Furious at their cowardice, he slapped one of them in the back of the head, yanking the RPG-7 from his grasp.

"Give me that!" he yelled as the T-72 fired over his head.

The sound of the shell reminded him of a cargo plane preparing to land. Yet the gunner undershot the target, and that allowed al Qatar to step out onto the road. He brought the RPG up to his shoulder, centering the reticle on the turret before pulling the trigger. The armor-piercing round shot from the launcher with a shriek and danced through the air before impacting the turret. The warhead hit the steel with a sharp *thwang* before punching through and exploding inside.

He yelled for another rocket just as the hatch flipped open, releasing a billowing pillar of acrid smoke. One of the crewmen appeared, looking dazed. His face was covered in blood and soot, and he tried to climb out of the burning tank, only to be shot in the head for his troubles.

Another RPG screamed from al Qatar's left as his men began to press the attack. The rocket slammed into the second tank but failed to pierce the armor.

"Allahu Akbar!" a dark-skinned fighter cried, hefting an American AT-4 antitank missile onto his shoulder. His tongue protruded from his mouth, and he carefully lined up the sights before depressing the red firing button.

The rocket shot from the green launcher in a rush of flame. The back blast jerked the launcher off his shoulder, knocking him off-balance. He stumbled, caught himself, and then cheered when the 84 mm rocket hit the tank and detonated—stopping it dead in its tracks.

The Iraqi soldiers suddenly found themselves without any cover—they tried to run back to the city, but the emboldened jihadists fell on them with a vengeance. Some of the soldiers had already dropped their weapons when the first mortar round arced silently overhead and exploded ten feet above the ground.

Shrapnel cut through the men like an invisible reaper, bowling them over in clouds of blood. The tide had turned, and over the roar of the battle, the fighters began chanting al Qatar's name.

By late afternoon, the killing finally ended. Al Qatar sat on a camo camp chair, studying the fat general kneeling before him. Automatic fire and the hollow *thump* of grenades marked the killing pits his men had set up. He held the blade before the trembling man's face.

"I thought my instructions were clear, General Husam. Was I mistaken?"

"You must understand, I have a family," the general pleaded.

"All of these men have families," al Qatar replied, motioning to the lines of men who were being forced to kneel on the edges of the hastily dug pits. "Does that make you special?"

"I . . . I . . ."

"You what?" he asked, sliding the blade under the general's chin. Firmly he raised the man's head until he was looking into his dark eyes. "You're special, is that what you are saying?"

"No, Emir."

"I have no use for a man who will not listen, and I believe that your family would feel the same."

"Please."

Al Qatar spat at the man's fat face, soiling his clean uniform. They had found him cowering in one of the houses, and, to his shame, he hadn't even tried to fight for his life.

Al Qatar slowly moved the blade into place on the man's throat, putting more pressure on the point until it broke through the skin. The general tried to edge away, but two of his own officers were holding him in place.

Behind them, Jabar had his pistol pressed to the back of one of their heads, and ominously pulled back the hammer with an audible click.

"Hold him tight, you two," he warned.

Al Qatar let off the pressure until he was sure that they had a good grip on their superior. Then he slowly pressed the blade all the way through his skin.

He yanked the knife from the man's throat, allowing the general to fall facedown on the ground. Blood rushed from the wound in a torrent of crimson spray, and Husam lay there, a ghastly, choking sound emanating from the back of his throat.

"Now, you hold him," he ordered, pointing at one of the officers, whose face was a mask of pure horror.

"I—"

"The emir said to hold him," Jabar said, pressing the pistol to his skull as the soldier slowly forced his comrade to his knees.

"Do you see what happens to people who betray me?"

CHAPTER 26

- - - - - - - - - - - - - - -

This is bullshit," SecDef Cage said, glancing out at the reporters packed inside the Pentagon's briefing room.

"Just stick to the talking points, and you'll be fine," Simmons replied, handing him the seating chart that identified those reporters who were considered safe and the ones he should avoid.

"Why don't *you* take this one?"

"'Cause it's not my job."

The first thing that Cage felt when he stepped onstage was the heat radiating off the high-intensity lights mounted to the ceiling. He started to sweat immediately as he took his place behind the shiny oak podium centered on the Pentagon's seal. Part of the reason was nerves, but there was more to it than just that.

Cage was about to force the president into a corner.

"Good morning," he began, glancing over at

the American flag, which stood proudly before the light-blue curtain hung behind him.

"Good morning, Mr. Secretary," the reporters replied enthusiastically, despite being crammed together in their tiny metal chairs.

The notoriously suspect press corps had been smitten with him ever since his very first press briefing, and Cage had no idea why. It was like a one-sided courtship, and the more he resisted their charm, the more they wanted to be accepted.

He found it strange because no matter how much affection they showed him, Cage hated the press.

"At approximately 0400 local time, the DOD, in collaboration with the CIA, launched a raid into Syria and eliminated two high-value targets. The mission was a success, and I am pleased to report that the objective was cleared with minimum casualties on our side. I will now take any questions that you might have."

"Can you tell us about the operation?" a pretty reporter from the *New York Times* asked loudly.

"Like I said, it was a combined DOD-CIA operation centered on two targets who had extensive links to al Nusra and a group calling themselves the Islamic State of Iraq," he replied over a barrage of snapping cameras.

He grabbed a glass of water from the top of the podium and took a sip, fighting the urge to wipe the sweat collecting on his brow.

"Yes, James," he said, pointing to a reporter from the *Washington Post*.

"Can you tell us a little about the intel that drove the operation?"

"You need to be more specific."

"Did the intel come from a drone, signal hit, or an asset on the ground?"

"We utilized all of those methods, and I have to say that the CIA did an excellent job collecting the necessary intelligence, which allowed the president to make an informed decision," he lied.

"Mr. Secretary?" a middle-aged woman asked from the edge of the room.

Cage didn't need to look at the seating chart to know who the woman was, because he had hand-picked her for this exact question.

"Yes, Wendy?" he said casually.

"Is there any truth to the rumors that an unknown group of fighters have conducted an armed incursion into northern Iraq?"

"I'm not sure where you are getting that information," he replied.

"Well, sir, according to my sources, combined al Nusra and Islamic State fighters have already taken Rabia and are currently besieging Tal Afar. Can you confirm that?"

"At this time, the Pentagon has no knowledge of any incursions, but as I have said before, the region as a whole, and Iraq in particular, have become a hotbed of insurgent activity since we left."

"Well, on that same note, a video was posted on Al Jazeera that shows what they claim is an American operative from the DIA having his head cut off. The video claims that this man was taken during the operation you spoke of in Syria. Does your office have any information on that?"

Cage took another sip of water, feeling the electric current arcing through the room. He knew he was playing a dangerous game, but he was all in, despite the cost.

"Wendy, on the record, I know nothing about the video. But off the record, I can promise you that it is just a matter of time before we get hit again. If we do not take a more proactive approach, there will be another attack—I can promise you that. The two groups you spoke of, al Nusra and the Islamic State, have had nothing to do but plot their next move since we pulled out of Iraq. Syria has become a breeding ground for radical jihad, and as much as we want to hide our heads in the sand, the fighters there are just waiting for an opportunity to strike."

Thousands of miles from Washington, David Castleman handed a roll of dinars to the taxi driver and stepped out into the street. He'd been traveling for most of the day, and he needed a shower almost as badly as he needed a drink.

There was a special place in his heart for Beirut, a city that had seen better days. The spy had his first posting here, and for some reason he had never let go of the apartment he had bought so many years before.

The smell of the ocean greeted him like a long-lost friend, and he wished he had time to walk down to the beach. Instead, he veered into an alley and headed west toward his destination.

Like everything else in David's life, the apartment was small and unassuming, and as he made his way up the familiar paint-chipped stairs, he had the feeling that he was finally home. He paused outside the light-blue door. Immediately he became alarmed when he noticed the seal he'd put on its side hinge was gone. His hand slipped to the Colt .45 stuck in his waist.

He brought up the pistol. The knob turned easily, and the door swung silently open on well-oiled hinges. The spy stepped silently over the threshold, the barrel of the .45 leading him into the entryway.

A solitary ceiling fan spun lazily in the center of the main room. The curtains billowed gently from the breeze coming off the ocean. The view was breathtaking, but his attention was absorbed by the man sitting on the couch.

"Hope you don't mind I let myself in," Captain Brantley said, holding up a bottle of beer.

"You could have locked the door," David replied.

"Yeah, sorry. I can't believe you still carry that old tack driver," Brantley said, getting to his feet.

"It's a classic, just like me."

"Hey, whatever works, boss."

CHAPTER 27

- - - - - - - - - - - - - - -

Mason sat in the passenger seat, trying to sleep as Zeus drove them east toward Iraq. Even though he was exhausted, sleep refused to come. Instead, all he could think of was finding Boland's disembodied head in that shitty farmhouse in Syria, staring sightlessly up at him.

The horrors of war weren't anything new, but this demon wouldn't let go. The guilt was the worst part, and he couldn't shake the feeling that it should have been him.

Mason knew that there had to be a reason, a link between the cause and the effect, but he couldn't see it. Both Renee and David had the innate ability to extrapolate the big picture from random bits of action, but he didn't dare call them. He still didn't know whom he could trust.

The question at the forefront of his mind was, why? Anderson had to have an angle, something that justified launching the mission in the first place. Mason knew that if he could just figure that out, he might be able to get in the game.

He had no doubts that someone had tried to kill him with the Hellfire strike. But that was nothing new. Mason knew he had more enemies than friends, but what in the hell could Anderson gain by killing Boland?

Opening his eyes, Mason glanced in the rearview mirror and caught the edge of the coarse blanket peeking over the backseat. Boland deserved a better shroud, but that was all they could find. As he stared at it, he felt a helpless rage boiling up inside him.

"Did you sleep?" Zeus asked.

Mason didn't answer. He bounced a smoke out of the pack of Pine cigarettes he had taken from Boland's pocket. He snapped open his dull gold Zippo and touched the flame to the end of the yellowed cigarette.

The first drag was acrid, burning the back of his throat as it rushed to his lungs. The smokes were made in South Korea, and they reminded him of his time in Afghanistan, when he'd first started smoking. Boland had bought a carton from a local man, and told Mason they were American. He'd never smoked before, and his teammate had laughed hysterically when he almost puked on the dirt floor.

"Mason, what are we going to do with Mr. Boland?" Zeus asked in Arabic.

"I don't know," he said honestly.

"We can't carry the body around with us. It's not exactly sanitary."

"I'm not burying him in this shithole."

"I'm not saying we should. I just think that his family might—"

"I hear you," Mason snapped.

He could tell by the patience in Zeus's voice that he wasn't finished. "Look, I know what you're going to do. I've seen that look before, but it's going to get bloody, and I don't think they are ready," Zeus whispered, motioning to the sleeping men in the back.

"Don't you even think about cutting me out of this," Grinch replied in his broken Arabic as he opened one eye. "T.J. was my friend too, and someone has to pay for what happened."

Mason cracked the window, letting the smoke trail out into the desert. Men like Boland were supposed to die in a pile of their own brass, he thought grimly, not tied to some fucking chair. Suddenly it all seemed so pointless.

Mason knew that he was slowing down, and even though he would never say it out loud, it scared him. He was only thirty-two, but he felt twice that. His leg bothered him every day, and there was only so much damage a man could take before his number finally came up.

But the worst part was that he didn't know anything else. If he gave it all up, what was he going to do? Mason had always wanted to be a soldier— that's what he was—and without that one constant, he knew he'd be lost.

"You have a family," he said, turning to look at Grinch.

"So? What the hell does that have to do with anything?"

"A lot. Zeus and I, we have nothing—this is all we know," Mason said, opening his arms to encompass the filthy truck. "Is that what you want?"

"Why don't you just call the colonel?" Blaine piped in. "You think he'd let this stand?"

"Anderson is the problem."

Blaine was surprised by Mason's harshness. "What are you talking about?"

"I've worked with Anderson, back before all of this, and he's not the guy you think he is." He turned himself halfway around, so the men in the back could see his face. "You guys know me, you know what I've done and what I've been through, so I hope you will listen to what I'm about to say. This mission has his fingerprints all over it, and you can bank on the fact that Anderson is in this just as deep as al Qatar. There is no way a colonel sends two strike teams into an unsecure objective, in broad fucking daylight, unless someone told him to."

The two men didn't respond, trying to process what Mason was saying. He had told them about his time in the Anvil Program, and his exploits during Iraq and Afghanistan were legendary.

David had let him handpick his recon team, and the first thing he'd done was to tell his men all about his time on the run. He had never lied to them and wasn't about to start now. Soldiers like Grinch and Blaine needed to believe in the men they followed and instead of alienating them,

Kane's honesty made them work tirelessly to earn his approval.

Mason went on. "I don't know how, but I am going to find al Qatar, and then I'm going to kill him—and anyone else who was involved. I'm warning you: we can't trust the task force, and nobody is going to be coming when we get in the shit. And after that's all done, if I make it out alive, I'm going to get Anderson." He wanted to make sure they realized that. "So, if I were you, I'd be on the next thing smoking, and I'd never look back."

He wasn't sure he liked their replies. "I'm in," Grinch said without hesitation.

"Me too. Just tell me what to do."

Mason looked over at Zeus, who shrugged behind the wheel. "I'd rather be sunning on the Riviera, but what the hell . . ."

Mason was glad it was all settled. This was the kind of team he wanted. "Okay, but before that, we have to get someone out here to recover Boland."

"How the hell are you going to do that without calling Anderson?"

"I'm going to use this," he said, holding up the dead man's beacon.

CHAPTER 28

- - - - - - - - - - - - - - -

Renee waited for as long as she could before slipping out of her room in search of Mr. David. She knocked softly at his door, but after getting no response, she headed to the operations area in hopes he might be there.

The ops center was quiet and dark, with the major source of light shining dimly from a laptop onto Dustin Toomes.

"Dustin," she said, approaching the man. He was wholly absorbed in some DVD that was playing on his laptop.

The analyst jumped as she put her hand on his shoulder. He yanked the bulky earphones off his head. "Renee, wh—what are you doing up?" he stuttered.

Toomes had been taking a lot of shit from the operators who'd returned from the mission, and he wore a resigned expression as he steeled himself for still another attack.

It was time to flip the script. "How's it going?" she began sweetly.

"It's been a shitty couple of days. Anderson's sending me back to the States," he said with a sigh.

"That sucks," she said, pretending outrage. "You've been a real asset."

Though it was a lie, he was grateful to hear it. "Thanks, that means a lot."

"What are you watching?"

"It, um, it's *Return of the Jedi*," he said sheepishly.

She knew exactly how to play the analyst. "That's my favorite one. You know, my dad loved *Star Wars*. We used to watch them all the time on VHS."

"Really, I never would have guessed," he replied.

"Look, I need a favor," she said, cutting to the chase.

A frown filled his face immediately. "Renee, I can't talk about—"

She raised her hand, cutting him off. "Just listen to what I have to say." She casually pulled over one of the rolling chairs and took a seat.

"People died," she said. "We trusted you, and the intel was wrong."

"I feel like shit, but there is nothing I can tell you about the source, or anything else."

She expected Toomes to say that. "I don't need you to tell me about the source. I already know who it is."

"That's not possible," he said.

"Al Qatar."

He was astonished, giving himself away. "How the hell—?"

"That's not important right now, Dustin," she said, leaning close. "Look, I know that someone fed you the source, and you were acting on good faith. You're not a bad guy, you didn't want this to happen, but the fact is that you're still responsible."

Dustin's shoulders began to shake. She laid a hand on his arm, consoling him. He tried hard to hold back the tears, but Renee's gentle touch had broken through the wall, and everything came tumbling out.

"Al Qatar was cleared by Boland. I checked him out before sending it up. He had the creds and had worked with the CIA before. I didn't know."

Renee kept stroking his arm softly. "What happened to Boland?"

"What do you mean?"

"Before the mission, Boland disappeared for a while. What happened? Where did he go?"

The analyst wiped his eyes on the sleeve of his sweater and then glanced over his shoulder to make sure they were alone. "You have to understand, this came from the top."

"Higher than Anderson?" she asked, feigning surprise.

"It all started in Washington. The DOD found a way to use cell phone towers to jam communications over a small area." The technology involved started to get him excited. "It's genius, really, and easy to use because it works off organic sources. All Boland had to do was plug them in and leave 'em."

"What happened?"

"Khalid grabbed him. No one has any idea how he knew they were even in country, but he grabbed Boland just as he crossed the border. Washington kept a lid on it, and when he managed to escape, he convinced someone that he could get the case back."

Renee did her best to hide her fury. "So that was the whole reason we launched the operation?"

"Exactly. I was given al Qatar's name and a bank account, and the agency wired him two million in exchange for the target location. You know the rest."

She sure as hell did. A lot of good men had died. "How do I find this al Qatar?"

"Shit, I don't know."

His excuse didn't sound convincing, and she probed further. "Isn't that your job?"

"Yeah, but I can't log into the system without leaving a trail. I'm already in deep shit as it is."

"This is your chance to make amends for the men who died out there," she pointed out, making herself sound stern, "and you're worried about your own ass? I thought you were better than that."

This argument hit home. "You have to believe me, there is nothing that I can do," Toomes insisted.

"What if I wire half a million into your account and then I tip off a guy I know in the FBI?" Renee was coming up with the plan on the fly, but she couldn't think of a better way to get the man to do what she wanted.

"Why would you do that?"

"The question is, why would you do it? You think they are going to put you in jail? Hell, no, what they will do is send someone like me to your house, and I will happily put a bullet in the back of your head."

"Jesus," he moaned.

She reverted back to the gentle approach. "Find al Qatar. I know you can."

Dustin saw the light at last. After exiting out of the movie, his fingers began flying across the keyboard. Different programs popped up on the screen as he typed prompts into the command line. Renee had no idea what he was doing, but as long as he got what she wanted, she didn't care.

She glanced around the TOC, praying that no one disturbed the man as he worked. The keystrokes sounded incredibly loud as he hammered away, his hands a blur. Soon one of the windows showed rows of numbers scrolling vertically through what she assumed was a phone-tracking database. Meanwhile, he opened another program and typed in his access code.

"What are you doing?" she asked.

"Boland had a program on his cell phone that captured any phone call made close to him. The program," he said, pointing at the scrolling window, "runs those numbers to an NSA database, looking for any patterns."

"What kind of patterns?"

"Once a number is captured, we are able to slave the originating phone, and capture all outgoing and ingoing calls. So even if it is not active, we still know who that person called or whoever called him."

She checked surreptitiously over her shoulder again, so he wouldn't get nervous. "How long is this going to take?"

He was entranced by the numbers. "Could take all night—I have no idea. Wait, here we go." He pointed. "A phone called this number in the States three hours before we launched. That same number called another phone the same day as the operation, and again today."

"Can you find out whose phone it is?"

"No, all it tells me is that one of the phones was purchased in Virginia."

That linked up Washington, DC. "Okay, what about the other number?"

"It's a satellite phone. One call originated in Syria, and the second call came from . . . it came from Iraq."

"What are the chances that it's al Qatar?"

"Renee," he said, like she didn't understand the complex world he lived in, "I can't give you an answer to that without a hell of a lot more time. I can track the phone, tell you where it is right now, but the only way I can tell you whose phone it is would be to have eyes on it."

Al Qatar was an Iraqi who had definitely been placed in Syria earlier that day. Where else would he go after the operation? Renee knew it was a gamble, but she had learned long ago to trust her gut. It was all she had, but she could work with it.

"How do I track that number?" she asked impatiently. "I want to know where the fuck it goes."

"Give me your iPhone."

"Don't tell me there's an app for that." She instantly pulled out her phone, before he could change his mind. Seeing it, he winced. "Just know that after that, it's your ass on the line, not mine."

"Fine, do it," she said. Already she knew the next phone call she was going to make: to Mason.

CHAPTER 29

- - - - - - - - - - - - - -

So how's your other boss?" David asked, placing his napkin on the table and reaching for the glass of Johnnie Walker Black.

"Still shady. You were right about him."

"Don't be too hard on him. Patrick was a good soldier and a good friend."

"Maybe so, but treason? Come on, the dude's a piece of shit."

The two men had finished dinner, and David was beginning to feel the effects of the long journey. More than anything, he wanted to lie down, but he still had work to do.

"You want some coffee?" he asked, draining the glass before getting to his feet.

"Sure, I'll take some."

The spy headed for the small kitchen. "So, fill me in."

"First off, how did you know?" Captain Brant-

ley asked as David opened a bottle of water and
poured it into a saucepan on the stove.

"Know what?"

"About Vann."

"He and I worked together in Iraq back in 2003,
when he was attached to JSOC. He was relentless—
hell, he was the main reason they found Zarqawi,"
David answered, pouring coffee grounds into the
bottom of an aged French press while he waited for
the water to boil.

"Yeah, we all know that story."

"He believed that we could reprogram some
of the detainees and use them as informers. I was
against the idea, but, as usual, no one listens to me."

"Okay, nice history lesson, but when you came
to me seven months ago, how did you know what
he was going to do?"

"The computer," David said.

"Your holy grail," the man said, looking over at
the laptop set on the wooden coffee table. "Are you
ever going to let me look at it?"

"Are you familiar with Pandora?"

"The online radio program?"

"No, the myth."

"Sure, she was the girl that opened the box and
let all the evil into the world."

"I see they are still teaching the classics at West
Point," the spy said with a smile. He lifted the
boiling water off the stove and poured it over the
grounds.

"Wasn't my best subject, but I did okay."

"That computer is my Pandora's box. There are

things stored in there that should never see the light of day."

"Fine, so your box told you that Vann was going to authorize a mission into Syria, seven months before it happened, and that someone was going to use an Iraqi that no one has heard about to kill one of our operatives?"

"No, but it did tell me who had any connection to the Anvil Program."

Brantley reared back in his chair, causing the legs to creak against the tile floor. "Vann was in on that shit show?"

"Yes and no, but the main point here is, your boss craves power. You put someone like that in the right circles, and he will do whatever it takes to ensure he never lets go off the brass ring."

"I'll buy that."

"There are people within the government who will never forget being forced to leave Iraq early. When Barnes was allowed to go into Syria, it wasn't just to start another war. It was a stepping-stone to a much bigger goal."

Brantley scoffed at this notion. "Iraq's over, and there is no way we are ever going back."

"That's where you're wrong," David said, pressing the coffee and pouring it into two cups. He placed the cups on the waiting saucers and carried them back to the table, careful not to spill.

"When Boland was picked up in Syria, no one knew a thing," he went on. "There were no records that he'd been sent on a mission, and no mention of what he was carrying across the border. Someone very high up wanted it that way, and I knew that it was more than a coincidence that he worked for General Vann."

"So it was all a setup, is that what you're saying? An American general sent one of his men into a rebel stronghold, with a very sensitive piece of equipment, and wanted it to be taken by a rebel leader?"

"Exactly."

Brantley waved a hand over his cup to cool down the coffee. "I'm sorry, David, but I'm not buying it. He did all of that so we can go back to Iraq?"

"Just wait—there is more to come. I just don't know what it is." He added in an undertone, "But I'm going to find out. That's why I have to go to Washington."

CHAPTER 30

- - - - - - - - - - - - - -

Al Qatar stared at the memory card he was holding. For a moment, it transported him back to the day the Americans had murdered his brother.

He could still remember his brother handing it to him and telling him to protect it with his life—a moment before Boland burst into the room and shot him in the face. That moment had started him down this path, and now that he was getting closer to his revenge, it seemed so surreal.

The Iranian in the seat next to him coughed, rudely yanking the jihadist from his painful memories.

"Is that it?"

"Yes," he said simply.

"Everything that you required has been done," Khalid said, holding out his hand.

Al Qatar closed his fist around his last connection to a life before war, and then ever so slowly handed it to Khalid. The sentimental moment had passed, and he was all business.

"Tell me about the mines."

"They are really very simple. My government knows that one day they must face the Americans, and our engineers have been working for the last fifteen years on how to sink one of their carriers. We have used small boats to get close, practiced shooting swarms of rockets, but to no avail."

"So, will this device work?"

"Oh yes. The answer, we found, was so very simple," Khalid said. "A very powerful mine was developed using depleted uranium that will cut through the bottom of the carrier like knife through a man's flesh."

"What is to keep them from seeing the mine?" al Qatar asked skeptically.

"We developed sensors to pick up specific frequencies: in this case the cavitations of the carrier's propellers. When the mines are emplaced, the sensors go active and wait until they pick up the target. Once the frequency is locked, the mine is released, and it follows the signal to the source. Quite simple, really."

"And they are powerful enough?"

"The charge is shaped to cut right through the hull. Are you familiar with explosive-formed projectiles?"

"Yes, like the IEDs you gave the jihadists in Iraq?"

"Precisely. A thin sheet of metal is placed over the explosives, and when the bomb goes off, a jet of metal cuts through the armor. In this specific case, once the metal has penetrated the hull, a second charge sends the explosives up into the breach, where it detonates."

"My many thanks," al Qatar said with a humble bow of his head.

"You know, they will hunt you to the ends of the earth for this."

"That is for Allah to decide. I am but an instrument of his will."

The Iranian smiled, slipping the memory card into his pocket. Then he placed his hand on al Qatar's shoulder.

"You are a brave man, and it has been my honor to work with you, but there is just one final thing, and then our deal is finished."

"Ahh, the name."

"Yes."

Al Qatar knew that he was making a deal with the devil when he had been introduced to Khalid al Hamas, but at the same time, he didn't have much of a choice. Killing a few Americans, while helping a bunch of zealots set up their own state, was one thing, but dealing a crippling blow to the Americans required an infrastructure he didn't have.

He knew that what Khalid was really after was his source. A man that high up, who was willing to betray his country, was worth way more than anything Khalid had given him.

"I still have need of this man," al Qatar said.

"And you shall have it, but you must give me the name—that was our deal. I must be able to protect myself when they find out the part my country played in this upcoming catastrophe."

"How do I know you will keep your word?"

"It is up to you, but without this"—Khalid held up a phone-like device—"the mines are useless to you."

Al Qatar knew he had no choice. Plus, in a few days, he would no longer need the man who had been feeding him information.

"His name is General Patrick Vann."

"The deputy director of the DIA?" the Iranian asked with a huge smile.

"Yes."

"By Allah, your reputation is well earned, my friend," he said, slapping the Iraqi on the back. "My people will be very pleased to learn this. Very pleased indeed."

"You might just get another house in the hills."

Khalid's smile froze on his face. Al Qatar knew he must be wondering how he knew of the gift he had received from the ayatollah.

"Yes, I know all about your houses and cars, and even where your son goes to school," he added.

"Are you threatening me?"

"No, I am just letting you know that even though our dealings are finished, I will be keeping a very close eye on what you do. Do not make the mistake of meddling in my affairs before it is time."

"I have no wish to ever cross you. I give you my word on that."

"Now give me the detonator."

The Iranian handed the device to the Iraqi but

couldn't help asking just one question before he left: "What is on the drive? I was never told."

"My friend, do you think Saddam would move all of his WMDs without keeping a list of where they went?" he said with a wink.

Al Qatar started the car and headed down the block before turning down an alley and heading north. He drove for ten minutes and then beeped his horn outside an ancient warehouse that still bore the scars of the American invasion.

Once his men opened the massive bay door, he drove the car inside and turned it off. Before getting out, he dug his phone out of his pocket and dialed a number from memory. The phone rang twice before his handler answered.

"Is it done?"

"Yes, he just left."

"Did you give him the name?"

"I did," replied al Qatar. "He bought it."

"Good. Is everything in place?"

"Yes, just send me the time."

"I will."

CHAPTER 31

- - - - - - - - - - - - -

Captain Chris Miller stood on the bridge, cautiously scanning the Iranian gunboat loitering a few miles off the bow. Every so often, he took his eyes from the binoculars and studied the helmsman, who had a death grip on the massive wheel, guiding the Nimitz-class supercarrier into the inbound clearway.

The Strait of Hormuz, only twenty-one miles wide, was the gateway for 20 percent of the world's oil. Due to the strait's narrowness, the International Maritime Organization had established inbound and outbound lanes of travel for any ship entering or leaving the Persian Gulf.

Tims had been through the Strait of Hormuz many times, but this was his first at the helm of the USS *George H. W. Bush*, and the last thing he needed was some Iranian captain trying to dick him around.

During his time as a naval aviator, he had played

chicken with Russian MiGs over the North Sea, but at 1,092 feet in length, the *George Bush* was a hell of a lot less maneuverable. It was well known that Iranian naval officers liked to act like assholes whenever a naval battle group entered the Persian Gulf, and Miller knew that without protection from the other ships, the carrier made an inviting target.

"Wouldn't you just love to blow his ass out of the water?" his XO—executive officer—asked, handing him a steaming cup of coffee.

Miller lowered the binos to his chest, and he could feel the leather strap biting into the back of his tan neck as he reached for the mug.

Born in Rhode Island, he came from a generation of navy men, and his grandfather had actually flown with George H. W. Bush during World War II. The navy was in Miller's blood, and he'd known that he wanted to be an aviator before he was even out of elementary school.

"Back during the first Gulf War, I almost got a MiG-29 right around here," he said, his pale blue eyes smiling as he took a sip of the coffee. "It's funny how everything comes full circle."

"What do you mean, Cap'n?"

"This is my last cruise. The last time through the strait and the last time I have to deal with assholes like that," he said, motioning to the gunboat with the mug that had his name emblazoned on it in gold script. "Seems like everything changes but stays the same over here."

"We're going to miss you, sir."

Miller was known as a fair skipper who took

care of his men, as long as they took care of his boat. His true passion was still flying, though, and he knew he was going to miss being in the air most of all.

"I'll miss you guys too. Not really sure what I'm gonna do. Hell, the navy's all I've known since Annapolis."

"Well, sir, I'm sure you'll think of something."

"You're probably right."

He was taking another sip when he felt a tremor run from the deck up through his legs. "What the hell?" he said, stumbling as a tearing sound screeched up from the bowels of the ship, knocking him off-balance.

Alarm bells sounded in the tight confines of the bridge as the lights flicked off for a second—before the backup generator managed to come online.

"Captain, the hull has been breached!" one of the sailors yelled as the general quarters alarm rang out over the ship's PA. Officers and enlisted men began rushing to their stations.

"What did we hit?"

"Sir—"

The ship reared up in the water as massive overpressure ripped through the bulkheads and blasted upward through the decks. It felt like an earthquake, and as the huge carrier settled back onto the surface of the water, a massive tidal wave washed over the deck.

On the bridge, sensors warned that the two A4W nuclear reactors had been breached, and Miller could hear screams coming from the engine room that told him his men were being boiled alive. Seawater poured through the massive breach, quickly overwhelming the ship's ability to contain the damage. A second explosion tore another hole in the bottom of the *George Bush*, and the carrier began to list to the side.

Nine levels below the bridge, Chief Petty Officer Jim Brands was slammed against the floor. The box of fuses he'd been inventorying was sent flying across the heavily reinforced room. All around him pallets of five-hundred-pound BLU-111 bombs rattled against their chains.

As he rose to his feet, he could feel blood dripping from his forehead. "Secure those fuses!" he shouted a second before a huge ball of flame blasted the door off the primary bomb-assembling magazine and rushed into the room.

His Nomex uniform burst into flames. The wall of flame melted the nozzles of the fire-suppression system, and the intense heat licked across the bombs, causing them to bubble.

The fuses were the first to explode, and a second later, the room evaporated in a blinding flash, gutting the hull as blue-and-white flames snaked topside in search of oxygen.

Two miles above the USS *George Bush*, Ensign Benjamin "Poppy" Speltz saw a flash of light off to his left. He looked out the side of his cockpit in time to see the first explosion rip through the flight deck of the carrier.

"Holy shit, what the hell was that?" he asked as he banked the F-18 Super Hornet into a tight left turn to get a better look.

"The ship is on fire," his wingman said in disbelief.

Flames were cascading out of the hangar bay, and he was forced to cover his eyes when the fuel depot exploded, ripping the deck in half. A column of black smoke rushed skyward, reminding him of the videos he'd seen of Pearl Harbor. The net came alive with chatter.

Coming out of the turn, he watched a CH-53E Sea Stallion helicopter thunder low across the water before the smoke swallowed it up. There was no room for the ships that had already made it through the strait to turn around, and as the carrier broke apart, he knew that no one else was getting through.

All the fuel that had not been vaporized by the explosion burned brightly on the surface of the water, flickering and undulating with the rise and fall of the ocean, burning the survivors as they bobbed to the surface.

The smoke began to envelope his F-18, forcing Poppy to climb or risk being swallowed up in the inky blackness.

He pushed the throttle forward, offering up a silent prayer to those caught beneath him, as the lip of the USS *George H. W. Bush* rose tragically into a vertical position before slowly disappearing beneath the ocean waves.

CHAPTER 32

Zeus dumped the Land Cruiser in a ravine on the far side of a small village, and Mason stood off to the side while Blaine and Grinch paid their respects to Boland.

He was the last one to grab his gear from the back of the truck. He found himself at a loss for words as he stared down at the blood-soaked blanket.

"We had some good times," Mason whispered, placing his hand on the shrouded body of his dead friend. "You were always there for me, and when you finally needed me, I couldn't get there. But I promise you one thing, brother," he vowed, his voice cracking with emotion. "They will pay what they owe."

Mason took the emergency beacon from his pocket and, after switching it on, laid it on Boland's chest. "Rest easy, bro."

He knew that the signal would be picked up by

the task force, and it wouldn't take long for them to send out a helo to investigate.

The men quickly loaded up into the Nissan Patrol that Zeus had stolen from a village a few miles away, and Blaine got behind the wheel, while Mason got in the back. He had just drifted off when the laptop dinged from his assault pack, alerting him to a message.

The Libyan spymaster, Ahmed, had done so much more than merely save his life after Mason's team had left him for dead. The man had taught him how to survive, and one of those lessons had been how to send messages when normal avenues of communication were unavailable. They set up a system of chat rooms, which allowed them to communicate in plain sight. This time, however, the message wasn't from the old spy, it was from Renee. "Why is she contacting me?" he wondered.

The little envelope at the bottom of the screen told him that he had an email. Once he opened it, a link popped up, inviting him to a garden forum that they had used in the past. For some reason, Renee loved to use the garden forums. The one time he'd asked her why, she simply smiled and said, "It reminds me of a simpler time."

It was an answer Mason could understand. The life they led stripped a person of the good memories and replaced them with the horrors of war. Sometimes a person needed to be reminded why they were fighting.

The message was simple and to the point, just like Renee:

"I hear you are looking for a gardener," it read. "I hear this one is all the rage—check out the link to his website."

Curious, Mason clicked on the link, and a separate window popped up showing a map and a blinking blue dot. He immediately recognized the program for what it was: the dot represented a captured phone. He had a very good idea whose phone it was. Using the touch pad, he double-clicked on the dot, and a ten-digit grid came up, which he quickly entered into the GPS unit.

The new route had them heading toward Mosul.

"Follow this," he said, handing the GPS to Blaine.

"Where are we going?" Zeus muttered without opening his eyes.

"Renee found al Qatar."

Kane felt like he'd just drifted off when the patrol came to a halt, and Zeus got behind the wheel. Mason gave up on going back to sleep, and after everyone had taken a piss, he moved to the front passenger seat. He lit a cigarette while Zeus pulled a CD from the visor and slid it into the player.

The American was able to ignore the music at first, but as the song kept hammering on, the Libyan got more and more into it. He began humming along. When he began drumming wildly on the steering wheel, Mason finally had enough.

"Dude, that shit is annoying," he snapped.

"What? I like this song."

"I'm not talking about the song, I'm talking about your terrible drum solo. It's making my fucking head hurt."

"Grumpy ass," Zeus muttered—before turning up the volume even louder.

The girl singer's voice blasted through the speakers, and Zeus ignored him, drumming even harder as he sang along.

"My loneliness is killing meeeeeee, and I must confess, I do beliiiiiiiiieve," he bellowed, singing along to Britney Spears.

"I'm going to throw that shit out the window," Mason growled, leaning forward to pop the CD out of the player.

Zeus swerved the SUV hard to the left, slapping Mason's hand away. The men in the back yelled for him to get back in his lane.

"Don't you touch it," the Libyan ordered, regaining control of the Nissan.

"Then turn it down!" Mason yelled.

"Fine, I'm turning it down," he replied, lowering the song to a human volume.

Mason was grateful for the gesture, but still something puzzled him. "Why does every car you steal have the same shitty music in it?"

"Because their owners all have excellent taste," Zeus replied, as though the answer were obvious. "Don't you worry about the music. When the time comes, how about you just find us a place to park? Can you do that, grumpy?"

As they drew closer to the blue dot, they began

to see smoke on the horizon. Mason used satellite imagery to find a rocky outcrop just shy of their target, and the decision was made to stop there and wait for the cover of darkness to make a move.

After hiding the truck, Grinch and Blaine set up a security position near the rocky apex, allowing Mason and Zeus to lie down in the shade. The remnants of old square-cut rocks surrounding an ancient cistern told Mason that this had once been a watering hole for passing caravans, but the water had long since dried up.

Mason rolled his battle shirt into a lumpy pillow and, after digging out a depression for his hips, quickly passed into the land of oblivion. The two most important lessons he'd learned in the army was to sleep when you can and to always eat whenever there's food to be had. He'd taken the lessons to heart, and they'd both served him well.

He was woken up by a hard shove on his shoulder, and as his eyes slowly fluttered open, his head was pounding from a lack of water. Mason could feel the sand fleas biting his arms, and the heat from the sun's rays burning his shins. Blinking rapidly, he realized that Zeus was looming over him.

"What the fuck do you want?"

"The dot is moving."

"What fucking dot?" Mason asked groggily as he sat up and pulled a Nalgene bottle from his assault pack. It was the last of his water, but as he greedily downed a mouthful, he swore that nothing had ever tasted so good. He wanted to drain the entire thing but refrained because he had no idea when he would find more.

"The dot is moving toward us," Zeus said.

"Real funny. You hate it when I sleep, don't you?"

"I'm serious: the target is coming this way," Zeus reiterated, turning the computer so Mason could see that he was telling the truth.

"Boss, you need to check this out," Grinch said over the radio.

"Shit, there is no way they could have spotted us, is there?" Mason asked, suddenly wide awake.

"Mason, you need to get up here, now," the sniper said urgently.

"I'm on my way."

Mason grabbed his rifle and crept up a path that had been washed flat by centuries of erosion. Realizing he could be exposed, he crawled carefully to Grinch's side.

The sniper had stretched his *shemagh* between a crevice, giving him some shade from the blinding sun overhead. Based on the shadows, Mason figured that it must be about noon.

"What's up?" he asked.

Grinch nodded to the desert floor only twenty-five yards in front of him. An old deuce-and-a-half cargo truck and a Humvee were pulling up. The dust still hovered in the air as four men got out of the Humvee and moved to the back of the large truck.

Mason breathed a sigh of relief, knowing that whoever was down there had no idea that they were hiding in the rocks. He lifted the rifle to his shoulder, sighting through the Trijicon ACOG mounted on top. The optic had a 4x magnification and a red chevron for a reticle. As he swept the optic over the back of the truck, he frowned at the mismatched group of civilians huddled in the back. Some of the men were bleeding heavily, and all of them look terrified as the men from the Humvee ordered them out.

Mason wasn't sure what he was watching, but if Renee was right, one of the men in the Humvee had to be al Qatar. As he scanned across the fighters, it became clear immediately what was about to happen.

The fighters yelled and cursed as their captives got to their feet and tried clumsily to climb down from the truck. Apparently they weren't moving fast enough for the fighters, and one of the men, who appeared to be in his early teens, reached up and grabbed an older woman, yanking her to the ground.

The back of the deuce-and-a-half was ten feet off the hard-packed ground, and the woman was unable to brace herself as she slammed headfirst into the ground. She lay motionless, her neck twisted awkwardly beneath her, as the man kicked her in the back. When he realized that the fall had killed her, he laughed.

Seeing the dead woman on the ground, one of the men began wailing and jumped awkwardly from the back of the cargo truck. He tried to move to her side, but the fighter struck him with the butt of his AK and pushed him around to the front of the truck.

"Zeus, refresh the tracker and tell me how close they are," Mason said into the radio.

"If this thing is right, they are no more than twenty-five yards away."

"Well, get up here. We have company."

Counting twenty-three civilians in total, Mason guessed that they were either Shiites or Kurds. Either way, it was obvious that the fighters couldn't care less if they lived or died.

A tall, thin man in clean desert fatigues got out of the passenger's seat of the cargo truck, and Mason placed the reticle on his target's head. This man must be in charge, and he assumed that it had to be the man who killed Boland.

The man began ordering the civilians to dig a hole near the lead vehicle. While they were handed shovels, he produced a small camcorder from his cargo pocket. After flipping open the screen, he panned the camera over the prisoners and then moved to get a better angle.

In the distance, artillery began banging away, and Mason could hear the rounds slicing through air before the detonations reverberated across the open desert with a deep *thump*.

"They are trying to take Mosul?" he asked in an undertone. "Who the fuck do these guys think they are?"

"Yeah, there was small-arms fire earlier, but I didn't give it much thought," Grinch whispered. "Guess they needed to take a slaughter break."

Mason lowered his eye back to the optic just as two fighters seized a young woman who stood huddled next to a middle-aged woman. She fell to her knees as they grabbed her shirt, and one of the men latched onto her arm, trying to drag her back to the deuce-and-a-half.

She screamed at them to leave her alone, but this only made them more aggressive. Amused, the thin man with the camcorder panned over slowly to catch the proceedings.

The first man lifted the young woman off the ground by her hair. The second man struggled to hold his rifle while grabbing her legs. The woman kicked and writhed in the man's arms, and his AK clattered to the ground, knocking up a puff of dust.

Mason heard Zeus scrambling up behind him as the thin man laughed and pointed at the fighter. Then the man came forward and slapped the girl hard across the face. The sound of the open-handed blow carried up to their position as the woman slumped to her knees.

"The man with the camera?" Zeus asked.

"It has to be," Mason answered.

He felt his stomach turn as he watched the woman kick her feet in the dirt and scream as one of the fighters grabbed her by the hair.

Mason could see the blood pouring from her nose as the fighter reached down to retrieve his rifle. Suddenly the older lady picked up a shovel, broke ranks, and rushed at him while he was shaking the dirt off the Kalashnikov. One of the guards yelled a warning, and the fighter turned casually and shot her in the face.

The shot reverberated off the rocks as the old woman was bowled over and fell in a heap at his feet.

"Boss?" Grinch said, settling his eye to his scope.

The fighter who had just shot the woman turned back to his original victim. She was still struggling to get free, and he ripped her shirt open, exposing her breasts. He gave her a sharp kick and motioned for the other man to throw her on the ground.

"Stand by."

Mason had no intention of watching the young woman get raped. As the fighter who had been dragging her by the hair pinned the woman's hands to the ground, and the other worked feverishly at unbuttoning his pants, he placed the reticle back on al Qatar's forehead.

"I've got the target," he said as the fighter tugged on his belt and fought to open the woman's legs.

"You have the target," Zeus replied, shouldering his HK.

"See you in hell," he said fiercely.

Grinch fired a second before Mason flipped the selector off safe and squeezed the trigger gently. The optic jumped as the HK bucked on his shoulder, and by the time he had reacquired his target, the man was down.

Zeus and Blaine fired at almost the same time, working their shots across the fighters while Grinch smoothly worked the bolt, got back on target, and shot the man who held the woman by the shoulders through his eye.

Mason finished the final fighter, and the only sound he heard was the woman's sobs down below.

"Blaine, you and Grinch provide overwatch. Zeus, you come with me," he said. "I'm going to put that bastard's head in a fucking box."

CHAPTER 33

- - - - - - - - - - - - - - -

What the fuck have you done now?" Simmons demanded, grabbing Cage by the shoulder and forcing him into one of the many offices outside the Situation Room. He'd just received word that the USS *George H. W. Bush* had been hit going through the Strait of Hormuz, and early reports weren't looking good.

Cage jerked his hand free with a violent tug, his fist shaking at his side as Simmons slammed the door.

"You think I had anything to do with that? You are the one running this shit show."

"Are you saying that Vann had our own men killed? Do you know how crazy that sounds?"

Simmons had put too much trust in the general, and the realization hit him like a kick in the balls. Vann had promised him that the attack would be surgical: just enough to get President Bradley's attention but not enough to do any real harm. Vann had promised him that he had the right guy for the job, but as more bodies began washing up in the Persian Gulf, it was obvious that Vann had chosen a psychopath to do his dirty work.

Jacob Simmons was a patriot, not a murderer, and right now all he wanted was someone to share the guilt he felt enveloping him. He knew without a shadow of a doubt that all those innocent Americans died because of him.

"In five minutes we are going to be standing in front of the president of the United States. You better get control of yourself, or we are both fucked."

The two warriors stared at each other, their anger filling the small room, as they fought to control their voices.

"How could you do that? How could you kill them?"

"I told you, I had nothing to do with that," Cage said. "I put you in charge of this, and somehow you let a simple operation get away from you."

Simmons felt used and, for the first time in his career, dirty.

"Don't you dare put this on me."

"Jacob, I told you that trusting Vann was the wrong choice, but you said you could control him. This is on you."

"I will kill you right fucking here," Simmons growled, starting forward.

"And then what? Who do you think they are going to pin this on? Me? Your fingerprints are all over this. They will bury you alive, and your daughter will have to live with the fact that her father was a traitor for the rest of her life. Is that what you want?"

"Fuck you," he spat, staring at the man he'd followed for his entire career.

Cage had changed, and suddenly the scales had fallen from Simmons's eyes. The man he knew was gone, replaced by a hard, hateful man who would sacrifice anything and anyone for his goals.

But Jacob's anger drained away at the mention of his daughter. He knew that Duke was right. He'd vouched for Vann and let him run with the operation instead of dictating what he wanted done. The plan was to disable the carrier, not destroy it, but no, Vann had given al Qatar too much rope, and now they were about to be hanged by it.

"What have I done?" Simmons moaned. "I just killed more Americans than any terrorist attack ever could."

"I've known you for a long time, Jacob. Hell, I've bled with you in more shitholes than I can count. Let me do the talking once we get in there."

"I can't believe I let you talk me into this. You accepting this job was never about America, it's always been about your son, about making them pay. When is it going to be enough?" Simmons demanded, bringing up the one thing he knew would cut right to Cage's core.

"Don't you talk about him," Cage hissed.

Simmons had been there when Cage found out that his son had been killed in Iraq. Cage's wife was sick when their son was killed, and she'd lost her will to fight after he was put in the ground. It was many years ago, but Simmons knew the pain was still there. He wondered if that's what all of this was about, avenging the death of his family, no matter the cost.

"You don't know shit, Jacob. How many more women and children have to die before we wipe those savages out? You want to shed a tear for someone, how about you cry for the hundreds they are slaughtering right now in Mosul?"

As the national security advisor, Simmons knew better than anyone what was happening in Iraq. He had the pictures from Tal Afar, showing the soldiers hanging from light poles, along with the mass graves they hadn't even bothered to cover up.

"How many more have to die before that pretty boy gets off his ass and wipes this evil off the map?" Cage demanded, pointing toward the hallway.

"No one cares about Iraq, Duke. They never did."

"Well, I care. I even cared about that shitbag Boland. You know that they cut his head off, Jacob, and put the video on the fucking internet. Do you have any idea how many hits that video has gotten in one day?"

"Fifty thousand," Jacob muttered.

"That's right, fifty thousand people have watched that video in less than twelve hours. So you tell me who's out of their mind."

"Duke, I—"

"It's too late for all of that. You can either eat a bullet or sack up and drive on, but the only way this is going to end is after we've killed every last one of them."

Jacob had already made his choice nine months ago, and he knew that there was no way out for either one of them. If he stayed the path, they had a chance to give America peace for the first time in a decade, but at the same time, he hated himself for what he'd become.

"What now?" he asked meekly.

"This shit is all over the news," said Cage, "and the people want blood. An eye for an eye, that's the American way, and I'm about to give it to them. The president will want me to hold his little hand and tell him it's going to be okay, and we're going to go in there and do just that. Before the end of the day, we are going to have a battalion of paratroopers in Iraq, and you know what? The people of the United States are going to be begging for more. But I need you with me. We have to see it through, or all the sacrifices are for nothing."

Jacob's head fell to his chest, and he closed his eyes before making the only decision he had left.

"Let's do it."

CHAPTER 34

- - - - - - - - - - - - - - -

Colonel Anderson stood with his back to Renee, watching the live news coverage coming out of the Persian Gulf. A pretty blond anchor had just been talking to a retired admiral, and then the picture switched to an aerial view of the rescue operations being conducted near the Strait of Hormuz.

A small fleet of boats was carefully navigating the watery debris field as it searched for survivors. Two huge salvage ships were anchored on the other side of the strait, and their crews were working feverishly to reopen the vital channel. The yellow news ticker along the bottom of the screen said that the president would be addressing the nation in the next hour, and then posted the estimated casualty rate.

Renee felt her heart sink as the figure floated across the screen. It read, "Two thousand, thirty-nine suspected dead in carrier attack." For some reason, her mind shifted to al Qatar. Could he have something to do with this? Was something like that even possible?

"Fuck," Colonel Anderson swore.

Parker had come to tell her that the colonel wanted to talk to her, and the look on his face was a mix of guilt and embarrassment, which immediately made her expect the worst.

Renee wanted to believe that Anderson was one of the good guys, despite Mason's constant warnings that there was more to him than she saw. The colonel had always been civil to her, but something told her that was about to change.

Anderson was unable to hide the anger glinting in his eyes. "Two questions, one chance: Where is Mason, and where in the fuck is David?" he demanded.

She knew all about Anderson's hatred of Mason, and she wanted nothing to do with that fight. "Excuse me?"

"Don't play dumb. I know David came to see you. He thought he was slick, landing without informing the tower, but the pilot had to file another flight plan, so I guess he's not as slick as he thinks."

Anderson was fuming, and as he spoke, bits of tobacco shot out of his mouth.

"A couple hours ago, I get a fucking hit on Boland's beacon. You want to guess what the search and rescue team found when they landed?"

"No idea, sir," she said honestly.

"They found his headless fucking body, that's what they found. Now, I need to know what those two are up to, and I need to know right now."

Renee was staggered by the fact that Boland had been killed. "Sir, I have no—"

"Cut the shit," he said, kicking one of the trash cans with a hollow boom; it rolled metallically across the floor. "I was there when you two went after Barnes, remember? I know David offered you a job, and then got you assigned to the task force. I'm not fucking stupid. But guess what? Unlike Mason, you are still in the military, and no matter what you think, you are still under my command."

Anderson paused to catch his breath. Then he pointed his finger at Renee. "So if you don't start talking, right now, I am going to have your ass locked up."

She knew that no matter what she said, Anderson wasn't going to believe her. Renee had never seen him like this, and suddenly she was reminded of her old boss General Swift. The only time the general showed this kind of rage was when he was being painted into a corner, and Renee suddenly had a sneaking suspicion that Anderson was involved in the attack.

"Sir, I promise you that I have no idea what's going on."

"Then how about we start with what you do know?"

She was going to treat the colonel like what he was: a venomous snake. "Like you said, David was here. He said that you kept him out of the loop on purpose, and that he had a job to do."

"Kept him out of the loop? He was in fucking Erbīl, for fuck's sake," Anderson spat.

Renee thought to herself, "And you deliberately launched the raid when he was in Erbīl." But she repeated yet again that she had no idea what was going on.

"Look," Anderson said, seeming to realize that she couldn't be bullied, "I know that some of the guys have been on your ass, but you've played the game before; you know how it goes."

Renee just looked at him, wishing she could comment on the understatement of the year, but she knew better than to say anything at this point. Her career was on the line.

"As much as you might want to blame me, we are on the same team, and I need to know where Mason is. This shit is a game changer," he said, pointing to the TV.

"I can't tell you what I don't know."

"Fine, you're done here," Anderson snapped. "I'm sending you back to the States."

"But sir."

"It's done," he yelled. "I am going to recommend that you be charged with insubordination, so you can kiss your career good-bye. Pack your shit and get your ass to the flight line. You are going home."

The news hit Renee like a kick to the gut, and she felt her knees go weak beneath her. The army was all she had ever known, and Anderson had just taken it away. It didn't matter if the charges went through. Renee knew she was done in the Special Operations world. She'd never be trusted again.

"Why the fuck are you still here?" he asked coldly.

Renee's eyes were burning from the tears welling up as she stomped from the ops area. She needed to get to her room before she lost it.

"Hey," Parker called from where he'd been waiting, but she kept going without looking up.

"Renee, hey, what's wrong?"

She knew Parker must have been the one who'd snitched her out in the first place; after all, he'd seen her with David. "Leave me the hell alone," she ordered.

"Whoa, hold on, what the hell happened?" he asked, jumping in front of her.

"Get the fuck out of my way. I don't want to see you," she yelled, pushing past him.

She hit the door leading to the sleeping area with both hands, and it slammed against the wall with a hollow thud. Turning the corner, she could see her room up ahead, and then Warchild stepped out into the hall.

"I'll tell you what happened," he said, leaning against his door frame. "Your girl got canned 'cause she thinks she doesn't have to follow orders."

"What the fuck are you talking about?" Parker demanded.

Renee felt something snap, and a white-hot rage fell over her.

She turned on Warchild like a wild animal, her fists flying out before he could step out of the way.

The first blow hit him in the solar plexus, doubling him over, and she stepped forward, snapping a vicious knee up toward his face. Warchild was caught totally off guard, and Renee felt his face bounce off her thigh. She was about to drop an elbow on the back of his neck when Parker grabbed her from behind and lifted her off her feet.

Warchild staggered backward, bleeding from his nose, but he recovered quickly and started toward Renee.

"Let that bitch go," he yelled as Renee kicked at his face.

"Fuck you," she spat. "I'll kill you."

"Chill the fuck out," Parker yelled, swinging her away from their team leader.

"You're dead, bitch. Do you hear me? You're fucking dead."

Parker kicked her door open and tossed her onto her bed. He held his hands up in the air, trying to signal peace, when Warchild came flying in the room. He lowered his shoulder and slammed into the master sergeant's back, knocking him to the ground.

Renee jumped to her feet. This time she was going to shut that big mouth of his.

"You want some of me, bleeder?" Warchild yelled.

Parker grabbed onto his leg, tripping him up, just as Renee launched a roundhouse kick to Warchild's head.

He stumbled out of the way, causing the kick to go wide. Meanwhile, more men piled into the room.

"What the fuck is this shit?" Sergeant Major

Jason Mitchell roared, pushing one of the operators out of his way and barging into the room.

His massive bulk filled the door frame, and his face was a dark shade of scarlet. He grabbed Warchild by the shirt and snatched him off his feet. "You stay the fuck out of her room," he yelled before tossing Warchild out into the hall.

Next he grabbed Parker by his arm, yanked him to his feet, and twisted his arm behind his back. "Get out of my sight before I break your neck," he muttered, shoving him toward the door. He then turned on the spectators: "The rest of you fucking gossips need to do something with your time—before I find you something to do."

The room cleared out in record time, and the sergeant major slammed the door so hard that the walls shook.

"Lock it up," he ordered, and Renee snapped to parade rest.

She could see the fire in his eyes and knew without a doubt that she was fucked.

"What is this bullshit?"

"Bad day, Sergeant Major," she stammered, trying to catch her breath.

"I couldn't give a fuck. What is your malfunction?" he yelled, stepping into her face.

Despite all the firefights and near misses she'd had, there was nothing as terrifying as the righteous anger on display in the tiny room. Renee felt her heart skip a beat as Mitchell's rage washed over her like a tidal wave, his massive fists trembling at his sides.

"You're pissed off because you got your ass in a sling, is that it? You think busting Warchild in the face is going to make it better?"

"Negative, Sergeant Major," she replied.

"I've watched you piss on this command since you got here. Do you think you're special? You think the rules don't apply to you?"

"Negative," Renee replied, the adrenaline draining from her body, leaving her feeling weak and exposed. She remembered that she'd just been fired.

"You think that bitch-ass CIA fuck is going to save you? You better answer me right now, or so help me, I will put you in a fucking box."

"Sergeant Major, I have no excuse," she said quietly. "Let me get my shit, and I'll be out of your hair."

Renee watched Mitchell take a step back as he tried to calm himself, but his blood was up, and he was still looking for a fight. His hands opened and closed rapidly. For some reason only he knew, that made his rage disappear.

"What the hell happened to you?" he asked finally, his voice even.

"I lost my shit," she said honestly.

"Jesus, Renee, I've been going head-to-head with the old man, trying to keep you on the task force, and you play right into his hands. I thought you were smarter than that."

"Guess not."

"You ready to quit?"

"What else am I going to do," she demanded.

"Stand at ease," he said, running his hand over his face.

Renee relaxed, suddenly feeling ashamed of herself.

"How fucked up are you?"

"Excuse me?"

"Don't give me that. I know what happened to you in Pakistan."

"That has nothing to do with this," she said defensively.

"You've seen a lot of shit in a short time. I get it, but if you can't get a grip, I can't use you."

It seemed like he was offering her a way out, although she didn't see how. "It doesn't matter. The colonel said I'm done."

"Fuck him, he won't be running shit pretty soon—not after that fucked-up mission he had us launch. Look, there is a war coming, and it's coming fast. You know what happened in the Gulf. You think the president's going to let that pass?"

"Looks like I'll be sitting that one out," she said glumly.

"You are so hardheaded," he said, exasperated. "You know, I've got a daughter like you: thinks she knows everything, but she doesn't have the sense to get out of her own way."

"I apologize, Sergeant Major," she replied formally.

"Cut that shit out. Look, we need people like you, but if you can't get your head right, I can't use you." He lowered his voice, making her aware that others might be listening in. "Tell me what the hell is going on, tell me what you know, and I will do everything in my power to keep you on the team."

Renee could see that Mitchell really cared, and as she sat down on the bed, she made the decision to trust him. In a voice just above a whisper she told him, "Mason said a guy named al Qatar is behind all of this."

"Who the fuck is al Qatar?"

"I don't know, but David does."

"I am so tired of the CIA and their bullshit," Mitchell said wearily, taking a can of dip from his pocket and cracking his finger across the lid. "If he knows, then where the fuck is he? Why doesn't he give us something?"

"I don't know."

"I swear to God, between him and Mason Kane, it's a wonder I have any hair left. You know, I was with ol' Mason in Iraq."

"I've heard you talk about that," she said, watching him shove a massive pinch of dip into his mouth before closing the lid.

"He's the real deal, maybe one of the best operators I've ever seen. Well, maybe besides Boland."

"I knew they were tight."

"Thick as fucking thieves. You know, Mason is a lot like you: kept to himself most of the time, but when he was on an op, he was one deadly motherfucker. Maybe he told you, but he had to raise himself when his dad split and his mom became a fucking drunk. Brought himself out of the fucking gutter." Suddenly the sergeant major turned and whipped open the door. No one was lingering out-

side. He closed it again and went on in a more normal tone of voice. "In any case, a lot of guys believe
that bullshit they said about him, but it wasn't true.
No way the guy I knew would kill a bunch of kids."

Renee simply nodded, glad that Mitchell's assessment matched her own.

"Where is he? I know that you know what he's
doing."

"He's going after al Qatar."

"Figured as much. David really knew what he
was doing when he latched onto our boy. It was
a smart play getting him to go after Barnes. What
he doesn't realize, though, is that he can't protect
Mason. He's got a lot of enemies, especially the
colonel."

"Why?"

"Because Anderson will do anything to win, and
if that means leaving some of our guys flapping,
then I can promise you he won't miss a wink of
sleep. Do you understand what I'm telling you?"

"Not really," she said.

"The only way you can help Mason is by getting
back in the game. If you really care about him, then
you have to stick around to watch his back. Because
I can promise you that there are people waiting for
him to slip up so they can drop the hammer on
him. Barnes had a lot of powerful friends."

"What do you want me to do?"

"I'm going to go talk to the boss, see if I can get
this shit sorted out. I'm not making any promises,
but I'm going to do my best," he said, turning toward the door.

"Sergeant Major," she said from the edge of the bed.

"Yeah?"

"Thank you. I owe you one."

"Don't get all excited yet. Wait and see what I can do."

CHAPTER 35

- - - - - - - - - - - - - - -

Mr. David had been expecting something big, but never in his wildest imagination had he considered that General Vann would allow al Qatar to blow up an aircraft carrier. The horror of what he'd seen on the TV monitors at Kennedy Airport had shocked him to his core, and even now, as he drove south toward Virginia, he couldn't believe it.

The usually implacable spy felt righteous anger overcoming the immense sadness as he listened to talk radio. The host was interviewing a retired general, and, as usual, their theories couldn't have been further from the truth.

"This attack has all the hallmarks of al Qaeda, there is no doubt in my mind," the host was saying.

David was tempted to pick up the prepaid cell phone he had bought in New York and call in to the radio station. But he knew that no one would ever believe that this attack originated in the nation's capital.

He checked the map spread out on the passenger seat and merged to the left to get off the expressway. It was raining, and the lights from the other vehicles made it hard to see as he slowed at the end of the ramp and turned onto the surface street.

After another twenty minutes, he pulled into a suburban neighborhood and parked the rental car four houses down from his objective. He opened the glove box and slipped the fake passport out of his back pocket and tossed it inside. After folding up the map carefully, he placed it on top of the passport and shut the glove box with a snap.

He reached into the backseat, grabbed the backpack, and opened the door, stepping out into a light rain. He'd already disengaged the dome light, so there was no chance of him being backlit as he closed the door, heading for a two-story brownstone.

At the back door of the house, he paused to don a pair of latex gloves. Then he slipped a headlamp over his forehead and activated the tiny blue light. Taking a lock pick set out of the bag, he inserted it into the door. He sensed his way until he felt the tumblers click into place.

The spy turned the knob slowly, listening for the squeak of the hinges, and stepped inside. He went straight to an alarm panel that chirped in the darkness. After typing the code into the panel, the beeping stopped, but before he closed the access lid, he hit the rearm button.

David wiped his feet on the rug before heading upstairs to the bedroom.

A stack of plates were piled in the sink, and a few cans of beer were nestled in the recycling bin, but other than that, the house was tidy. He knew that the owner planned on cleaning before his wife got home, but David was going to make sure he didn't have that chance.

Climbing the stairs to the bedroom, his shoes sank in the plush carpet lining the staircase. The steps creaked. Blue moonlight cast a soft glow over the walls. He entered the master bedroom and approached a neatly made bed flanked by two high end tables.

David placed the backpack on the floor next to a chair with a towel draped over the back. He took the towel, folded it in half, and placed it on the edge of the bed. Before taking a seat, he turned off the headlamp, stowed it back in the bag, and then lifted out a Beretta 92F.

He'd never liked the gun, and thought it was a bad idea when the military chose it as its service pistol, but as David screwed the suppressor into the barrel, he knew it would do the job. Once the suppressor was secure, he placed the pistol on the side table, checked his watch, and got comfortable.

Thirty minutes later, David felt the vibrations of the garage door opening through the floor.

The spy was sure that recent events would have kept his target at the office until much later, but there was something to be said about small mercies. He heard the door slam, and the alarm beep as the man typed in his code.

Five minutes later, he heard footsteps coming up the stairs. David grabbed the pistol off the table and closed his eyes so the lights wouldn't blind him.

The overhead light came on with a flash, and the spy opened his eyes, the pistol pointed at the man who jerked to a halt as he was about to throw his jacket on the bed.

"Hello, Patrick," he said.

"What the fuck?" General Vann exclaimed.

"Have a seat."

"David, why the hell are you in my house?"

"I think you know. Now have a seat before I put a bullet through your kneecap."

"Look, don't do anything—"

The pistol spat in his hands, and the bullet struck the general in the side of the knee, knocking him to the ground. David was up in a flash, his left hand sweeping the towel off the bed and forcing it over Vann's mouth.

"Don't scream. It's beneath you."

He might as well have saved his breath, because the general immediately began to yell beneath the towel. David hit him expertly in the back of the neck with the pistol, and the muffled screams immediately stopped as Vann fell unconscious.

CHAPTER 36

Mason didn't know what to expect as he approached the woman flanked by his two fresh kills, but he was still surprised to find no fear in her eyes. She stared up at him defiantly as he slung his rifle over his shoulder.

"I am not going to hurt you," he said in Arabic.

"I need a new shirt," she replied, wiping the blood off her face with the torn edge of her ripped blouse. "Do you have one?"

Mason slipped the assault pack off his back and squatted painfully to the ground. After digging around in the pack, he found a faded brown T-shirt and tossed it to her.

He couldn't help but notice that she was very pretty but also very young. Mason guessed that she was maybe eighteen, maybe younger or older. It was hard to tell out here. Her eyes, though, held an ageless quality that he'd seen far too frequently. It spoke of a loss of innocence and a familiarity with death that most people could never fathom.

Mason knew that while soldiers were forced to witness untold horrors, the civilians caught in the middle suffered the most.

She pulled the ruined blouse over her head, making no attempt to cover her firm breasts. Anger blazed on her face as she got to her feet and spat on the two dead men lying before her.

"Who are you?"

"My name is Mason, and I'm an American."

"Why are you here?"

"I—" He stopped in midsentence, not really sure how to answer her.

She probably understood the desire for revenge all too well, but for some reason, he was ashamed to tell her that he was engaged in a mission of death. The young woman was still a child, and she didn't have to know about the horrible aspects of war that were so common to his life.

"I am looking for someone," he said finally.

"Hey, Mason!" Zeus called. "We need to leave before more of them come."

Off to the side, the Libyan had a small camera out and was taking pictures of what was left of Anu al Qatar's man's face. He forced open the dead man's remaining eye and snapped a picture before moving to check the rest of the bodies.

"Where can you go?" Mason asked the young woman.

"My uncle has a house not far from here. He will want to know that his sister is dead," she replied, motioning to the older woman, whose blood lay fresh upon the ground.

"Vehicle coming," Grinch said over the radio, ending the conversation.

"How many?" Kane responded.

"One, maybe two."

"Blaine, grab the truck." He addressed the girl: "You need to get them ready to move."

She walked briskly over to her aunt's corpse and struggled to lift the body. Zeus joined in to help her. As he did, he ordered the survivors into the back of the deuce-and-a-half.

Meanwhile, Mason walked over to the body he was hoping was al Qatar's. He ran his hands over the corpse and felt a bulge of papers in the man's pocket. He stuffed them down the front of his assault shirt, not having the time to check what they were, and flipped the man onto his stomach.

"Have fun in hell," he muttered, taking a frag from his kit and yanking the pin free. Still holding the spoon, he jammed the frag into the sand, ensuring that the spoon was held down by the dead man's weight, and then pulled his hands free.

He spit on the man's body and scanned the ground for anything he might have missed. Zeus yelled for him to hurry. The young woman jumped behind the wheel of the cargo truck and cranked the engine.

Mason completed his hasty search, but as he made his way over to the Humvee, he had a nagging feeling that he was forgetting something. Raising his rifle, he put a burst through the engine block, hoping it was enough to disable the vehicle, and jogged to the heavy cargo truck that was already rolling forward.

He hauled himself up into the cab, slamming the door behind him. He was going to ask Zeus why he wasn't behind the wheel, but the Libyan shrugged.

"She wanted to drive," he said simply.

"Where are we going?" he asked her.

She slammed the vehicle into third gear and gently let off the clutch before mashing down on the accelerator. "To my uncle's."

"I know that, but where does he live?"

"Not far from here."

Mason shook his head. That's what he got for expecting military precision from a civilian. He glanced over his shoulder to ensure that all the passengers were sitting down.

"Well," he said, "if you're going to drive, you better drive fast."

CHAPTER 37

Al Qatar was heading back to his command post when heavy machine gun fire kicked up from the east. The radio came alive with reports that Kurdish Peshmerga troops had just overrun the units he had sent to take the bridge. To top it off, al Qatar couldn't get Ali to answer the radio.

The day had gone well up to that point. His men had discovered fifteen Stryker armored fighting vehicles, twenty 120 mm mortars, and a hundred armored Humvees in a truck depot just south of the airfield. He knew that the Iraqi army hadn't bothered to destroy the ammo dumps before retreating south toward Baghdad, its soldiers having left behind crates upon crates of javelin missiles, AT-4 antitank weapons, and Mk-19 grenade launchers. But the sudden counterattack made it impossible for him to reach the airfield where the bunkers were housed.

News of his stunning victories had spread already, and men were flowing in from Syria and other parts of Iraq to join his army. The video he had released, taking credit for having sunk the USS *George H. W. Bush*, made al Qatar an instant celebrity among the violent jihadists lurking around the Mideast. He knew that it was only a matter of time before America brought its might to bear, but instead of being afraid, he was already making preparations for his final act of revenge.

"Where is Ali?" he demanded as he strode into the command post.

"They sent him to supervise the executions," Jabar said, pointing at the bearded mullahs seated around a dusty table. "I have sent a man to retrieve him for you."

Al Qatar ignored the men and instead began searching for his satellite phone.

"Where is the phone?"

"That is the least of our worries right now," a round-faced man, dressed entirely in black, said from his place at the head of the table.

"It is *my* worry," al Qatar replied.

"Forget the phone and sit down," the man said harshly.

Abu Bakr al Baghdadi brushed a fleck of dirt off the sleeve of his black robes, willing al Qatar to respect him.

The self-proclaimed head of the newly established Islamic State of Iraq made no attempt to conceal his condescension, and al Qatar felt a spark of anger ignite within his chest. The bearded cleric had begged al Qatar to bring his fighters to Iraq after he chased the Syrians from Aleppo, but now that Mosul had fallen, he felt he needed to show who was really in charge.

"I believe we agreed that I would do the fighting, and you would handle the . . . *politics*," al Qatar said, pronouncing the word with disgust.

"And nothing has changed. But why antagonize the Americans?"

"My desire has always been to destroy them, and my resolve is as strong as ever."

"You have done an excellent job," al Baghdadi commended him. "You have killed thousands of them without losing a single drop of Arab blood. Do you think that your luck will hold when they come here in force?"

Al Qatar had no patience for the mullah.

"As I have said, many times, I have a plan, and it isn't finished yet."

"Very well, but remember that Allah does not bless the proud."

Al Qatar hid his disdain for al Baghdadi's remarks. He knew his accomplishments thus far had come from careful planning, not from anyone's blessings. But at the same time, he knew he still needed Baghdadi's support.

"What would you have me do with *my* men, then?"

"We need to take the oil fields," the mullah replied.

"I do not need any oil. There is plenty of fuel here."

"The oil is not for you. It is for the movement.

We need the money we shall receive from its proceeds."

Al Qatar knew in an instant what all of this was about. These bearded sycophants were using him to build their own state, just as they used the Koran to control the mindless youths they convinced to turn themselves into martyrs.

A truck came to a grinding halt outside the building, and al Qatar could hear some of his men yelling as they slammed the doors. A man covered in blood rushed into the room.

"Ali has been killed," he shrieked, holding up a bloody camera.

Al Qatar felt his face pale and was aware that the men at the table were staring at him. "I am afraid that I must attend to this," he said softly, fighting to hold his composure. "I want you to know that I remain your most faithful servant and promise that I will not abuse the faith that you have placed in my hands."

"We can ask for nothing more," Baghdadi said, getting to his feet.

Al Qatar waited for everyone to leave. Shouts were coming from the next room, and as he walked through the door, his men refused to meet his gaze.

"What happened?"

"They placed a grenade under Ali's body, and it killed Oman when he went to check on him," Jabar said, standing next to the man who had blood covering his shirt.

"Who did this?"

"I do not know, but they brought this back with

his body," the man replied, holding out the mangled camcorder.

Al Qatar snatched the black recorder from the man's hands, noticing the melted edges and the bloody fingerprints smudging the casing. The lens was shattered, but when he punched the Play button, the device came to life.

The screen showed a young girl on the ground and two of his men ripping her shirt. She spat at one of them, and he heard Ali's unmistakable chuckle as one of the men slapped her across the face.

"Is she too much for you?" Ali asked with a laugh.

"You bitch," one of the men cursed, punching her in the face before throwing her to ground.

The camera bobbed as Ali focused in on her face. The man closest to her head grabbed her hands and pinned them under his knees. Another hand came into view, and twisted her nipples hard before slapping her across her breasts.

The man's belt jingled as he unbuckled it, and a moan of desire escaped from the fighter's throat as he fumbled with her pants.

Suddenly there was a dull smacking sound, and as Ali panned up to the man who was holding down her hands, a jet of blood splattered across his face.

In the next instant, the clear image became jumbled, and the screen shook as Ali fumbled to turn the camera. His fingers must have brushed across the internal microphone, because the sound became hollow and distant. Then the camera lens was pointing up at a mixture of sky and brown earth.

The picture bounced as something fell in front of the camera, but the autofocus kicked in, and a second later, al Qatar was staring at the side of Ali's shattered face.

Al Qatar clutched the camera tightly, praying that the man who had killed his friend would show himself. His fingers were wet with sweat against the plastic body of the camera, and he could feel his heart beating in his ears.

Out of the silence came a voice, and a man was standing in the frame.

"I am not going to hurt you," the man said.

"I need a new shirt. Do you have one?" the girl replied.

The man knelt down, the wires of his radio snaking up to the headset attached to his forehead. Al Qatar at first thought he must be a Kurd, but then he saw the man's rifle, and knew he was from the West.

"Who are you?" the girl demanded.

"My name is Mason, and I'm an American," he said.

Al Qatar wanted to smash the camera as the battery indicator beeped on the screen before cutting off. How could the Americans be on his trail already? He had just released the video that very day. There was no way they could react that quickly.

"Where did they go?" he demanded, turning on the man who had found the camera.

"Answer the emir," Jabar barked, slapping the man in the back of the head.

"They headed north in one of our trucks. I sent

men after them, but I think they might be heading to the border."

"If they cross the border, I will kill you, do you understand? Take as many men as you need, but find them and bring them back to me," al Qatar screamed.

"Yes, Emir."

"Find them before the sun goes down."

"Of course. Consider it done."

For the first time in a long while, al Qatar felt a surge of fear as he turned his face away from the men. If the Americans were already here, then he had to get to work before they launched an attack. Almost as an afterthought, he rushed into the room where he kept his gear and snatched his bag off the floor.

"How did they get find us so quickly? Were we betrayed?"

"I do not know, but we still have much work to do," Jabar replied. "Ali was a brave man, and he knew what was expected of him."

"I need you to take this," al Qatar said, grabbing from the bag the black box that Khalid had given him.

"Already?"

"I do not know how much time we have left. Take as many men as you need, but be sure that you emplace all of them," he said, holding up what looked like a USB drive and showing it to Jabar. "Plug it into the port that is labeled 'Transmit.' Do you understand?"

"What do I do after I plug them in?"

"Come back and help me prepare the attack on the airfield."

Jabar took the plastic box and headed out of the room, leaving al Qatar on the bed.

He began digging his fingers in his face. He felt his nails cut into his cheek before he balled up his right hand and shoved it into his mouth, biting down hard to stifle the scream building inside him.

No matter what happened, he promised himself, he would make the American bleed for what he had done to Ali.

CHAPTER 38

- - - - - - - - - - - - - - -

The area outside the task force hangar was alive with activity as a pair of V-22 Ospreys flared above the tarmac. Their huge turbo props blasted up a cloud of grit as they settled to the ground.

Renee had never seen the tilt-rotor aircraft before, and since she didn't really have anything to do, she had become a de facto liaison for the different units flying in. She still didn't know if she was staying or going, but Sergeant Major Mitchell had told her not to pack her stuff up yet, so she was trying to stay busy until she was given an answer.

The Pentagon had sent word to Anderson that it planned to use the airfield as a staging base, and for the time being, the task force was back under the Joint Special Operations Command's control. Something big was in the works, and their tiny corner of the airfield had become a very busy place.

C-17 transport planes and Chinook helicopters had been dropping off men and supplies for the last ten hours, and already more than four hundred members from the US Army's 82nd Airborne Division's First Battalion, 504th Parachute Infantry Regiment, were housed in the hangar next to Task Force Eleven. The paratroopers had been working all night, unloading pallets of parachutes and ammo in preparation for what Renee assumed was an invasion.

"Excuse me, ma'am, I need you to step away from the aircraft," a marine said, holding up his hand as he strode out of the back of the Osprey.

"Are you in charge?" she asked, stifling a smile.

"No, ma'am, but I seriously need you to take a few steps back," he said as his hand slipped down to the pistol on his hip.

"What the hell is going on here?" a tall, rangy man with a thick, grayish goatee and a scar running up the side of his face demanded from the back.

"I was just telling this lady that she needed to take a few steps away from the Osprey, Chief."

"Do you have any idea where you are right now, son? Do you think they are going to just let any chick walk around here if she ain't cleared to be here?"

"Uhh, I didn't think—"

"That's right, son, you didn't think. Go grab the rest of the gear and try not to piss anybody off," the man said, jumping off the ramp and sticking out his hand.

"Please excuse him, ma'am. He's new and partially retarded. My name is Gunny Jeremiah Charles, but you can call me Chief."

"Pleasure to meet you, Chief. My name is Renee. I'll show you guys where to drop your gear."

"Damn fine to meet ya, Renee," he said, taking a plug of tobacco out of his assault shirt pocket and biting off a chunk. "Can I offer you some? It's the good stuff, not that store-bought shit," he said with a smile.

"No, thank you, Chief, maybe later," Renee said with a laugh.

The tall marine reminded her of actor Sam Elliott, and she imagined that in another life he could have been a cowboy. His laid-back demeanor and the warmth in his eyes put her at ease, and she took an immediate liking to the man.

"Where are you from, Chief?" she asked as the rest of his team began unloading from the Osprey.

"I'm from California but spent most of my youth around Colorado. My family owned a little place around Sterling. Ever heard of it?"

"Can't say that I have, but I've only been out West a few times."

"Well, hell, ma'am, maybe when this is all over, you should go check it out. It's God's country."

"I'll keep that in mind," Renee said, glad to hear a cheerful voice for once. "How many men did you bring?"

"I've got six plus me. The captain had to head stateside because his brother was on the *George Bush* when it went down."

"Did you see it go down?"

"Yes, ma'am. We were on the amphib ship when she sank. Damnedest thing I've ever seen.

Word on the street is that the boy responsible is just over there in Iraq."

The operators were members of the Marine Raiders, an elite force that traced its ancestry back to World War II. The unit was skilled in direct action and deep reconnaissance. The Raiders were the new kids of the Special Operations community, but by no means untested. The Marine Corps Special Operations Command (MARSOC) pilot program, or Detachment One, had made their name in Iraq, and when the unit was officially stood up, it conducted combat operations in Afghanistan.

"The brief is scheduled for 2100. If you can follow me, I will show you where to put your gear," Renee said.

"I'd appreciate it."

The hangar was bustling with activity as Colonel Anderson and his staff worked through the operation timeline while team leaders pored over the maps and imagery. Gear and weapons were spread out in orderly piles, with men checking their equipment or relaxing before the brief.

Renee's thoughts drifted to Mason, and a knot of worry drifted up from the pit of her stomach. She had been trying to get ahold of him since sending the intel she had gotten from Dustin, but he wouldn't answer.

Her iPhone chirped in her pocket, telling her that she had a new email, and she was just about to check it when she saw Warchild striding toward her.

She cursed silently, continuing to look down at the iPhone, hoping he would leave her alone.

"Hey, can we talk?" he asked as he drew near.

He was the last person in the world she wanted to talk to right now.

"I don't have anything to say," she said with a sad smile.

"Well, then, just listen. Parker told me what happened, and I just wanted you to know that he didn't tell me shit."

"Why should I believe you?"

"Why the fuck would I lie? I have no idea what he sees in you," he said with a laugh, "but I just wanted you to know that it didn't come from him."

Renee knew when she was being played. Parker was the only one she'd told about David.

"He made his choice."

"Hey, just trying to look out for my buddy," he said, holding up his hands before turning to leave.

"Hey."

"What?"

"Sorry I whacked you in the face."

Warchild smiled and reached up to touch his black eye. "I guess I deserved it. You're all right."

"Okay, you two, save it for the enemy," Sergeant Major Mitchell rasped as he strode into their midst. He turned to address everyone assembled. "The briefing has been moved up. I need all team leaders and squad leaders to give me an 'up' on men and equipment in thirty minutes."

"Roger that," the men chorused.

Renee stepped to one side and finally checked

her phone. The email contained a picture and a short message from Mason:

"Found the gardener. Please confirm."

She felt the breath catch in her throat at the sight of the mangled body. Yet enough was intact that she could confirm the identity. She slipped over to the operations area to see if she could use one of the computers. Renee found an open laptop and quickly typed in her pass code.

"Hey, what are you doing at my station?" Sergeant Judson, one of the intel guys, asked from his place near the coffeepot.

"I need to check this," she said, holding up her phone as she furiously logged in to one of the databases the task force shared with the CIA and the NSA. If there was any information on al Qatar, the program was the best place to look.

"Renee, you're going to get my ass in a sling," Judson said as he came up behind her. "What the hell are you looking at?"

"I just got a hit on one of our targets. One of ours thinks that al Qatar might be dead," she sort of lied.

"Who told you that?"

"Just let me check it out real quick, and I'll get out of your hair."

"Can you at least let me sit down, so you don't piss off Anderson?" he begged.

Renee got up, letting Judson have his seat, before forwarding the pic to his email.

"I sent it to your email."

"Okay, hold on."

He clicked on his mail folder and saved the image to the desktop. Once the icon popped up, he uploaded to the database and hit the Search button.

"This could take a minute," he said.

"I've got nothing but time," she said, staring at the computer.

She settled in for the long haul and watched the screen as it flashed face after face of known terrorists. Renee knew that the database was massive, and willed it to go faster as she looked over at the men checking their equipment. It hurt having to ride the bench on this one, but she knew she was lucky even to be allowed in the hangar.

Renee was about to go grab a cup of coffee when the computer dinged, and a face popped up on the screen.

It wasn't al Qatar.

CHAPTER 39

General Vann opened his eyes. Realizing that he was tied down, he tugged desperately on the restraints holding him to the chair.

"Don't worry, you didn't get any more blood on the carpet," Mr. David said.

Vann said something that couldn't be understood behind the duct tape placed over his mouth.

The spy rose to his feet. "I will make sure I clean up the other spot before I leave. I'd know how upset Katy would be," he said, stepping closer. "Unfortunately, neither one of us has a great deal of time, and while I will be leaving soon, you will not. But before I kill you, I am going to give you the opportunity to choose how much pain you want go through."

David tucked his pistol into his waistband and lifted a roll of clear painter's plastic from the backpack. He began unrolling it beneath the chair, ensuring that he slipped it under the general's legs.

"I know what you've done, so I hope you won't lie about it," he remarked. He took out his knife and cut the plastic before unrolling another section. "What I don't know is who you are working with and how far up this goes. That's where I need help."

Once the area beneath the chair was covered, David placed the roll back in the bag. In one vicious swipe, he tore the tape off the general's mouth.

"You've made a mistake," Vann blurted out. "I have no idea what you're talking about."

The response was a hard, ringing slap to the man's temple. "Do you remember when we were in Iraq?" David asked. "You used to observe the interrogations I would conduct? They called them interrogations, but we know what they really were, don't we? It was torture."

"Don't do this, please, David."

"The CIA taught me how to break a man. But it was what I learned on the job that was the most effective. You've seen the results for yourself. "

"Look, there has to be a way we can work this out," Vann begged.

"Right now I have a gun and a knife," David said lightly, "but if I go down to your garage, I bet I will find all sorts of tools. Hedge clippers might be interesting. How about a jigsaw—do you have one of those?" David watched the general shrinking in his seat. He adopted a harder tone. "Why don't we start with who you are working with?"

"I can't."

David placed the tape back over Vann's mouth and shrugged.

"I'll be right back. You know, any man worth his salt owns an electric drill."

The spy took his time going through the garage, knowing that the longer he was away, the more Vann would panic. He found a milk crate on the floor, into which he placed a hammer, a pair of bolt cutters, needle-nose pliers, and a small blowtorch from the workbench, and headed to the door.

He wasn't going to enjoy this. He was hoping that Vann would tell him what he wanted to know without putting himself through a great deal of pain. But David had been doing this long enough to know that they always resisted at first.

"Sorry I took so long," he said, placing the crate on the floor next to Vann's feet. "So, here's what I found," he said, taking out the tools and placing them on the floor.

David saved the blowtorch for last. He lifted it out and held it before the general's eyes.

"You know who is really good at this? Mason Kane. And by the way," he added, "if you are wondering, he is very much alive."

The gas came on with a hiss that startled Vann, and when David gave it more gas, it flickered from a light yellow to a rushing blue. Vann's forehead began to sweat as David moved the flame closer to his face.

"I hate that you're making me do this," he said before placing the flame on the center of the general's chest.

Vann jerked in the chair as the room filled with the smell of burning flesh. He tried to flip the chair backward, but David held him roughly as he flicked the flame down to his abdomen.

Vann's eyes bulged as he screamed, and the veins in his arms rippled as he tried to break free.

David pulled away the blowtorch. "Now, let's try this again. Who are you working for?"

CHAPTER 40

- - - - - - - - - - - - - - -

"D o you have a phone?" the young woman asked Mason as the truck bounced across the undulating desert floor. From up in the cab, the ground looked flat, but the rocky ride told another story altogether.

The deuce-and-a-half had been a stalwart of the American military since World War II, and like the Willys Jeep, it was renowned for its reliability—but not for its comfort. Mason felt like he was being beat to hell, and he longed for the comfort of the Land Cruiser that was trailing them.

"I have a sat phone," he said as he pulled the bulky Iridium out of his pocket and switched it on.

The phone took a few seconds to come on, and when it finally began tracking the satellites, he saw that he had four missed calls from a number he didn't recognize.

"Whose number is this?" he asked Zeus, holding out the phone so that the Libyan could read the number on the tiny LED screen.

Zeus looked up from the cigarette he was trying to light, his face a mask of annoyance. "What am I, a telephone operator?"

"Do you know the number or not?"

"By Allah," he muttered before looking at the screen. "It's Renee's," he said, and then refocused his attention to connecting the flame of his lighter with the tip of the cigarette.

"Can I use your phone, or are you going to tease me with it?" the woman asked.

"First, tell me your name," Mason demanded.

"It's Sara."

"Okay, Sara, you know my name, and the grumpy one back there is Zeus."

"Great, can I see the phone now?"

"One more question. Where the hell are we going?"

"I told you we were going to my uncle's. Now give me the phone."

Mason was trying to figure out his next move. With al Qatar out of the picture, he figured his job was finished. He knew that after he made sure the civilians were safe, he had to get Grinch and Blaine back to the task force. But he wasn't sure what he was going to do himself.

Boland's death had changed things, in that it had set him down a path with no way out. He needed Zeus at his side, but a part of him knew that he was condemning his best friend to death. Now that al Qatar was dead, he felt a sense of relief.

He handed Sara the sat phone, and she punched in a series of numbers while trying to drive the truck. She was beautiful in that Persian way. Her dark hair and pale skin gave her an exotic elegance. Yet it was her fierce green eyes that really attracted his attention. They shone with an inner strength that drew him to her, and for a second he allowed himself to dream of a life outside of war.

"Hello?" she said after placing the phone to her ear. "Yes, yes, I am fine."

Mason could hear a man's voice on the other end of the line, and he forced himself not to listen in.

"Yes, we are coming, but I have some Americans with me," Sara said, pulling him away from his thoughts.

Mason knew that the Kurds and the United States had a complex relationship, with America doing much of the taking. Fighting for the most powerful nation in the world entailed a certain burden, in that America wasn't always the most faithful ally. US policy was usually a one-way street. If you could help its interests, then America would help you, but Mason knew better than anyone that the United States was a fickle friend.

"Good, we will be there soon," Sara said, hanging up.

"I hope your uncle likes Americans," Mason said as he took back the phone.

"No one likes Americans," Sara replied, garnering a chuckle from Zeus.

"What are you laughing at?" he asked the Libyan.

Zeus poked his shoulder from the backseat. "She is right, no one likes you."

"I'm not talking about me," he said, but in reality, he knew he was.

Sara was quick to clarify her statement. "I am in your debt."

"Can you tell me what happened?"

"The same thing that always happens," she said bitterly. "Men come from the south, and we are left alone to fight them."

"Okay, but why?"

"Because this is our home."

"All right, but what were you doing in Mosul? You are a Kurd, are you not?"

"My uncle sent me to get his wife," Sara said softly, "but she was killed by those men."

"Why would he send you? You're just a—"

"Just a what?" she demanded angrily. "A girl? Can not a girl fight just as well as a man?"

"That's not what I meant," Mason backpedaled. "Whoa," he thought, "have to watch out with this one." Then she muttered something under her breath.

"What was that? I missed it."

"I said you are all the same. You think that only men can fight for what is theirs."

"Oh, is that right?" Mason said, getting a little heated himself. "If men are all the same, then why did we save you back there?" Zeus groaned behind him, and he turned around to see the Libyan shaking his head.

"What?"

"That is not something you want to say in a situation like this," Zeus said.

"She started it. I just wanted to know where the hell we were going," Mason protested.

"You must forgive my friend," Zeus said to Sara. "He is a good man, but he does not understand women."

"Fuck him," she said, wiping a tear from her eye.

"Ahh, shit, look, I didn't mean to say that, I just . . ." He trailed off, not knowing what to say next.

"It is fine," Sara said, her voice cracking. "If you had not showed up, I don't know what I would have done."

"Those men, where did they grab you?"

She explained, "My uncle is a powerful man in Erbīl. When he learned that the fighters were coming north, he tried to warn the US, but they didn't listen. He sent my brother to Mosul, and when he didn't hear back from him, he sent me. I was told he never made it to my aunt's house."

"And the others?" Mason asked, motioning to the back of the truck.

"The fighters had lists of people given to them by the Iraqi police. They were going from house to house, rounding up the undesirables and taking them outside the city. These new fighters have only been there for a few days and have already killed so many. Baghdadi is a terrible man."

"Who?" Mason asked, not recognizing the name.

"Abu Bakr al Baghdadi, the man responsible

for bringing the Syrians into Iraq. He is a brutal, hateful man."

It was the same story Mason had heard years ago when they were looking for Abu Musab al Zarqawi, the Jordanian militant who'd inherited the al Qaeda mantle in Iraq. The clerics had learned long ago that they could cloak their violent rhetoric in the Koran and get their followers to conduct unspeakable horrors in Allah's name.

He was thinking how things never changed, when the Iridium vibrated in his hand.

"It's not him!" Renee said breathlessly as soon as the call connected.

"What do you mean, it's not him? He had the phone."

"His name is Ali Hasa. He is a Syrian national. I checked it in two separate databases."

Zeus was leaning forward on top of the seat, but Mason ignored him.

"Are you sure?"

"A hundred percent, but that's not the worst part. The *George Bush* was sunk in the middle of the Strait of Hormuz, and al Qatar is taking credit. The president wants blood."

"Wait, what?" Mason cried, appalled. "How does a militia leader sink an aircraft carrier?"

"No one knows. They think he used some kind of mine. Things are crazy around here. There is a huge operation in the works."

"Ah, shit, don't tell me that," Mason said, although he realized that, of course, the United States couldn't let that ride.

"Look, I'm kinda out of the loop right now, but we have guys coming in from everywhere. We need you back here."

"I can't right now," he said.

"Look, I will help you find this guy, but the task force is going to need you."

Rejoining the task force meant that Kane would have to take orders, and they wouldn't be directed toward putting al Qatar's head in a box. "I have to go," he said impatiently.

"Mason, don't—"

He hung up the phone, cutting her off, and announced to Zeus, "It wasn't him."

"Fuck. I thought for sure I was going to get a vacation."

But Mason wasn't listening. All he knew was that al Qatar was still alive. That meant his mission ahead was crystal clear.

CHAPTER 41

- - - - - - - - - - - - -

Jacob Simmons drained the glass of Bushmills whiskey, and he was considering pouring another when his phone began vibrating across his desk. He checked his watch—it was only eight thirty in the morning, but he had been drinking since well into the night, and he knew that the wife was probably pissed that he hadn't come home.

He was drunk, and in no mood to talk to her, especially since he was expected to be in the Situation Room in an hour. Deciding that another shot of Irish whiskey wasn't going to hurt, he poured another finger into the glass and ignored the phone.

"Sir, I have your packets," his secretary said as she entered the room and placed a thick binder on his desk. "Can I get you some coffee, sir?"

"That would be nice," he muttered, running his hands over his face as he headed to the bathroom.

Simmons closed the door behind him and flipped on the light. He knew that Cage would go ballistic if he showed up to the briefing looking like a drunk, and a part of him almost didn't care. But he knew that he was walking a fine line with his old friend right now and couldn't afford to push it.

He turned on the water in his personal shower, and as it heated up, he ran a razor over his face. The steam clouded up the mirror, forcing him to wipe it off to finish up the shave. In the rough oval he cleared out, he realized that he hated the man staring back at him.

"How has it come to this?" he asked, running the blade over his chin.

He undressed and stepped into the shower. The water felt great as it splashed over his body, and he let the heat wash over him for a few minutes. "Now to get sober," he told himself. He turned the hot water all the way off and forced himself to stand under the suddenly freezing spray.

The cold water stung his skin, and yanked the breath from his lungs, but he forced himself to take it until his skin began to turn blue. No matter how much he drank, or the amount of pain he inflicted on himself, the fact that he was responsible for almost three thousand American deaths would not go away.

"Damn it," he sobbed, turning the hot water back on.

If not for his wife and daughter, he would have

used the pistol he kept in his desk last night, but he knew that he'd already caused his family enough harm—even though they knew nothing about what he'd done.

As Simmons began to warm back up, he knew that his part in the plot was going to get out eventually, and then what the hell was he going to do?

He still felt a little drunk when he got out of the shower and dressed in the fresh suit he kept on standby. A cup of coffee sat steaming on his desk, and as he reached for it, his phone beeped, telling him he had a message.

Jacob expected it to be an angry voice mail from his wife, but as he slid his finger over the phone, he saw it was a text message from his daughter. He took a sip of the coffee, clicked on the message—and then felt his blood turn cold.

The coffee burned his hand as he dropped it, and he barely had time to grab the trash can before he vomited. The whiskey burned his throat with scalding force, and his secretary came into the room, a look of concern on her face.

"Sir, are you okay?"

"Get the fuck out," he screamed. His hands scrambled for the phone, where the picture of his daughter's tear-streaked face was still displayed starkly.

A large arrow was centered over the strip of cloth tied across her mouth, and as soon as he pressed his thumb over the icon, her screams filled the room. The video had been shot in his dining room, and the camera slowly panned over his daughter, who was tied to a chair, before moving to his wife, who was similarly bound.

Around her neck a note was attached to her blouse that read, "Come Home—Alone."

CHAPTER 42

- - - - - - - - - - - - -

"Can you fix it?" Mason asked the back of Grinch's legs as the sniper tinkered with the cargo truck's engine.

"Hell no," his muffled voice replied from under the hood. "This thing is fucked."

"Damn it. Well, it looks like we're walking," he said to Sara. "You mind telling me where we are going now?"

"There is a village a few miles from here," she said anxiously. "My uncle has people there who can get us across the river."

"We need to hurry," he said, gazing over at the group of civilians who were still sitting in the bed of the truck.

"Boss, looks like we have company," Blaine called out, his arm pointing to the south, where a dust cloud was growing in the distance.

"Shit, we need to move, *now*."

Mason raised the ACOG and tried to see how many vehicles were speeding toward them, but all he could make out was the sun flashing off glass. He had known that it was only a matter of time before the insurgents found the bodies they had left behind, but he'd hadn't planned on the truck breaking down.

"How far is the village?" he asked again as Grinch hopped down from the front of the truck and wiped his grease-soaked hands on the front of his pants.

"A few kilometers," she said with a sinking voice.

The civilians in the back of the truck began pointing at the billowing cloud of dust. Their panicked cries filled the air. Mason knew there was no chance that they could break contact and keep them safe.

"I need you to take as many people as you can fit into the Land Cruiser and go," he said to Sara.

"You want me to leave you here?"

"It's either that, or we all die. Grinch, grab our gear and find a suitable position to fight," he ordered as he hurried to the back of the cargo truck.

There was no way everyone could fit in the truck, so Mason was forced to play his final card.

"Get them to cover. I'm going to call Anderson," he told Blaine, trying to judge how much time they had before their pursuers arrived. The medic began herding the civilians into the wadi, leaving Mason to swallow his pride and make the call.

"I wondered if I was ever going to hear from you again," Anderson said sharply after picking up. "Where in the fuck is David?"

"No idea, but we can talk about that later. Right now I need help bad," Mason said, looking down at his wrist-mounted GPS.

"What makes you think I'm going to help you?"

"'Cause you're going to need me to pull off your little operation."

Anderson processed this claim for several moments before replying. "Fine, but if I do this, you play by my rules from now on."

"Whatever you say, boss man, but if you don't launch an attack in the next fifteen minutes, I'm not going to be able to help anyone."

"Send me your grid."

Mason read the coordinates off the Garmin and then added, "I have five foreign nationals with me. They are going to need a ride too."

"Fine, but Mason?"

"Yeah?"

"If you fuck me on this, I'm going to put you down. You hear me?"

"Yeah, I got it."

He was putting away the sat phone as the Libyan walked up.

"How hard was that?" Zeus asked.

Mason's old friend never failed to make him smile. "You don't want to know," he replied.

"What is happening?" Sara asked, looking at both of them.

"You need to go with the others," Mason said simply.

"Sometimes we must do what we have to so that we can survive," she said inscrutably, and he realized she was paying him a compliment.

"That's true," he replied.

"You are not like all the rest."

"I told you people liked me," Mason replied. "Now please, go join the others."

"You know," Zeus pointed out, "she is just being polite."

"Shut the fuck up," Mason said, slinging his assault pack. He and Zeus walked over to the edge of the wadi, where Grinch was setting up their makeshift position.

It was a good spot, several dozen feet north of the disabled cargo truck, where two of the dried rivulets came together to form a Y. Near the front of the trench was a small shelf that Grinch was already standing on, and just below him, the depression was deep enough for Sara and the other refugees to hide.

Blaine had them crouched down along the gravel-lined bottom, and he was trying to find cover for them to use.

Where the two fingers of the wadi came together, Mason realized, it was tight enough for them to set up a 360-degree perimeter, with enough cover for them to shoot from. It was too wide for a truck to drive over, so they didn't need to worry about being flanked, but he knew that if he wasn't able to direct fire from two sides, they couldn't deny the fighters freedom of movement.

"You guys hold here. Help is on the way," he said, yanking an M18 claymore mine from the big pocket.

"What the hell are you going to do with that?" Grinch asked.

"I'm going to leave them a little surprise."

"Well, you better hurry your ass up—they're getting close."

"Don't worry about it. Zeus, no matter what happens, get them on the bird," he said before moving back to the truck.

The broken-down deuce-and-a-half was parked perpendicular to the wadi, and Mason quickly opened the claymore's scissor legs and slammed them into the hard-packed sand near the back tire. He screwed the blasting cap into the mine, but after looking at the firing wire, he knew it wasn't long enough to stretch back to the wadi.

The only place for him to hide was in the cab, and after covering the wire with a long pile of sand, he began walking backward, paying it out. Then he climbed into the passenger side of the truck.

"Mason, what the hell are you doing?" Grinch asked over the radio.

"I don't have enough wire. Just cover my ass."

"You can't fucking stay there."

"It's the only way. Shut up and get ready."

"Forget the claymore—" he said, but Mason turned down the radio's volume, and silence filled the cab.

He had set up a lot of ambushes, and Mason

knew that the first deadly surprise would be the most crucial. All he had to do was hold out long enough for the cavalry to arrive. If he could do that, he might just make it out alive.

Kane tried to get himself set in the passenger seat. He plugged the wire into the firing device and jammed a fresh magazine into his rifle. He could hear the trucks getting closer, and he nudged his head up to look through the back window.

Approaching were two Ford F-250 pickups with their Iraqi markings painted over and a Humvee with a .50 caliber machine gun mounted to the top. Mason ducked back down and focused on slowing his heart rate.

He knew that if he didn't take out the machine gun, it was going to be a short fight.

The Humvee's supercharged engine whined as it struggled to keep up with the lighter Fords. He guessed that there would be at least twenty fighters in all and clicked the transmit button attached to his vest.

"Grinch, you have the fifty cal."

"Time to make the grass grow," the sniper whispered back.

Mason wiped the sweat from his palms, making sure he had a good grip on the detonator.

The lead vehicle began to slow as the driver spotted the stranded cargo truck. Instead of stopping short, the vehicles kept coming until they were just ten feet away.

Mason realized that he hadn't considered what

to do if the trucks flanked him. He felt a whisper of panic creep up his spine. It was too late to move.

"Time to roll the dice," he muttered, gripping the olive-green firing device firmly.

At the last minute, the heavily armored lead vehicle slammed on its brakes and the tires skidded across the rocky desert floor before finally coming to a stop. A cloud of dust washed over the area, obscuring Mason's vision of the kill zone.

He felt the sweat dripping down his back as the smell of exhaust drifted up to his position, and the heavy diesel engines rumbled behind the dust cloud. There was a metallic *thump* as one of the armored doors was unlatched, followed by the sound of voices.

The dust cloud began to dissipate, revealing a knot of men walking up to the truck, clutching American M4s.

"Check the truck!" one of the men shouted in Arabic.

"Shit, c'mon, I need more than one," Mason murmured as the fighter moved forward cautiously.

He knew that if the first man saw the claymore, the ambush was fucked before it started. Luckily for him, the fighters were undisciplined, and instead of checking the area and setting up a base of fire, they began milling around.

The range of the antipersonnel mine was about 110 yards. At that distance, the 680 grams of C4 plastic explosive would send the ball bearings out in a 60-degree killing arc. He flipped the safety bale off the M57 firing device. All he had to do now was squeeze the top and bottom halves together to detonate the mine.

It was hot inside the cab of the truck, and his neck was beginning to hurt from craning backward. He wanted to see what was going on but knew he couldn't risk exposing himself. Mason could hear the fighters' boots crunching on the gravel, and he tried to visualize where they were.

"Is it empty?" one of the men demanded.

"Are you going to give me time to check?" another one asked, his voice no more than a foot away.

Mason switched the detonator to his left hand and placed his right hand on the pistol grip of the HK416. Using his thumb, he snapped the selector switch to fire. The tiny *click* sounded incredibly loud in the tight confines of the cab, and he felt the truck sway as his target climbed up on the running boards and turned the door handle on the driver's side.

The door swung open with a groan, and then a head appeared. It took a second for the fighter's eyes to adjust to the dim interior, but when he finally saw the barrel of Mason's rifle, it was too late.

The suppressor coughed as the round shot out of the barrel and plowed through the man's forehead. Mason didn't wait for him to fall. He gave the detonator a hard squeeze and ducked his head.

The claymore went off with a flash of angry orange and a thump that jarred Mason's teeth. He had aimed the antipersonnel mine about waist height, and the ball bearings sliced through the air at almost four thousand feet per second, but he didn't have time to admire his handiwork. He climbed up to his knees and slammed the muzzle through the back window just as the gunner's head erupted and his body dropped into the Humvee.

Mason had to use the fixed sight, mounted atop the ACOG, due to the distance between him and his targets, and as soon as he got a decent sight picture, he began firing. He hit his target with a tight pair to the chest, but instead of going down, the man leveled his AK and began spraying the deuce-and-a-half.

The rounds cut easily through the thin aluminum skin, blasting out the rest of the window and showering Mason with glass. He ducked behind the seats, flipping the selector to full auto, and fired back through the truck while trying to turtle down into the floorboard.

A shard of glass sliced into his palm as he shifted to grab a fresh mag, and the rest of the fighters opened up on the cab of the truck.

"Little help!" he yelled into the radio.

Suddenly he smelled fuel drifting up into the cab. Then an RPG screamed from the back end of the truck. The warhead hit one of the cross beams that spanned the troop compartment and exploded in a cloud of shrapnel and black smoke.

Mason kicked the passenger side door open and turned his body so he could see out. Fire from the RPG crept slowly toward the cab. His only option was to throw himself to the ground.

Glass cut through his battle shirt as he pulled himself toward the opening. He was just about to throw himself to the ground when the .50 caliber opened up.

The heavy machine gun ate lazily through the belt of ammo, sending its large-caliber rounds blasting through the cab. One of the rounds hit the open door, ripping it from the hinges, and Mason lifted himself up just as a fighter came into view.

He was so close that Mason could see the muscles in his forearm as he worked the trigger, sending brass arcing from the AK. The first shots were high, and they shredded the dashboard, filling the interior with chunks of yellow padding. The suppressor of his HK got caught on the seat, and he tried to jerk it free when a round slammed into his chest.

The impact knocked the air out of his lungs, and he saw blood splatter up from the wound a second before the fighter crumbled to the ground. Mason felt a dull throbbing, and then a sharp pain cut through his collarbone.

"Fuck," he said, grabbing at the wound. His fingers came back bloody, but it was the intense heat from under the floorboards that really concerned him.

Ripping a frag from its pouch, he tried to pull the pin with his right hand, but he found his arm wouldn't work. He switched the grenade and grimaced as he pulled the pin with his left.

The flames had made it to the cab, and they licked at his pants as he pushed himself toward the open door. He tossed the frag through the back window before heaving his upper body over the jamb. Mason used his left hand to pull himself to the point of no return, and then he was falling.

Mason tumbled out of the truck, contorting his body so he wouldn't land on his head. Suddenly his rifle sling snagged on something, jerking him upright and crushing his wounded shoulder.

He was hanging awkwardly from the sling, and out of the corner of his eye, he saw Grinch running from the wadi.

"No," he yelled, waving his good arm to stop him.

The frag exploded behind the truck, and Mason struggled to get to his knife while Grinch ran toward him. He got out the blade and managed to slice through the sling just as his sniper got hit.

Mason hit the ground like a bag of rocks, his HK clattering down beside him. He grabbed for the rifle as the .50 caliber traversed away from the deuce-and-a-half and began engaging another target. His finger found the pistol grip, and he swept the rifle low across the ground, firing under the truck.

The bolt locked back with a snap, and he was forced to let go to grab a fresh mag. Holding the HK between his legs, he ripped the empty mag out and awkwardly shoved a fresh one in. He engaged the bolt release with the flat of his hand, and got shakily to his feet, keeping low as he moved to the front of the truck.

Grinch's body lay still ten feet from his position, and he knew from the amount of blood already pooling around his teammate's body that he wasn't going to make it.

Mason was just about to step into the open when an explosion slammed into the ground, knocking him off his feet.

He lay flat on his back, ears ringing, and the smell of burning flesh filling his nose. Looking up, he caught a glimpse of an A-10 tank buster leveling off, flame spitting from its 30 mm cannons. The pilot brought the Warthog so close to the ground that he could see it shudder as it fired.

Wuuuummmmppp.

Empty casings rained down all around him as the pilot punched the throttle, yanking the A-10 upward into a slow arc. Soon he flipped it over and rolled back on target.

Mason used his rifle to push himself to his feet and staggered to where Grinch lay bleeding on the ground. Pushing the pain out of his mind, he focused on his motionless teammate, ignoring the rounds snapping past his head.

"I'm here," he yelled over the hateful roar of the A-10's GAU-8 cannon.

Grinch's face was pale with a tinge of blue, and Mason knew right away that he wasn't getting enough oxygen. He shoved his hands beneath the man's kit and immediately felt blood pouring from the exit wound five inches below his shoulder blade. Mason pulled his hands from under the sniper's body armor. With his fingers covered in blood, he yanked the man's knife from its scabbard.

As he began cutting Grinch's kit free, he screamed for Blaine, hoping his voice carried over the firefight. He stabbed the knife into the ground and began fumbling to unzip the trauma kit attached to the man's vest.

His bloody fingers kept slipping off the zipper. "Goddamn it," he muttered over the rounds cracking over his head. Finally, he threw his body on top of Grinch's, shielding him from the fire.

"Fucking shit," he yelled as a round hit the sniper's rifle with a metallic slap before ricocheting into the air.

The A-10 whirled around for another pass, but instead of running, the fighters were holding their ground, still trying to kill the American who was stuck out in the open.

In the distance, he could hear the deep *thump, thump, thump* of rotors beating the air. Blaine came sprinting out of the wadi, but Mason knew the bird wasn't going to make it in time to save his friend's life.

Mason could feel Grinch gasping beneath him as he began CPR. He had lost too much blood.

"Move," Blaine yelled, diving to the ground, his chest heaving from the short sprint.

Mason finally got the sniper's trauma kit open and dumped it on the ground. He snatched the Asherman chest seal from the pile of medical supplies, tearing at the plastic with his teeth, while Blaine cut the bloodstained shirt away from the wound.

"Hurry the fuck up," the medic shouted, grabbing the chest seal from Mason.

The seal was a flat disk about the size of a coffee can lid, with a gray valve sticking out of the center. Blaine stripped the plastic cover off the seal, exposing the medical-grade adhesive, before pushing the valve through the wound, flattening the clear pad flush against his chest.

"Fuck," Blaine cursed as Grinch convulsed violently beneath him. "Stay with me."

The bird was getting closer, and Mason awkwardly stripped the pin off a smoke canister.

The pain in his shoulder caused his vision to swim, making it hard to focus on the radio as he switched to the air-to-ground net.

"Any station this net, this is Ronin 6. I have an urgent surgical patient and need extract now."

"Roger, Ronin 6, let us clear the area," came the reply.

"Negative, put the bird on the ground now, or he's going to die," he yelled back.

"Ronin 6, this is Road Dog 1. This next one is going to be danger close. I need you guys to get to cover."

"Road Dog, Ronin 6, drop it. I've marked my position with red smoke. You are cleared to engage danger close," he replied, looking up at Blaine.

The medic bent down to shield his patient as the A-10 lined up for its final run.

"Uhh, roger that, Ronin. Coming in hot."

"Easy day, brother," Mason said to Blaine with a grim smile.

"Wouldn't want to be anywhere else."

CHAPTER 43

- - - - - - - - - - - - - -

Mosul was vital to the control of northern Iraq, and the American forces that had been stationed there during the war had learned the hard way that the city was always on the verge of chaos.

While it had fallen easily enough during the 2003 invasion, keeping the peace was a different story altogether. The airfield had been a crucial linchpin in the supply system that had kept the American soldiers fed, armed, and protected, but this time it was supplying the jihadists.

Al Qatar knew that the Americans had left more ordnance and ammo in the bunkers than almost any place in the country, and as his convoy approached the main gate, he was still surprised that the Iraqi army hadn't attempted to defend it.

The concrete barriers placed along the road leading into the airfield forced his driver to slow as he serpentined his way toward the towers that guarded the approach. Like two reinforced sentinels, the towers dwarfed the metal gate, which stood open for the invaders. Their looming shadows played across the hood of the Ford F-250 as he passed beneath them.

If the Iraqi army had put up even a half-assed defense, al Qatar knew he would have lost a lot of men just trying to breach the outer defenses. Even now, he could see the unmanned barrels of the .50 caliber guns poking out over their sandbags, silently observing his men as they drove past.

Everywhere he looked, the signs of the American occupation were stamped on the airfield like perfectly preserved ruins of their technological advances. The tan exteriors of the modular housing, stacked row after row in orderly lines, offered a glimpse of how many soldiers had been stationed on the base, and he knew from his time in American captivity that, day and night, this area would have been filled with infidels preparing to run operations in the city.

In the distance, sunlight glinted off the glass of the control tower in flashes of red and orange as his driver headed for the flight line. All along the road stood concrete shelters built to shield the soldiers from the nightly harassment of rockets and mortars that his brothers had rained down on the Westerners.

Al Qatar's plan was coming to fruition, and despite the lingering loss of Ali, he felt a tinge of excitement as he read the gray letters identifying the salmon-colored terminal as the gateway to the Mosul airfield.

The recently repaved tarmac lay like a reptile soaking up the sun beneath a neat row of six Black Hawk helicopters, parked with bowed rotors before the tidy hangar.

"Get the trucks that we need," he said into a small radio he held in his hand. A group of vehicles came to a halt behind his truck.

"Yes, Emir," came the reply. Jabar drove around the helos and headed to their destination.

Al Qatar had been watching the news almost every day since his attack on the American carrier, and he knew that no matter how much the US president wanted to avoid another war in Iraq, his people were demanding blood. Last night he had addressed the nation and promised a swift and deadly response, which had put al Baghdadi and the rest of his clerics on edge.

They were scared of what was about to happen. There was talk of going back to Syria, but al Qatar was having none of it.

"What will happen when the Americans come?" Jabar asked, pulling his boss from his thoughts.

"They will bomb us first," he replied, watching his second-in-command out of the corner of his eye.

Al Qatar wanted the Americans to come back to Iraq. The airfield that he now held provided the perfect staging. Still, he wasn't sure if his men would be able to stand up to the bombardment that would precede the main assault.

"We will need much more of that," Jabar replied, motioning to the large bag of methamphetamine lying on the floor in the backseat.

"The men will have more than they need," al Qatar replied with a satisfied nod.

His plan was simple: he was going to dope his men up before the attack. Once the Americans were committed, he was going to destroy them with their own bombs. To do that, though, he needed to get into the ammo bunkers, which rose like ancient burial mounds on the horizon to the south.

"Do you see them?" he asked, pointing.

"Yes," Jabar replied.

The convoy stopped short, and one of his men jumped out with a pair of bolt cutters. He snapped the lock off the section of heavy chain securing the silver fence that enclosed the neat rows of bunkers. Stretching around the perimeter of their target was a roughly eight-foot-high dirt berm designed to protect the airfield in case of an explosion. Once the gate swung open, al Qatar's truck rolled along the gravel road that led to the first row of bunkers.

The heavy doors slid silently open on well-oiled tracks, revealing pallets of ordnance stacked neatly along the concrete floor. The first bunker was full of small-arms ammunition and grenades, and he waited while the rest were opened one after another. Each one contained different ordnance, all arranged by type, and he could hear his men marveling at the amount of ammo they had just seized.

"Rockets, Emir," one of the men exulted, stepping out of the way as al Qatar peered inside. Stacked against the southern wall were case after case of AT-4 antitank weapons and LAW light antitank weapons. On the other side, he made out the distinctive markings of portable surface-to-air missiles.

The first of a line of heavy cargo trucks pulled in behind him. He commanded the men to take all the surface-to-air missiles out of the bunker and then continued on to the next one.

Inside was what he had been after all along, and he motioned for one of his men to drive one of the vehicles over to him. As the driver pulled up, he stepped inside and ran his hand over the tips of the 155 mm artillery rounds, weighing almost ninety pounds apiece, stacked from front to back inside the magazine.

"Load as many as you can onto each of the four trucks," he told Jabar.

He knew it would take the men most of the morning to load the heavy shells, but it didn't matter. While the rest of his fighters were securing weapons and ammo, the most important thing he had to do was load the trucks with the rounds. After that, all he needed to do was send them to the Mosul dam and wait for the Americans to attack.

CHAPTER 44

- - - - - - - - - - - - - -

Mason opened his mouth wide to prevent his eardrums from bursting, and he squeezed his body tight over the wounded sniper as the 500-pound bomb passed overhead. The fins of the Mk-80 whistled as they cut through the air, floated gently over the disabled deuce-and-a-half, and slammed into the group of fighters who refused to break contact.

Cruuump.

The explosion struck like an invisible hand, slapping Mason in the back. Its heat licked savagely over his unprotected neck. He felt his body being lifted off the ground, and for a moment, he was weightless. The world slowed around him. The air rushed from his lungs in a ragged gasp as a black, noxious cloud enveloped him in darkness. Then he crashed back to the earth.

He vaguely heard someone calling his name over the radio as his eyes fluttered open. Mason's face was buried in the ground next to Grinch's, and he saw the terror in his teammate's eyes as he gasped for breath.

"Mason," the voice yelled again.

He shook his head in a vain attempt to restart his addled brain. His hand searched for the rifle that had been ripped from his grasp. Next to him, Blaine forced himself to a sitting position.

Suddenly the air began to clear, and he looked up to see a V-22 Osprey floating down above him. The heavy twin rotors beat the ground, swirling smoke and grit all around. As soon as it touched down, a group of marines charged down the ramp and quickly set up a 360-degree perimeter. The A-10 remained orbiting above the chaotic scene.

Mason groaned as he got to his knees and wiped his hand across his face in an effort to clear the dirt from his eyes. A corpsman was suddenly in his face, shouting "Are you good?"

"Help him," he croaked, pointing down at Grinch.

"Hold on, buddy," the marine said.

Mason was struck by how young he looked as he went to work on Grinch, checking his wounds with a precision born of countless repetitions.

"Mason." He recognized the voice: Zeus.

"I'm good—get them to the bird," he said.

"I need a litter," he heard the corpsman yell into his radio.

Mason looked around, taking in the mangled deuce-and-a-half, and then the blackened hulks of the fighters' vehicles, still burning among the twisted remains of the dead jihadists. It was a hellish scene, and he felt his stomach turn as the men loaded Grinch onto the stretcher.

"We have to go," Blaine yelled, helping him to his feet.

Mason ducked his head, stumbling amid the prop wash of the massive blades turning about his head. As they neared the ramp, he pulled himself free of Blaine's grip and waited as Zeus and the civilians they had saved rushed into the cargo hold of the Osprey.

Sara had her arms wrapped around another woman, who was obviously terrified to board the aircraft. Mason could see her mouth moving as she spoke encouragement into the woman's ear, and Mason found himself marveling at her strength. Her face was a mask of dirt and grime, and she ignored the thin rivulet of blood streaming down her scalp and over her cheek. A grim smile passed over her face as she walked up the ramp, and then she was inside.

Mason took one final glance at the battlefield. For the second time in the last few days, he swore to avenge those who had fallen.

Blood had already soaked through Grinch's stretcher, and in the dim light of the cargo compartment he looked pale and small. His breathing was increasingly erratic, in contrast with the sound of the Osprey thundering through the air.

Most of the civilians stared blankly at the floor,

refusing to look at the half-naked American who had saved them. Mason wanted to hate them, wanted to blame them for the unequal trade-off that was occurring before his eyes.

"Look at him," he ordered over the roar of the engines.

Sara was the only one who met his gaze, and he could see the mix of anger and sadness in her eyes.

"Look," he ordered, trying to get to his feet while pointing down at his dying teammate.

Zeus grabbed him by the shoulder, trying to pull him back, but Mason shrugged him off. By now, tears were falling freely down his face. But he knew that no matter how angry he got, what had happened to Grinch was on him.

He had failed him just as he had failed T.J., Boland, and so many others that he almost couldn't keep count.

The marines were staring at him, but he didn't care what they thought.

Sara got to her feet, shielding the woman who was crying next to her. "This is not their fault. Blaming them won't save him," she yelled in Arabic.

Suddenly Grinch began convulsing on the stretcher, and Mason stood by helplessly as Blaine and the corpsman started chest compressions. Zeus's arms closed around him and pulled Kane back onto the nylon bench.

"Don't do this to yourself, not now," he said, placing his mouth next to Mason's ear. "It's not what he would have wanted."

The Osprey began to descend, and Mason felt his heart sinking into his chest. It was all over. Blaine reached for a solar blanket from the aid kit, but the corpsman held up his hand, motioning for him to stop. The young marine got to his feet, and headed to the front of the aircraft, where an American flag hung from the ceiling. Taking a knife from his pocket, he cut the 550 cord attaching it to the metal strip before turning back to Grinch. Ever so carefully, he draped the flag over the dead warrior's body, tucking the edges beneath him so that they wouldn't touch the ground.

Blaine wiped a bloodstained hand across his face, leaving a crimson trail mixed with sweat. The medic locked eyes with Mason for a moment before dropping his head.

Mason would have gladly traded his life for Grinch's, but for some unknown reason, it was his fate to live while those closest to him died.

The landing gear locked into place with a thump, and the massive engines rotated upward as the bird hovered, stabilizing before dropping to the tarmac below.

The wheels touched down with a distinct bump, and as soon as the bird settled, the marines got to their feet and reached down for the litter. The ramp lowered with a mechanical whine, and they lifted the fallen soldier from the floor and carried him toward the ramp.

From his place near the back of the aircraft, Mason watched the wind catch the edge of the flag. A group of men from the base rushed low under the spinning blades of the Osprey. Yet once they saw the flag-draped body, they stopped short, assuming the position of attention. Mason heard one of them yell, and, in unison, they saluted the fallen soldier.

CHAPTER 45

Like the rest of the troops at the airfield, Renee felt restless. The initial excitement that came with prepping for a mission had long dissipated, and while the paratroopers passed their time by checking and rechecking their equipment, she tried to read a book.

Sergeant Major Mitchell had managed to persuade Colonel Anderson to let her stay, but instead of going into action with one of the strike teams, Renee was going to be jumping in with the main assault. She had set up a cot near the back of the hangar the troopers were using so that they wouldn't have to find her if something new came down. She was lying on her back, trying to pay attention to her book, when she heard Parker yell her name.

"Yeah?" she called, dog-earing the page.

"Someone's been hit on Mason's team. They're coming in now."

"What? Who was it?" she asked, getting to her feet.

"No idea. C'mon."

She threw the book onto the cot and followed Parker out onto the tarmac.

A medical team was already standing by, ducking against the downdraft driven by the Osprey's massive rotors. The ramp was lowering, and she felt her heart catch in her throat as soon as she saw the flag-draped litter being carried from the back of the bird.

"Oh shit," she murmured. "Please don't be Mason." She prayed silently as the marines stepped onto flat ground and loaded the body into the back of a Chevy Silverado pickup.

She didn't even realize that she was running toward it until one of the ground crew stepped forward to intercept her.

"Wait till the rotors stop," he yelled as she fought her way past.

"It's okay," Parker shouted. "Let her go."

Mason appeared at the top of the ramp, with Zeus following a step behind. Renee felt a wave of relief as he made his way down wearily. His kit was filthy, and a huge bloodstained bandage covered his shoulder.

She ran to his side, keeping her head low as the engine spooled down.

"I was so worried," she said. Noticing the tears cutting through the blood and grime caked on his face, she asked, "What the hell happened?"

"Bad day," he said as she went to hug Zeus.

That's when she noticed the civilians trembling at the top of the ramp. "Who are they?"

"We ran across an execution squad when we were looking for al Qatar," he began. "I . . ." Too exhausted to continue, his voice trailed off.

"They were slaughtering civilians," Zeus said, motioning for Sara to come down and join them.

"It was my fault," Mason said. "We shouldn't have been there in the first place, but when we tried to exfil, we ran into some trouble. That was when Grinch got hit."

"Mason," Anderson's voice rang out from the shadows.

Renee turned to see the colonel and Sergeant Major Mitchell standing by.

"Yes sir," he said, heading toward them.

Renee noticed that he was limping, and it was obvious that he had been hit more than once, but Mason betrayed no signs of pain as he made his way over.

"Good to see you alive," Anderson said, holding out his hand.

Mason winced as they shook hands.

"You hurt?"

"Just a scratch," he replied.

"Looks a little more serious than that. Go get your ass checked out. We need to debrief you."

"Roger that, sir. What about Grinch?"

Colonel Anderson lowered his head, and it

was obvious that even though he didn't care for Mason, he still cared about the men under his command.

"We can talk about that later. Once we get him cleaned up, we are going to send him stateside. We'll take care of your guy."

"He deserved better than me," Mason said as the Silverado pulled away.

Mitchell, taking over for Colonel Anderson, commanded, "Parker, take his gear, and get these people something to eat and a place to stay. I'll make sure Mason gets cleared by medical."

"You did a helluva thing out there," the colonel said sincerely, patting him on his good shoulder before turning to head back to the hangar.

"Don't worry about Anderson. Just get yourself checked out," Sergeant Major Mitchell said once he was gone. "None of this shit is on you."

"Shouldn't have been there in the first place," Kane muttered.

"What was that?"

"I said . . ."

"I heard what the fuck you said."

"Mason," he said firmly, "I told you that this wasn't your fault. You need to get that out of your head right now. Boland, T.J., and Grinch were all soldiers, and they knew what was at stake, just like you do. Don't try to make this into another one of your crusades."

"T.J., Boland, and Grinch are on me, and you know that."

"Bullshit," Mitchell said sharply, taking a step closer.

Renee could see that Mason was hurting, and she knew that he would take this to heart. She also knew that Anderson wanted him in the fight, and as long as he could still stand, he would be going back in.

"You saved these civilians, and that means something. Remember that when you want to feel sorry for yourself. Now go get yourself patched up. We have work to do."

Turning to Renee, Mitchell pointed his finger and said, "You make sure he sees the doc."

"Roger that, Sergeant Major."

A woman whom Renee had never seen before moved to Mason's side and asked, "What is going to happen now?"

Renee noticed that unlike the rest of the civilians, she wasn't scared.

"This man will get you something to eat, plus a place to rest," Renee replied in Arabic.

"I have to go see a doctor," Mason said. "I will find you when I am finished."

The woman translated for the rest of the civilians what was happening and then walked over to Parker for further instructions.

"Who is that?" Renee asked, curiosity getting the better of her.

"He saved her life," Zeus said simply.

"We all saved her life," Mason corrected.

"Come on, you," Renee said as she reached

for his rifle and led him to the medical area inside
the hangar.

"You're lucky that your collarbone isn't broken,"
the Special Operations medic said after he finished
suturing Mason's shoulder.

Renee stood in the corner, unwilling to leave
her friend until the doc checked him out. The bullet wound to his shoulder looked terrible, and the
wound to the back of his arm would have stopped
any other man.

The first time they met, she had expected a
monster, but the more time they spent together,
the more a deep respect had formed between them.
She knew that Mason was in a dark place mentally, and she felt for him. "What comes around
goes around, though," she thought. He had been
there when her team was wiped out in Pakistan and
had been extremely supportive during her grieving
period.

"How's the knee?" the medic asked as he placed
a gauze pad over the wound.

"It's still fucked up," Mason replied.

"I'll give you some Percocets to take the edge
off," he replied. "I would tell you to take it easy, but
we all know where that would get me."

"Doc, I need you to clear me," Mason demanded.

"You can't be serious," Renee interjected. "You
are exhausted, and banged to shit."

"If either one of you thinks I'm not going on

this mission, you're smoking crack," Mason replied harshly. "Just patch me up and give me the pills—that's all I need from you two."

The doc raised his hands in mock surrender. As for Renee, she knew she had overstepped her bounds, but she was legitimately concerned for Mason.

"Don't look at me like that," she said. "Just because I'm worried about you doesn't make me the enemy."

"I'll go get the pills and leave you two to it," the doc said, hurrying out of the room.

"Don't try to keep me off this op," Mason warned, wincing as he pulled on a fresh battle shirt.

"I'm not. I just want you to take care of yourself. When was the last time you slept?"

"I'll sleep when I'm dead."

"I know what you're going through, and it's not your fault."

"I don't want to talk about it."

"Well, then, you can fucking listen. The mission was fucked up from the beginning, and if you and Zeus hadn't done what you did, I wouldn't be here right now. I don't know what the hell happened out there, but I know you did everything you could. Hell, you saved their lives," she said, pointing out toward the hangar.

"Damn it, Renee, I don't want to talk about this shit right now."

"If you want to carry this cross by yourself, then there is nothing I can say to stop you, but I'm not going to sit here holding your hand while you have a pity party."

Mason grew sullen. He knew she was right.

Renee was smart enough not to push the issue. She was well aware of what happened when you backed Mason into the corner.

"When are they planning to launch?" he asked suddenly.

"The briefing is later tonight," she said as the doc came back in the room, holding a bag of pills.

"You know what to do with these," he said, tossing them to Mason.

"Yeah, but I'll save them for later." He struggled to his feet.

"Look at yourself, you can barely stand up. You need to get some sleep. Maybe you should try taking care of yourself for once," Renee said as he stumbled and then caught himself.

"Do me a favor, both of you," Mason said, looking from Renee to the doc. "Don't get in my way on this one. I am taking down the guy who killed Boland, and that's final."

He roughly stuffed the pills in his pocket and headed for the door. She shook her head, knowing that he was operating from a place of pure hate.

"How bad is he?" she asked the doc once the door had closed behind her friend.

"His knee is swollen, his arm is messed up, and he's fractured his clavicle. Other than that he's in tip-top shape."

"Are you going to clear him?" Renee asked, concerned.

The medic looked at her glumly, and Renee knew the answer before he even said anything.

"Look, you've been around long enough to know how this thing goes. He's not going to sit on the sideline, no matter what I say."

"I realize that, but his head's not right."

"Is yours?"

"What?"

"How many guys out in that bay *aren't* fucked up? They go through Ambien like they are fucking Skittles. If we had a psych doc on hand, none of them would be mission ready."

"But your job is to make them sit on their asses, not to patch them up and send them out to the grinder again," she replied, feeling a wave of heat crawl up her face.

"Let me ask you something: If you were in his shoes, would you take a seat on the bench?"

Renee knew he had her.

"Your silence speaks for itself," he said before turning away to clean up the bloody gauze pads.

There was a chance that Anderson or Mitchell might not let Mason go out, but she knew it was a small one. If they said he was too bad off to go on a mission, they would all have to admit to themselves that they were human, and that was something that none of them was comfortable doing.

Being the only woman on the task force gave

Renee a unique view of the male psyche, but what the doc had said about her own head being fucked up had hit home. She knew she wasn't over what had happened to her team in Pakistan, and Mason had always stood by her. Renee was faced with a terrible decision, and without David around, she knew she had to make it for herself.

CHAPTER 46

Simmons grabbed the pistol from the desk drawer and slid it into his jacket pocket before heading to the door. He rushed past his secretary, and his shoes echoed on the floor as he ran down the hall to the garage. He didn't care what the cameras saw as he burst through the glass door and yanked the keys out of his pockets.

He started the black Chevy Suburban SUV and dialed his home phone as the tires screeched across the black asphalt. The phone rang five or six times before the answering machine picked up, and the prerecorded message his daughter, Daisy, had made came through the phone.

"Shit," he yelled, barely waiting for the wooden security arm to raise as he hit the gas and sped into traffic.

Simmons knew better than to call the police. He felt his stomach churn as he blew through a red light, knowing no one could help him now.

The national security advisor had no idea who was holding his family hostage, but he knew without a doubt that if he called anyone, they were dead.

He raced home in less than twenty minutes, and only by God's grace did he avoid being in an accident or pulled over. He slammed on the brakes as he skidded into his driveway. He slammed the SUV into Park without waiting for it to come to a halt. Jacob ran to the back door, which lay open before him.

"Megan. Daisy," he yelled, yanking the Sig Sauer P229 from his pocket and barging into the den, heading for the dining room.

"Stop where you are and place the pistol on the ground, or I will blow your daughter's head off," a voice commanded.

Simmons froze as he came around the corner. The only thing he could see was the black suppressor pushed against his daughter's head.

"I am not a savage man, Mr. Simmons, and it would pain me to kill her, but I need you to know that I will not hesitate if you don't follow my directions."

His daughter screamed from behind her gag as the man pressed the suppressor into the side of her head. Shaken by the muffled cry of terror, Jacob tossed the pistol to the ground.

"If you hurt them, I will kill you," he warned.

"Unlike you, I do not kill innocent people. Now put these on," the man replied, tossing a pair of flex cuffs at Simmons's feet.

Jacob placed the black plastic cuffs over his left hand and pulled it tight with his right. "It's going to be okay," he said to his daughter before using his teeth to pull the other loop tight around his right hand.

"Get on your knees," the man ordered.

As soon as he complied, David Castleman stepped into view. "Mr. Simmons, do you know who I am?"

"Yes, I met you last year at the White House. Why are you doing this?"

"Then you know what I do?" David asked, ignoring his question.

"Yes, I know who you are, I know what you do. Please, just let them go, and I will tell you whatever you want to know."

"I'm sure you will do exactly that, but before we go there, I want you to know that last night I was at General Vann's house. We had a very interesting and, unfortunately, very violent conversation. He told me many things after I burned the skin off his chest, but none of that needs to concern you." David spoke in a measured tone, letting the menace speak for itself.

"What I need you to focus on is this: if you lie to me, I will not hurt you, I will hurt her."

"Daisy, look at Daddy, it's going to be okay."

"I need you to know, Mr. Simmons, that for you to keep that promise requires that you tell me the truth."

"I'm going to fucking kill you," he said, spitting at David.

"Mr. Simmons, I want you to stand up and come into the dining room."

Jacob got to his feet, walked past his daughter, and took a seat across from his wife.

"Place your head back against the chair."

As the president's national security advisor leaned back his head, David walked behind him and looped another zip tie around his neck. He used his left hand to run the free end through the plastic buckle and cinched it.

"Is that too tight?" the spy asked courteously.

"No, it's fine."

David walked around to the other side of the table, where a large white napkin was draped over a row of objects. He pulled the napkin off slowly, revealing a long kitchen knife, a pair of pruning shears, and a clear plastic bag.

"I need to know who you are working with," he said, taking the large plastic bag off the table and holding it up with his left hand. "Please resist the urge to lie."

"Secretary of Defense Cage and General Vann."

"What about Colonel Anderson?"

"He isn't involved in anything other than planning and execution."

"And what was your plan, exactly?"

"SecDef Cage has been using his influence to direct national policy through the president of the United States. He used al Qatar to force the president to send the USS *George Bush* into the Gulf, and then alerted al Qatar to when it would be going through the Strait of Hormuz."

"So you wanted the carrier destroyed to garner support for another invasion into Iraq?"

"Yes. But just disabled. Not sunk."

"And then what happens?"

"After the invasion, we take enough losses on the ground to validate the use of more troops."

"What did you two hope to accomplish by this?"

"Destroying the jihadist threat in Iraq and Syria."

Jacob noticed that tears were flowing down his wife's face, and said, "Baby, I am so sorry. I never meant for it to get so out of hand."

"Your wife didn't believe me when I informed her of your complicity," David said, taking a tape recorder out of his pocket and turning it off. "But I promised to both her and your daughter that we would get to the truth." David held up the recorder like a prize. "It is such a tragedy. You had everything a man could want, right here in this room."

CHAPTER 47

- - - - - - - - - - - - - -

Al Qatar was overseeing the emplacement of a ZPU-4 on the south side of a hangar when the phone in his pocket went off.

"Yes," he said as one of his men took a seat behind the four-barreled antiaircraft gun and rotated the adjusting wheel until it was pointing skyward. They had found boxes of night-vision scopes in one of the armories. He shook his head in disgust as the gunner looked through the scope and said, "It is not working."

"It is a night sight, you idiot," one of the men berated him.

"The trucks are loaded and fueled," Jabar said over the phone. "Are you sure you do not want them closer?"

"They will be fine here. I don't want the American drones to find them," he replied.

"Has he called yet?"

"No, but he will. You just make sure the men are ready." With that, al Qatar hung up.

He was annoyed that his source hadn't called yet to tell him when the Americans were planning to launch. He had to wonder if the man was going to keep his word. Forcing the thought from his mind, he gazed across the airfield, lost in thought momentarily.

Even if the man didn't call, al Qatar knew that he had more than enough guns for the Americans, and once the trucks were staged, there was nothing left for him to do but wait.

Sticking his hand in his left pocket, he could feel the remote control that would activate the electromagnetic pulse his man had hardwired into the cell towers. Khalid had told them that the device would slave itself to antennas, and when he activated it, they would destroy any electronic equipment the Americans had. The only problem was that it wouldn't take them long to figure out what was going on. So, in essence, he had only one shot to destroy the initial assault.

He knew this was his last battle, and all he had to do was live long enough to blow the dam and kill all the soldiers on the ground. It had been Ali's plan to blow the massive Mosul dam, and al Qatar thought that this would be the perfect tribute to his fallen comrade.

"Do not leave your position," he ordered the men as he headed for the ladder that led down to the tarmac. Still the phone didn't ring.

CHAPTER 48

- - - - - - - - - - - - - - -

think it is a mistake," Zeus said. The olive-drab cot squeaked beneath him as he turned onto his side.

"Why?" Mason asked wearily. He had slept for more than twelve hours but still felt like crap.

"Because we don't know anything about her," Zeus replied.

"If you can think of another way, then let me know. But as I see it, this is our only chance to get al Qatar."

"Is that all you care about, your precious revenge?"

"Excellent question," Renee said, stepping into their makeshift home. She had a tray of coffee in one hand and a black plastic bag in the other.

Mason got to his feet with a grimace and took the coffees from Renee before handing one to Zeus.

"What's in the bag?"

"Don't try to change the subject. What are you guys conspiring about?"

"The girl Sara," Zeus offered.

"Fuck, man, you ever heard of operational security?"

Zeus rolled his eyes as Renee tossed the bag onto Mason's cot.

"I got you both fresh uniforms, but if you don't want to tell me what's going on, you can keep wearing that ratty shit."

That was a good enough bribe for Zeus. "The girl's uncle has connections with the Peshmerga," he began, ignoring Mason's icy stare, "and Rambo here wants him to sneak us into Mosul so we can kill al Qatar."

"Are you fucking out of your mind? Just let them bomb the shit out of it and call it a day," said Renee.

"Seriously?" Mason asked. "It doesn't matter how many bombs they drop or who they put on the ground. I need to see him die."

"I know you blame him for Boland and Grinch, but—"

"He blew up a fucking aircraft carrier," Mason almost shouted.

"For once in your life, let someone else help you."

"Not going to happen," he replied.

Zeus took a sip of coffee, frowning at the blind need for revenge. "Who made this shit?" he asked, pointing at the cup.

Renee laughed, "Is it that bad?"

"It is terrible. You Americans just don't know how to make coffee."

"Whatever." Renee laughed again. "Have you run your little scheme by Anderson yet?"

"Yes and no," Mason replied. "I told him I could get eyes on the target, but didn't tell him how."

"Well, I want you to hear it from me before anyone else says anything: I advised against you going out," she said, refusing to meet his eyes.

"What the—?" Mason said, but she cut him off by raising her hand.

"Look, I'm not trying to screw you. I just think you're too banged up."

"I told him it was a bad idea also," Zeus muttered from his cot.

"Maybe you should listen, for once," Renee said.

Mason rolled his eyes. "If I wanted to talk to my mom, I would go back to LA."

"Whatever. At least someone cares about you, and I know if the roles were reversed, you would do the same for me. So stop looking all betrayed."

"Fucking women," he grumbled, lifting his soiled battle shirt and taking out his smokes. He lit the cigarette with his trusty Zippo and looked up at Renee through the haze of smoke.

"Oh, fuck you," she said in exasperation. "If you don't want to listen to reason. I'm just trying to save you from yourself. And you're not supposed to smoke in here."

"Okay," Mason replied, taking another drag.

"So what are you doing on this little jaunt? You still attached to that psycho?"

"Don't try to change the subject," she said.

"I'm not."

"No, I've been moved to the main assault."

"The airborne assault?" he asked, almost choking on his coffee. "When was the last time you did a static line jump?"

"A long-ass time ago, but they sent me through a mini refresher."

"Jesus. Too bad you're not on the dark side, or I would take you with me."

"Yeah, I know."

"Anyone seen Blaine?"

"Last I saw of him, he was headed over to the morgue. He looked like hammered shit," Renee said.

"What do you expect? He and Grinch were tight."

Mason grunted in pain as he got to his feet and gingerly wind milled his arms before grabbing the battle shirt.

"How's the shoulder?" Zeus asked.

"Fine," he lied while slipping the shirt over his head. "I know neither one of you agrees with my decision, but I'm standing by it."

Zeus squinted from the cigarette smoke and studied his friend before answering. Mason couldn't meet his gaze. He knew that lately their relationship had been very one-sided, and deep down he wasn't sure why the Libyan stuck with him. He knew that he owed the man his life, and that by all rights, it should be the other way around.

"You know I'm with you, but I think Blaine is . . ."

"What?" Mason asked, taking a seat beside him.

"He's done, man."

"I know, but I can't order him to stay behind."

"Whatever you're gonna do, you better think of it fast, because here he comes," Zeus said as Mason heard footsteps to his rear.

Just like Renee had said, Blaine looked terrible, with red-rimmed eyes and the same bloody uniform he had worn the previous day.

"I found you a new sling," he said after dumping the medical supplies on the bed. He tossed the tan piece of nylon into Mason's lap.

"Where have you been?" Mason asked.

"Took a walk. Word is, they are going to bomb the shit out of Mosul before we even hit the ground. So, what's the plan?"

Mason grabbed his battered rifle, and, noticing the blood spatter on its upper handguard, shielded it with his body to keep the others from noticing.

"We were just talking about the op," Renee said, trying to distract Blaine as Mason snatched his old battle shirt off the ground and used a sleeve to wipe off the blood.

"Fuck, man," Blaine said softly, sinking onto his cot, his eyes locked on Mason's rifle. "I can't believe he's gone. Did you know that Grinch's wife was pregnant? It was going to be his first kid.

How am I supposed to tell her she has to raise it by herself?"

Renee placed a hand on his shoulder as he lowered his head into his hands and began sobbing.

Mason knew that every man had his breaking point, no matter how hard he was. Some soldiers never bounced back from seeing their friends die, and in just a few days, Blaine had lost two of his brothers.

"We're going out again," Mason said finally, knowing that the sullen shadow that had fallen over the group was unhealthy. "And you're not going."

"Fuck that, Mason," Blaine cried. "Who do you think you are, making that call for me?"

Mason knew he was being hypocritical, especially after the argument he'd just had with Renee and Zeus, but he wasn't about to put Blaine in harm's way when his head wasn't in the fight.

"Easy, bro. Someone has to take Grinch's body back to the States, and I don't want it to be a stranger."

Zeus nodded at Mason, telling him that he was making the right call.

"I can't let you guys go out without me. What if one of you gets hit?"

"We'll have medical coverage. But that's not your concern," Mason stressed. "You need to be the one who takes him home."

The anger in Blaine's face dissipated as the logic of the idea sank in. A single tear trickled down his cheek before he nodded his assent.

"Okay," he said finally.

"Get a shower and change out of that shit. I'll let the bosses know that you're going to help us out on this," Mason said, walking over to Blaine and placing his hand on the top of his shoulder. "You did all you could. Don't ever forget that."

CHAPTER 49

- - - - - - - - - - - - - - -

As the Chinook raced across the ground, Mason used a red-lensed headlamp to check the map on his knee. Flashing the light onto the wrist GPS unit, he realized they were about twenty miles from the landing zone. He was more than ready to get the hell off the bird. His knee was hurting from bracing himself against the pilot's erratic maneuvers, and he cursed aloud as the helo suddenly surged up in the air and then dropped back down again.

Zeus sat up next to him, giving up trying to go to sleep now that they were across the border. "This is intolerable," he yelled over the engine noise.

Mason pointed at his watch and held up ten fingers.

A group of US Army Pathfinders was seated on the nylon benches that ran the length of the Chinook. Unlike their World War II namesakes, the modern Pathfinders unit was part reconnaissance and part air-to-ground liaison. The men of

Fox Company's Red Platoon had once been members of the Eighty-Second's long-range surveillance detachment, but during their last deployment to Afghanistan, they'd had been attached to an aviation unit.

The young paratroopers were instilled with the esprit de corps that comes with belonging to an elite unit, and they had a swagger that Mason appreciated. The men were masters at their jobs, but they had never operated on this side of the fence. He could tell that they were nervous, despite the fact that most of them had spent their entire adult lives in combat.

He turned away, and his mind drifted back to the conversation he'd had with Sara before leaving Turkey. She had wanted to accompany him on the mission, and it had gotten to the point where she'd almost refused to help unless he allowed her to go.

"You can't go; there is no way," he'd told her, but the woman stared defiantly at him, her chin raised, her arms crossed over her chest.

"Then you figure out how to get my uncle's help."

"Look, I can't take you with me even if I wanted to," he tried to explain, but she wasn't having it.

"I am going."

"If you go, then who is going to take care of all of them?" Zeus asked, jerking his finger toward the refugees.

"What do you mean?" she demanded.

"If we are not here, who is going to look out for them, make sure they get food?"

She considered that complication before finally lowering her head in defeat.

"Fine, give me the phone."

The call lasted fifteen minutes, and at first, it seemed like her uncle was in no mood to help. From what Mason could gather from the one-sided conversation, the man had his hands full dealing with al Qatar's fighters, and he was afraid to send any of his men to aid the Americans. But Kane had to hand it to Sara. She seemed to always get what she wanted, and by the end of the call, her uncle had agreed to help.

As Mason studied the map, he hoped that the Kurd was a man of his word, because he had no idea how they were going to get to the airfield without him.

"Ten minutes," the pilot said over the internal net.

Mason switched off the headlamp and took a deep breath. He could feel the effects of the previous days just on the edge of his consciousness. Renee had been right when she said he was running on empty. He was exhausted both mentally and physically. Still, this wasn't the first time he had forced himself past his limits.

Mason reached into the pocket sewed on the sleeve of his battle shirt and pulled out a vial of "go pills." He shook one of the orange tablets into the palm of his hand before passing the small plastic bottle to Zeus.

"What's that?" one of the troopers asked from the other side of the Chinook.

"Vitamins," he replied, flicking the pill into his mouth and washing it down with a sip from his CamelBak.

"Really? No way," the man yelled back.

"It's speed. You want one?"

"Speed? Isn't that bad for you?"

"Probably, but it will keep you up," Mason replied, taking the vial back from Zeus and snapping the cap back on.

"Shit, I've never done drugs," the soldier yelled back.

"First time for everything." Mason smiled as the helo began to slow.

The crew chief got up from the ramp and paused to untangle himself from his safety line before moving over to the control box. His thumb jabbed a button, and the ramp began to lower, letting in a burst of fresh air.

"Well, if you need one, let me know," Mason said, getting to his feet.

The pilot waited until the last minute to flare the bird and then gently set the rear wheels on the desert floor. As soon as Mason felt the front wheels touch down, he flipped down his night vision and hustled down the ramp.

He kept his head low, holding his breath as the rotors beat down on him. The exhaust felt hot against his neck, and specks of debris slapped him in the face as he rushed out beyond the spinning blades and took a knee. The other soldiers piled out beyond him and moved expertly to their initial positions.

Mason scanned the terrain slowly as the pilot pushed the throttle forward, and the bird thundered into the distance. He checked to ensure that they had 360-degree security set up and then depressed the illumination key on his GPS. The digital arrow pointed southwest, toward the coordinates where they were supposed to meet up with members of the Peshmerga.

He rose to his feet with a muffled groan. Back at the hangar, he'd heard one of the Pathfinders refer to him as the "old guy," and it made him realize that he'd been at war for a very long time. The desert had become such a big part of his life that Mason almost couldn't imagine leaving it. What would happen the day he had to let it all go?

The Pathfinders' squad leader made his way over to Mason and whispered, "What's the plan?"

"We pray the Kurds show up," he said simply.

"And if they don't?" the sergeant asked uncomfortably.

"Then we figure it out."

"What about you? You want one of my guys to take point?"

Mason placed his hand on the squad leader's shoulder. "Don't worry about me, Skippy. You just try to keep up."

There was a definite divide between the Special Operations world and the "regular army," and Mason knew that the soldiers he was about to lead into harm's way were counting on him to keep them safe.

During his time in Afghanistan and Iraq, he

didn't have a great deal of contact with regular army troops, and when he did, they were always supporting Delta. The men of the 82nd referred to all Special Ops, especially the Delta operators, as "cool guys," and longed for the freedom that came with not having to shave or deal with the spit and polish of their daily lives.

Mason knew that they were seasoned warriors, but he wasn't sure what would happen when the shit hit the fan. Being a capable, conventional soldier was one thing. In the fight to come, though, his biggest fear was that he was going to let them down.

CHAPTER 50

A ll right, listen up," the colonel said as he turned to the large screen and pointed the red laser up at the Mosul airfield. "Real quick, we are going to go through the phases of the operation."

Renee stood off to the side as Anderson went through the key leaders' briefing that preceded the mission. Warchild and Parker were standing with their teams, but she saw no sign of Mason.

Next to her, the platoon sergeants and company commanders of the airborne assault stood nervously as they listened to the brief. Most of them had green notebooks in one hand and bottles full of dip spit in the other. This was going to be the largest airborne operation since the United States invaded Panama to overthrow dictator Manuel Noriega in 1989, and none of them wanted to be the one who screwed up.

"The Ronin element and the Pathfinders from the 82nd have already inserted here," Anderson said, pointing at the northeastern edge of Mosul. "They will link up with members of the Peshmerga and move down to objective Johnnie Walker, which is here." He pointed to a spot on the map near the airfield.

The colonel motioned for his executive officer to switch slides. "Once they hit their rally point, the Pathfinders will break off and secure the primary drop zone in preparation for the drop, while Ronin moves onto objective Jack Daniel's to locate HVT one."

"Who is going to be controlling the air assets?" Warchild asked.

"Strike Team Texas," Anderson said, pointing at Parker, "will insert with members of the Marine Raiders at objective Wild Turkey, and set up an overwatch position, while Strike Team Nevada, augmented by Team Utah, will set the blocking position to the north.

"Once the high value target—call sign Elvis—is located, Warchild, it is up to you to prosecute the target."

"Parker, I need steel on steel, you got me?" Anderson said, pointing at the bearded operator, who was trying to catch Renee's eye.

"Roger that, sir," he replied, focusing his attention back on the colonel.

"Good. The first flight of C-17s will be over the drop zone no later than 0345, so the window to set up security isn't very big. I've been told that they will drop no matter what, so that area has to be clear."

Anderson waited for the slide to change, revealing a satellite image of the airfield. Random gun emplacements dotted the perimeter of the tarmac, and groups of trucks were bunched up near fighting positions.

"We have preplanned targets on these known positions, but other than that, we have no idea what they have in store for us. I imagine we will take some fire on the initial assault, but the idea is to bomb the shit out of them and get them running for the hills. We will have an AC-130 Specter gunship on station, as well as a full complement of F-15s and F-18s coming out of Turkey. Parker, if you need them, we will also have an eighty-one-millimeter mortar section, but we need to leave that organic to the troops on the drop zone."

Colonel Anderson dropped the pointer and looked hard at the soldiers under his command. "I want you to remember what these pieces of shit did," he said fervently, "and all the Americans who are without loved ones because of them. There are no rules of engagement. If it moves, you kill it, and if it stops moving, make sure it stays dead."

CHAPTER 51

The stark stillness of the desert night invited doubt, and Mason found the utter isolation unnerving. Waiting had never been his strong suit, and he knew that the Pathfinders were getting edgy. Mason was well aware that fear could kill a man faster than any bullet, and while he wasn't afraid of death, he was terrified by the specter of his own failures.

"Do you think they will come?" he whispered to Zeus.

"I've never trusted the Kurds. They are a flighty people," the Libyan whispered back.

Mason checked his wrist-top GPS for the tenth time, more out of frustration than anything else. He knew he was at the correct grid, but the Kurds were late, and the main assault was less than an hour away. If they didn't show up soon, he would have to move on without them.

Shifting the sling off the back of his neck, he

squeezed his shoulders up toward his ears, holding the stretch for ten seconds before releasing it. The relief was immediate but lasted only a few seconds. He was running over the contingency plan again when a tiny flash of light emanated from a rocky outcrop to his south.

Kane waited to ensure that he wasn't imagining things, but when the light flashed again, he lifted his red lens map light and flashed two short beams in response.

Mason headed toward the outcropping. Zeus joined him, matching his pace to the right. Only the sound of their feet crunching over the desert floor filled his ears. When they were five feet away, a man materialized out of the shadows.

"Peace be with you, brothers," the Kurd said, letting his AK-47 dangle from the sling around his neck.

"And to you," Zeus replied in Arabic. "We were not sure you were coming."

"Ahh, yes, we were held up on the road, but we took care of the problem," he replied.

"What kind of problem?" Mason asked, lowering his rifle as they embraced in the traditional manner.

"We came upon a patrol coming from the city, but do not worry, they will not be coming back," he replied, kissing the sides of Mason's cheeks.

The Kurd was the same height as Mason, with strong shoulders and a jovial, honest smile lit by the green hue of night vision. He pounded Mason firmly on the back as the American rotated his monochromatic NODs up onto his helmet and took measure of the men standing before them.

"I am forever grateful for what you did for my niece. It is a terrible situation, what is happening in Mosul."

"Allah allowed us to be of service," Zeus replied as he too embraced their new ally.

"His name be praised. You may call me Joe," the man said.

Mason signaled the Pathfinders that it was safe for them to come up. "Okay, Joe, my name is Mason, and this is Zeus. What can you tell us about the defenses around the airfield?"

"The terrorists have been working hard since they took the city. We have been hard-pressed to keep them on their side of the river, but even now, they threaten to crush us. When the army fled, they left behind many big guns and tanks. It will not be easy getting close to them."

"Can you do it?"

"Yes, but as I told Sara, the man that you seek does not leave the airfield."

"Have you seen him?"

"I have not, but my son"—he paused to point at one of the fighters who appeared from behind the rocks—"he has seen him. They call him the Lion of Syria. He is an evil man."

"Yeah, he's a real asshole," Zeus said.

The Kurd was appraising them as well. "We can get your men to where they want to go, but for you two, taking out the Lion will not be so easy."

"Well, Joe, if it was easy, everyone would do it," Mason said.

That made Joe laugh. "As you say," he replied. "But we are wasting time. I have brought trucks if you wish to leave."

Mason followed Joe to the backside of the outcrop, where four pickups were waiting. The Pathfinders crammed into the beds of the last two, and the Peshmerga dispersed quickly between the vehicles.

"You will ride with me," Joe said, motioning to the first truck, which had a 240 Bravo machine gun mounted to the roof.

Mason and Zeus squeezed themselves into the back while Joe got in beside his son, who quickly lit a cigarette.

"We took the machine gun off one of the fighters," Joe noted. "It is much better than what we had."

"I assume they have gotten into the armories?"

"Oh yes. All of their fighters are much better armed now than when they came. Your government has seen to that," he said sadly. "Maybe next time, your president will take all of his guns with him."

"Yeah, that would be nice," Mason admitted.

"I cannot figure America out," Joe's son finally spoke, blowing a cloud of smoke into the air while struggling to start the old truck. "They armed the Iraqis after they fought them but give us old trucks and battered AKs. How does this make any sense?"

"I have no idea," Mason said honestly.

The route Joe took sent them wide of their final objective, but twenty minutes later, Mason could see Mosul's lights as the small convoy bumped along. In the front seat, Joe worked a handful of radios, checking in with the men he had scattered at various observation points around the city. Every time one of the outposts would tell them that an area was clear, Joe's son would steer the convoy in that direction, only to be waved off as they drew near.

Al Qatar's men were roaming the edges of the city in armed bands that seemed to pop up every time Mason thought they had found a way through. Finally, Joe ordered one of his commanders to make an armed feint four kilometers to the north of their current position, while the convoy moved south.

His well-trained men avoided getting pinned down by the enemy and also managed to open up a lane for the convoy to maneuver through.

Mason knew they were cutting it close. He was already trying to visualize how they were going to locate al Qatar before the bombardment began.

"Do not worry, my friend, I will get you where you need to be," Joe yelled from the front seat, noticing the American checking his watch. "The man you are looking for isn't going anywhere, especially after all the time he has spent setting up all of his guns."

"What do you mean, all the guns?" Mason asked, suddenly concerned.

"Oh, they have been quite busy."

"That's kind of important information," Mason said.

"Everyone knows this."

Mason flipped his radio to the air-to-ground net, hoping to relay the intel before the jets got on station, but before he could key up, a voice filtered over the net:

"Able 7 to Tomahawk Base, we are on station, how copy?"

"Roger that, Able 7, you are cleared hot. Good hunting, boys."

"Good copy. Able 7 to Able flight: let's get some."

Zeus looked at him, his eyes wide with disbelief. The timeline had been pushed up, and no one had bothered to let them know.

CHAPTER 52

- - - - - - - - - - - - - - -

Al Qatar stepped onto a small porch that ran the length of the terminal building and lit a cigarette. The flame from the lighter briefly illuminated the PVS-14s hanging around his neck. A welcome breeze wound its way over the hangars and through the hidden gun emplacements that his men had worked so hard to camouflage from the American drones. It had been a hot day, and the temperature was beginning to drop as the residual heat evaporated slowly into the night.

He could hear faint snatches of nervous conversation along with the occasional *tink* of metal-on-metal contact while his men waited for the Americans.

Al Qatar raised the PVS-14 night-vision monocular to his eye and scanned the horizon. He could see the lights coming from the Kurdish encampment to the east, but the sky itself was still empty, like an endless, inky-black ocean.

The tip of the cigarette burned brightly when he took another drag, and the small amount of light caused his NODs to flare as they greedily gobbled up the extra little bit of light.

"What if they don't come?" Jabar asked.

Al Qatar hadn't told him that his source had never called, and the question sparked an uneasiness the jihadist had been fighting all day.

"They will," he said, feigning a confidence he didn't have.

The Americans had to come.

"I have always hated the waiting," Jabar said, refusing to leave al Qatar alone with his thoughts. The Iraqi was just about to go back inside when he heard a faint rushing sound emanating from the north.

"Quiet," he snapped.

Al Qatar raised the night-vision optic toward the sky and surveyed the sky in a frantic arc, the stars coalescing in shiny green blurs. The city lights blossomed yellow as he searched for the source of the sound, and he almost missed the flashing light cutting across the sky.

The Americans had come.

"Get to the trucks," he commanded even as a part of his brain screamed at him to run.

He was caught in the open, not sure if he should run back into the terminal building or head toward the concrete bunker fifteen feet in front of him.

Jabar took off in a sprint, and al Qatar was just about to follow when an explosion detonated a hundred feet to his rear. The concussion shoved him forward, knocking him off his feet. Al Qatar tried to brace for the fall, his arms shooting out as he was twisted into the air.

He hit the ground and felt a sharp pain in his wrist as his hands skidded across the gravel. Shrapnel clattered, and a fierce heat washed over him a second before a fireball engulfed the airfield.

DShKs clattered to life from the roof of the terminal building, sending a trail of tracers bending into the sky. Al Qatar had instructed the gunners to wait until he gave them the signal to engage, but apparently they were too amped up to remember.

His brain yelled for him to get to cover, and his boots scratched the rocky sand as he scrambled to his feet.

The first missile screamed overhead, a flaming streak of light that slammed into the roof of the terminal, vaporizing the crew in a shower of sparks. Al Qatar shielded his face, changing directions to avoid being hit with the debris that geysered into the air.

A second fireball blossomed near the south end of the field, and the concussion washed over the row of Black Hawks, sending a wave of glass tinkling across the asphalt. He screamed in terror. Fuel from ruptured helos splashed across the tarmac to his left, and the gentle breeze he'd been enjoying a moment ago now carried the earthy scent of burning blood.

He felt like an animal caught in a trap. He wanted to activate the towers and save himself, but al Qatar knew that it was too early. Worse than that, he knew that this was only the opening salvo.

The bunker appeared before him like an open grave, and he dove headfirst into its black embrace, trembling as he crawled to safety. The radio jammed into his belt went clattering across the ground, and he heard a voice yelling "Fire, Fire, Fire" from the speaker.

His fingers clawed through the darkness, vainly seeking the radio. When his hands finally closed around it, he pushed the transmit button, hoping it was not too late to get his gunners to hold their fire. The radio beeped loudly, informing him that his transmission hadn't gotten through, and he cursed loudly—waiting for them to clear the net.

The men manning the weapons knew their job was to die, and they had all sworn to sacrifice themselves to Allah in exchange for an eternity in paradise. But most of them were high on amphetamines, and one of them was "hot miking" the radio, which meant no one else could use it.

He needed to get them to stop shooting, but as more jets rolled in to drop their payloads, more of his men tried to shoot them down.

One of the pilots came in so low that al Qatar could see the heat coming out of the F-15's engines a second before the bombs dropped from the pylons beneath its wings. They seemed to hang weightless in the air as the afterburners kicked on with a *thump*, and the aircraft shot back into the night sky.

The ordnance blasted into the already burning terminal, and the bright explosion backlit the chunks of concrete flying like matchsticks. Al Qatar saw a man's torso tumbling through the air.

Terrified by the slaughter, some of his men decided that it was time to run.

He got to his feet, moving to the front of the bunker, and bellowed for them to take cover. They knew better than to expose themselves to certain death, but as he raised the radio to his lips, he realized suddenly why they were running.

There was no mistaking the low droning sound filtering down from the darkened heavens, and al Qatar felt a wave of unadulterated fear wash over him the moment the AC-130's Vulcan cannons came to life in a roar of leaden death.

The powerful rotary cannons sent his mind reeling back to the dark night in Iraq eleven years before. It had been the AC-130 Specter that had kept him trapped inside the building and forced him to witness the death of his brother.

Once again, he found himself at the gunship's mercy, forced to watch the steel rain falling on his men.

The AC-130's Vulcan cannons suddenly fell silent, and he knew from past experience that inside the massive aircraft, the pilot was switching to another weapons platform. During his time in captivity, he had come into contact with mujahedeen who had faced the fearsome predator and managed to survive. They had all told the same tale: there

was nowhere you could hide from the sophisticated gunship, but if you were bold enough, you
could exploit its weaknesses.

Al Qatar raised the NODs to his eyes, scanning the night sky to see where the AC-130 was in
its orbit. Through the PVS-14s he saw an infrared
targeting laser settle on one of the hangars, and a
second later the gunship opened up with its 105
mm howitzer, firing a high-explosive round right
through the center of the building.

He realized the Americans must have someone
on the ground designating targets for the aircraft.
For whatever reason, he decided immediately it was
the man who'd killed Ali.

"There is someone spotting targets for the air-
planes," he shouted into the radio. "Use your night
vision and follow the laser!"

Al Qatar sprinted from the bunker, gripped
with a sense of purpose that exorcised the fear
holding him in place.

The gunship fired another round through the
roof of the hangar.

"Allah, be merciful," he prayed, running toward a stack of crates hidden under a camouflage
netting.

"I see him. I see him," an excited voice shouted
excitedly as the gunship switched over to its 40 mm
Bofor cannons, and began decimating the positions
he'd worked so carefully to hide.

"Kill him," he yelled.

The rounds hit the ground in rhythmic bursts

of threes and fours, as a fighter fired an RPG toward the source of the laser.

Al Qatar heard another RPG scream toward the east side of the airfield as one of his men began engaging the gunship. He managed to get off two long bursts before a missile slammed into the position, cutting the man and his gun into a hundred pieces.

The terrorist had no way of knowing if they had hit the AC-130, but he heard its engines roar as the pilot throttled up, yanking the bird out of its lethal arc. Al Qatar could see the camo netting now, and forcing a last burst of speed out of his tired legs, he dove through the opening.

His hands shook as he tore the lid off the wooden crate and grabbed the plastic launcher from within. The Stinger surface-to-air missile weighed almost thirty pounds, and it was awkward to get into action in the dark. Al Qatar activated the PAS-18 thermal imaging sight before slamming the battery coolant unit into the hand guard and lifting the unit onto his shoulder. Sweat was pouring down his face, burning his eyes, as he waited for the sight to come online.

"Hurry, hurry," he urged himself, raising the missile skyward. The thermal sight kicked on, revealing the heat from the AC-130's engines as it struggled to gain altitude.

"*Allahu Akbar*," he shouted as the sensor acquired the target. Gas rushed into the firing system, and a growl told him that the missile was locked on.

The missile's ejection motor spat it from the launcher, and a second later the rocket engine kicked on, rushing skyward in a flash of exhaust. Its contrail bent in the air, the infrared seeker head tracking toward the target, but he was already throwing the empty launcher to the ground when the missile disappeared.

The men he had set up along the edges of the airfield began to fire, and he knew that the paratroopers were about to be dropped. His hand shot to his pocket, searching for the device that would activate the EMPs, but it wasn't there.

Al Qatar felt the massive rip, torn through the bottom of his pocket, and quickly turned to see where the activation device had fallen out. He frantically retraced his steps, not even noticing the explosion in the sky.

Bombs and missiles were hammering every inch of the airfield, and he ducked instinctively as he searched the ground. The fuel that had leaked across the tarmac ignited in a whoosh, sending a wall of flame leaping into the sky.

All around him, his men were dying, their screams filling the air as more ordnance rained down like a plague. Another explosion went off near him, scorching his face and knocking him back to the ground. He struggled to breathe, crawling across the ground. The night suddenly turned to day—and then he saw it.

The flames danced off its shiny black case, and al Qatar greedily snatched it off the ground, flipped it open, and mashed down on the red button.

He watched the tiny LED light blink as it sought to connect with the first receiver, and he knew that in a few seconds it would all be over.

CHAPTER 53

- - - - - - - - - - - - -

Renee sat on the nylon bench seat, trying to think of anything besides how bad she had to pee. Her assault pack was nowhere near as heavy as the rest of the paratroopers' oversized rucks, but her legs were going to sleep.

The jumpmaster stood next to the troop door, his grim face bathed in the red light emanating from the ceiling. He extended his arms and held up both hands, showing the jumpers ten fingers, while yelling, "Ten minutes."

"Get ready," he shouted a second later.

She felt the C-17 begin to slow. He pointed at her stick and yelled, "Outboard personnel, stand up."

Struggling to her feet, she almost lost her balance when the bird hit a pocket of rough air. Holding her static line in her left hand, she grabbed at the skin of the aircraft with her right, steadying herself as she bumped into the paratrooper behind her.

"Inboard personnel, stand up."

Renee felt like she was going to puke as the rest of the jumpers got to their feet, and the jumpmaster instructed them to "Hook up."

She clipped the static line snap hook into the metal cable that ran the length of the aircraft, holding on to the yellow static line like her life depended on it.

The jumpmaster held up both of his hands, making two small Os with his thumbs and forefingers, which told the jumpers to check their static lines. Then he patted his chest, signaling them to check their equipment.

Renee was trying to focus on the man giving the commands, but as the air force loadmaster knelt down at the bottom of the troop door, rotated the lever, and pulled it up and open, she found her attention diverted by the view of empty sky.

The sounds of the huge engines, along with the rush of outside air, blasted into the interior of the C-17 like a tornado, carrying the smell of exhaust with it. From her position as the first jumper, she could see a hazy cloud of exhaust floating against the backdrop of lights rushing below the bird. Her adrenaline spiked, racing through her body like a jolt of electricity and forcing her attention back to the jumpmaster who yelled, "Sound off for equipment check."

From the front of the plane, the last jumper slapped the man in front of him on the ass, signaling that he was good to go. The nonverbal communication was sent all the way to the rear of the plane, and when she felt the slap on her ass, she knifed her hand in front of the jumpmaster's face.

"All okay, jumpmaster!" she yelled.

The jumpmaster slapped her hand out of his face and yelled, "Stand by."

Renee took a step forward, handed him her static line, and positioned herself in the door.

Renee's heart went cyclic, beating so fast that she thought she was about to have a heart attack as she stood staring out into the night. Her legs were shaking, and her stomach churned as the wind buffeted her face.

There was no going back now.

She was about to jump out of a perfectly good airplane, right into the middle of a firefight, and Renee was terrified.

The pilot pushed forward on the throttle to keep the C-17 from falling out of the sky just as tracer fire burned past the troop door.

"Turn green, motherfucker," the jumper behind her yelled, and suddenly every paratrooper on the plane started going wild, working themselves into a frenzy that echoed loudly inside the C-17.

The sudden explosion of emotion gave her chills, and she let herself go, screaming in unison with the men, who held no fear of what lay outside the door.

"We're coming, motherfuckers," the jumpmaster yelled just as the green jump light came on.

Renee stepped forward into the night sky, heaving herself clear of the C-17 with one big leap.

The jet blast slapped across her face, shooting her legs up in front of her. She tucked her head into her chest to keep her helmet from getting ripped off.

"One thousand, two thousand, three thousand," she yelled, and then the canopy ripped free of the pack tray, slamming her to a sudden stop as it deployed above her. The risers slashed the sides of her face before snapping tight beneath the canopy. Suddenly everything was still and silent, and she was floating five hundred feet above the earth.

The C-17 was ahead of her now and disgorging jumpers from both doors. Their parachutes blossomed in the night air, defying the gunfire that erupted below.

"Fuuuck," a paratrooper yelled as he came slicing in from her left. His feet danced across her canopy, and it began to collapse as he stole her air.

Renee had been so focused on what was going on that she had forgotten to pay attention to the fact that there were already two hundred jumpers in the air, and they were all much heavier than her. Weighed down by their gear, they began falling past her.

She felt her stomach fly up into her throat as the canopy above her collapsed completely—sending her into a free fall. Desperate, she yanked the metallic rip cord grip and let it fall free. She slapped the front of the reserve chute with the palm of her hand. The reserve chute shot out, assisted by a large spring, and immediately caught air, slowing her rate of fall dramatically.

For the second time that night, the jolt from the opening chute yanked her to a halt, jarring her body. Below, the ground rushed up to meet her. Renee hit the quick release on her assault pack and shoved the weapons case away from her body before mashing her feet and knees together and preparing for a parachute-landing fall.

All the while, tracer fire crisscrossed the drop zone. Rounds zipped past her face, cutting holes in her chute, as the ground rushed closer and closer.

The balls of her feet hit first, and then she slammed into the ground, her bent knees buckling as she shifted her weight away from her right side, and she felt her back hit the earth. Rolling her legs over her head, she came to rest in a pile of riser cord and dust. She felt a bolt of pain surge up her back but blocked it out as a sharp breeze forced her canopy open and began to drag her.

Quickly snapping her left riser release, she struggled to get out of the harness while staying below the bullets snapping overhead. Somehow, she untangled herself and quickly began searching for her rifle.

To her left, a muzzle flashed in the darkness. A massive explosion slammed into the ground five hundred meters to her north. As she threw herself onto her face, the man fired again, getting closer. Then she heard the distinctive *pop . . . pop . . . pop* of an M4 a few feet away. The shooter hit the ground with a grunt.

At last, Renee's hands closed on her weapons case, and she yanked her HK-416 free.

Smaller explosions, mixed with heavy machine gun fire, erupted from every direction. She slammed a magazine into her rifle and yanked back on the charging handle. Staying low, she pulled her NODs from beneath her shirt and snapped them into the mount on her helmet. She flipped them on with a twist of the small knob and suddenly she could see.

The scene unfolding around her was chaotic, with paratroopers struggling to free themselves from their harnesses and get into action all while taking fire.

"You good?" a voice said, and on her right appeared the man who had saved her life. He paused to fire another shot into the fighter who was lying five feet away from her before moving to her side.

"Holy fuck," she panted, trying to catch her breath.

"Alpha Team, on me," someone yelled, swinging an infrared chem light over his head.

"C'mon, that's us. Let's go." The man slung his ruck onto his back and jogged over to the man with the chem.

Squad leaders and platoon sergeants shouted orders over the gunfire while paratroopers grabbed their gear and worked to get their weapons into action.

"Get those fucking guns up," a team leader

commanded as Renee scooped up her assault pack and trotted toward the chem light.

An RPG screamed low across the drop zone and exploded between a group of soldiers who were just getting out of their harnesses. The flash of light temporarily blinded her, and she felt herself stumble.

"Medic," a voice begged before a 240 Bravo opened up, drowning out his cries.

Renee's breathing was ragged, and she was already sweating hard as another formation of C-17s came over the horizon. She dropped to a knee next to the Alpha Team squad leader and ripped open her assault pack, yanking her body armor free from the bag. As she struggled to put it on, she heard the transport's powerful engines go silent in the sky above.

"What the fuck?" one of the soldiers exclaimed. She looked up in time to see one of the C-17s dipping toward the earth.

"Sarge, radio's dead," one of the soldiers yelled as the stricken bird screamed toward the ground, paratroopers still jumping from the doors.

"Did you put a fucking battery in it?"

"Hey, we need to move, now," Renee yelled, seeing the plane's nose angle sharply toward the ground.

It was obvious something was wrong when the second bird followed suit and began to lose altitude.

"Let's go . . . Let's go," the team leader yelled, watching the stricken aircraft. "Follow me."

Renee left her assault pack lying on the ground

and got to her feet, her right arm still wrapped up in her kit.

"Everybody, clear the drop zone," she yelled, running toward the airfield, which burned like an orange beacon in the night.

CHAPTER 54

- - - - - - - - - - - - - - -

Mason ducked his head just as the RPG exploded. He had just taken his eye out of the SOFLAM, or Special Operations Forces laser acquisition marker, when he saw the fighter launch the first rocket. He felt the sophisticated laser designator bounce against his helmet as it was knocked off its base.

Using his elbow, he propelled himself backward off the slight rise he had been using as an observation post right before a second RPG came screaming in. The rocket rushed over his head, so close he could hear it cutting through the air, before slamming into one of the Peshmerga's vehicles parked on the downward slope.

"Way too close," Zeus said amid the rounds buzzing like hornets over their heads.

The Toyota pickup burned brightly as the ammo in the bed began cooking off, and Mason knew they were backlit. He could hear some of the Pesh fighters moaning in the darkness as he tumbled down to the low ground.

The radio blared in his ear, and something exploded high above the airfield.

"Hammer 21 is hit," the pilot of the AC-130 hollered over the air-to-ground net.

Zeus slapped him on the arm and pointed to the sky, where they could see the gunship breaking apart.

"Hammer 21 is going down," the pilot yelled, his voice losing all traces of calm.

"Aww shit," Mason said, knowing that their mission had just gone to hell.

"That's not good," Zeus replied, the corners of his mouth turned up in a wry smile.

"Yeah, ya think?" Mason replied.

Anderson had underestimated al Qatar's ability to mount a credible defense, and the Specter couldn't have been hit at a worse time. In the distance, Mason could barely hear the second wave of C-17s coming in over the drop zone.

Mason snatched the laser designator off the ground, knowing he had to find a better position, when he noticed that the lens was shattered. He realized the buckled olive-drab body of the designator had saved him from taking a face full of shrapnel.

"SOFLAM is done," he said, tossing the million-dollar piece of equipment to the ground.

"Ronin 6, Steeler Base, I need you to secure the crash site—" The radio squelched loudly in his ear, the sound distorting, before going dead.

"What the fuck?" Mason asked, ducking below the rounds cracking sharply around the position they had just abandoned. He yanked the radio out of his pouch. He knew it had a fresh battery, but for some reason the radio was dead.

"My comms are down," he yelled at Zeus.

The Libyan was on a knee, slamming his hand into the battery pack of his own radio. A frown crinkled his face.

"I just changed the damn batteries," he said, forcing another battery pack into the radio. "It's dead," he said a second later.

Mason raised his rifle, pushing past the Libyan, and began searching for a break in the high ground that would give him a better view of the airfield. He found a small pocket of terrain and cautiously poked his head out in time to see a large explosion on the edge of the drop zone.

It was hard for him to make out the cause of the fire until he raised the ACOG to his eye, and saw the tail section of a C-17 burning on the edge of a jumbled debris field.

"What the hell is going on?" he wondered aloud.

"Get down," Zeus yelled, pushing him out of the way as a shadowy black object blotted out the night sky and hurtled toward the airfield.

Mason hit the ground hard, almost losing control of his rifle. A heavy gun opened up on the dark shape. There was a thin flash of light, and his NODs were knocked askew, causing him to lose sight of the object.

A loud explosion boomed over the gunfire. It

was much louder than an RPG, and by the time he got to his feet, he could already smell the distinctive odor of burning jet fuel.

"Another bird is down," Zeus yelled as Mason refocused his night vision.

A chill ran up his spine, and his mind raced to process what he was seeing. The airfield was awash in burning fuel, and above the flames a solitary figure floated on a red and white canopy, drifting aimlessly down to earth.

Mason realized the flash of light he had seen was the pilot punching out of the bird, but he hadn't seen an explosion or anything else that would suggest that the aircraft had been hit by ground fire. He was still trying to figure out what had knocked the jet out of the sky when a group of fighters ran out into the open, their rifles raised toward the falling pilot.

CHAPTER 55

- - - - - - - - - - - - - - - -

David was exhausted when he finally lay down to sleep. He had gotten the answers he needed but had gone as far as he could. Taking down Cage would be as easy as releasing the tape to the media, but that would accomplish only so much, and David wanted the man to truly pay for what he had done.

He lay in the darkened room, looking up at the ceiling, and realized he wasn't sure what his next step needed to be.

The way forward was going to require a great deal of planning. David knew it wouldn't take Cage long to learn what had happened to Vann and Simmons. There was no way the SecDef wasn't going to hit back. He'd just scratched the surface, and he was unsure whom he could trust. With Renee and Mason still in the Middle East, he was going to have to wait until an angle presented itself.

He wanted to go to the president, but once

again he knew no real justice would be done if he did. David had spent his life defending the Constitution and the United States, but now that the country was in dire need, he was helpless to do anything other than place a call to Colonel Anderson, warning him about the EMP al Qatar had in his possession.

He picked up the phone and dialed the number to the task force operations center. As he waited for someone to pick up, he felt so very tired.

CHAPTER 56

"Someone get me these fucking comms up," Colonel Anderson yelled, kicking his chair across the operations center.

The black swivel chair spun as it rolled across the plywood floor before smacking into the wall and flipping onto its side. Above the chair, the monitors that had been transmitting the drone feed blinked from white and gray static to a dark screen that said, "No signal."

"Any station this net, this is Steeler Base, how copy?" the communications sergeant repeated into the radio as he flipped through the tactical command nets.

"What the hell is going on?" Anderson demanded. "Someone better tell me something. I have men dying out there."

"Steeler Base, this is Variable 1, I read you loud and clear," a voice replied over the speaker, attached to the side of the radios.

"Variable 1, identify."

"Steeler Base, Variable 1 and 2 are a flight of F-15s bearing 328 degrees out of Qatar. How copy?"

"Good copy, Variable. We have lost contact with all elements in the vicinity of AO Mosul."

"Yeah, we can't get anyone on the horn either. Request sitrep."

"Tell them to stay out of the area until we figure out what in the hell is going on. Someone get on the horn with Centcom and see if we have any satellites in the area."

Anderson had experienced commo problems during an operation before, but never to this extent. He was totally cut off from what was going on with his men on the ground. Yet the fact that he could communicate with assets outside the battle space led him to believe that the commo problem was local.

"Sir, David Castleman is on the horn," an NCO said, handing him the phone.

That was the last person he expected to hear from. He snatched the phone and pressed it to his ear. "Go for Anderson."

"I don't have time to go into it," David informed him, "but I've learned that al Qatar has a jammer that he's hooked into the cell phone towers."

"How do I kill it?"

"You knock one out, and the others will fail."

"Are you sure? Where did you get this intel?"

"I just finished having a chat with Jacob Simmons. He didn't speak very highly of you or of

General Vann. When I get back, we are going to have a little chat. Won't that be nice?"

Anderson slammed the phone in its cradle. He felt his skin go cold as he turned to his men.

"Sir, are you okay?"

"We need an electronic countermeasure bird on station. Tell them to jam all the cell traffic coming out of Mosul," he ordered.

"We are going to need clearance."

"That doesn't matter right now. Just make it happen," he ordered, moving to his chair and taking a seat.

He knew he needed to focus on the operation, but the room was suddenly spinning. If David Castleman knew, he was screwed. The colonel lowered his head between his knees, hoping he didn't pass out.

CHAPTER 57

- - - - - - - - - - - - - - - -

In a matter of moments, the drop zone had been transformed into a cauldron of death. The wrecks of the C-17s burned brightly against the backdrop of the savage firefight, casting dancing shadows across the open terrain and, in the process, negating the night-vision capabilities of the paratroopers.

Everything that could have gone wrong had done so in the blink of an eye. For the time being, Renee realized, no one was coming to the rescue.

The last decade of war had given the military a false sense of security in its almost total reliance on technology. But now, without air support, GPS, radios, and the ability to evacuate the wounded, the paratroopers were forced to fight through the fog of war like their forebears at Normandy.

Noise and light discipline were thrown out the window. Seasoned NCOs bellowed orders over the staccato bursts of machine gun and small-arms fire. Company commanders were forced to send runners across the kill zone in search of squad leaders and platoon sergeants. Amid this chaos, the paratroopers went back to their roots, banding together in small groups as they pressed the attack.

"Ammo. Ammo," the 240 Bravo gunner yelled as he began laying suppressing fire onto a fighting position to his east. Renee lay flat on the ground to his left while an RPK returned fire at almost point-blank range.

The gunner fired a long burst, showering a wave of white-hot shells down her back. Most of them hit her battle shirt, but the ones that found skin stuck to the sweat running down her back, giving the sensation that she was lying in a pile of fire ants.

Tearing her eye from the optic of her HK, she tried to shake the burning brass free. Another burst of fire snapped overhead, and she was forced to bury her face in the sand.

To her right, Renee could see that the linked 7.62 feeding into the 240 was growing shorter by the second. The position needed more ammo. She used her elbows to propel herself backward and went in search of more ammo.

The ground was littered with torn bodies, discarded equipment, and the billowing canopies of unsecured chutes. Some men yelled for medics, while others rushed forward to get into the fight, only to be cut down by shrapnel from exploding RPGs or machine gun fire. The fighting had lost all of the sexiness that most of the men had come to expect from twenty-first-century warfare. They were experiencing combat at its most basic, cruel level, and while some were able to push through, others simply shut down and waited to be killed.

A group of paratroopers gathered around an 81 mm mortar system that the gunner was snapping into action. He secured the bipod legs to the cannons with a metallic snap and quickly mounted the sight. Meanwhile, his team leader struggled with a handheld mortar ballistic computer.

"Fuck this piece of shit," he fumed, throwing it to the ground. Two of his soldiers yanked high-explosive rounds out of their plastic tubes.

"I need 7.62 ammo," Renee said, coming to a knee.

"Well, I need a beer. If you find one let me know," the sergeant said calmly.

The gunner feverishly spun the elevation knob attached to the bipod, raising the mortar toward the sky.

"Guess we are both out of luck," she said as an errant round ricocheted off the tube.

"Ahhhh, fuck," one of the men yelled, dropping the mortar round he was holding to clutch his face.

"Malone," the squad leader yelled, moving over to his soldier.

"My face—they shot my face off," the paratrooper screamed.

"Dude, you're good," the gunner said, pulling the man's hands away from his wound, revealing jagged cuts but no significant damage.

"Buss, get back on the fucking gun. I've got this," the squad leader commanded.

"Shit," the gunner cursed, pulling away from his wounded squadmate and moving behind the mortar.

Renee pushed ahead, yelling in vain for ammo over the cacophony of the battle unfolding around her.

The fighters guarding the airfield's perimeter used grazing fire to keep their attackers' heads down. The only tactic they cared about was pouring fire into the ranks of paratroopers.

Squad leaders gathered as many men as they could, and these teams began bounding forward under hastily emplaced support by fire teams. Grenades and machine guns were the weapons of choice on both sides, and explosions boomed while tracers crisscrossed the drop zone.

Renee heard a weak voice yelling as the mortar boomed to life behind her. She finally caught a slight movement a few feet in front of her. As she crawled closer, she saw a paratrooper lying on his back, bleeding heavily from a chest wound. Like many of the jumpers, he had packed his body armor in his ruck, and she could tell he had been trying to don it when a round found his unprotected flesh.

"I've got 7.62," he said, trying to sit up.

"Stay down," Renee ordered. "Medic. I need a medic."

She ripped open the small trauma kit attached to the body armor that lay uselessly next to the wounded paratrooper. She quickly pulled out a packet of blood-clotting gauze.

"You're going to be okay," she said as she packed the wound.

"Take the ammo—don't worry about me," he replied.

Renee knew that the paratroopers valued the lives of their brothers and the mission as a whole more than their own lives, but this was the first time she had actually experienced the fabled self-lessness for which the division was famous. Despite the fact that the young soldier knew he was dying, he was more worried about getting ammo to the men who needed it than his own life.

"Medic," she yelled again.

"Just go," the young paratrooper repeated. He yanked a belt of ammo from the ground next to him and pressed it into her bloody hands.

"Hold on," Renee said, continuing to dress his wounds.

Suddenly, out of the corner of her eyes, she saw a man running low through the hail of fire pouring in. Zigzagging across the drop zone, in apparent disregard for his own safety, the soldier ran straight for the downed paratrooper.

"I got you," he said, sliding to a halt beside his patient. He tossed his aide bag on the ground and addressed the wounded paratrooper. "You going to be fine, bro."

"You got him?" Renee asked.

"Yeah. How you feelin', troop?" he asked, checking the wound.

"Doc, go help someone else, I'm fine."

"Hey, I've got nothing but time," the medic replied as he worked to control the bleeding.

Renee felt a wave of emotion bubbling up inside her as the medic caressed his patient's face. Done here, she grabbed the bloody belt of ammo off the ground. She knew that no one would ever understand the sacrifices of these men—the powerful sacrifices that were unfolding all around her—and despite the horror of the battle, she knew she was witnessing something sublime and noble.

Taking the ammo, she headed back to the front. On the way, she passed the mortar crew, whose cannon was almost vertical as it fired in support of the assaulting element.

"Hang it," the gunner yelled while his assistant stood up and placed the tail fin of the round into the barrel.

"Fire."

The round fell down the tube with a scraping sound before hitting the firing pin and blasting skyward. The assistant gunner had another round in his hand already, waiting for orders as Renee hustled past.

"Ammo . . . Ammo." The 240 gunner was still yelling as she dove beside him and tried to snap the slippery belt of ammo into the links already feeding into the gun.

The rounds twisted in her hands, and her fingers slipped on the blood, but she somehow managed to snap the metal link into the last round. The gunner laid down on the trigger.

Braaadaaaaappp. Braaadaaaaappp.

As he let off the trigger, another 240 opened up from the south, picking up the rate of fire as the first one let off. The two gunners couldn't see or hear each other, but they had managed to interlock their fields of fire without being able to communicate. Their rounds were keeping the fighters' heads down long enough for a squad to maneuver into fighting position.

Cruuuuump.

A mortar round exploded on the edge of the airfield and two paratroopers rushed at the fighting position. The 240 gunners shifted fire before one of the men tossed a frag ahead of him and hit the ground.

The explosion lit up the horizon. One of the squad leaders got to his feet and yelled, "Follow me."

"Let's go . . . Let's go," the 240 gunner said, lifting the machine gun off the ground and running foward.

Renee fell in step behind him, her rifle up, searching for a target. She caught up quickly with the lead elements. When a fighter popped up out of a trench, she snapped the safety off and fired two quick shots into the man's face. Figuring he had friends, she snatched a frag off the front of her kit.

"Frag out," she yelled, yanking the pin out with her left hand, while still cradling the rifle.

She let the spoon flip off, hearing the paratroopers closest to her echo the fact that she was about to toss a grenade, and then flipped it into the trench ahead of her. Renee took a knee and waited for the frag to go off. A moment later, it detonated amid screams of agony.

Renee sprinted forward and jumped down into the trench. A fighter lay writhing in pain at her feet, and she shot him in the top of the skull. She cleared the right side of the trench, her chest heaving from the short sprint, sweat running into her eyes, and her heart hammering in her ears.

The trench had been dug hastily, with the dirt from the hole used to form a berm along the lip. Renee stepped over a box of ammo, noticing the grenades and RPGs stacked at intervals along the trench line. A boy no older than fifteen was crouched near one of the cases of ammo, trying to yank an empty magazine from his AK-47.

Renee didn't hesitate as she settled the reticle of her Eotech holographic sight on the boy's forehead and pulled the trigger. The round snapped his head back, blowing his brains across the sandy floor of the trench.

"Allahu Akbar," a man yelled behind her, and she turned to see a fighter running at her with a grenade clutched in his hands. She tried to get the rifle up on target, but knew she was too slow.

Suddenly a shadow fell across her. The 240 gunner appeared at the edge of the trench and fired a short burst across the fighter's chest. The jhadist fell forward, the frag still clutched in his hands.

Renee threw herself to the ground and prepared herself to eat the blast by tucking her head low into her chest and opening her mouth so it wouldn't blow out her eardrums. The wait seemed like an eternity, and when nothing happened, Renee looked up slowly.

"Holy shit, it was a fucking dud," the paratrooper said. "I can't fucking believe it. I thought you were done."

Renee saw the grenade sitting harmlessly less than a foot in front of her head. Slowly she got to her feet—she was shaking and felt like she was going to vomit. Then the sound of gunfire quickly brought her back to reality.

"Alpha Team, on me," the team leader ordered from the other side of the trench. "You two get the fuck up here. We're moving out."

She climbed out of the trench and saw that the edge of the airfield was only a few yards away.

"I'm staying with you; I think you might be good luck," the 240 gunner said, falling in beside her.

Renee managed a smile before a secondary explosion erupted near one of the hangars. She had met death, and it felt awfully good to be alive. Now all she wanted to do was link up with Mason and get the fuck off the objective.

CHAPTER 58

Mason heard trucks idling on the other side of the metal shed and he crept around the corner carefully to get a better look. The vehicles had their lights off, and through his NODs, he could see artillery shells mounted to the back.

A tangle of wires dummy corded the rounds together, and he realized immediately that he was looking at a massive vehicle-borne IED. Next to the lead vehicle, a man stood smoking, in the shadows, oblivious to the shells.

"We need to go," the driver said, poking his head out the window.

"We wait for the emir," the man replied.

"We do not have time. We will never make it to the dam if we don't leave now."

"We wait," the man shouted, throwing his cigarette to the ground and shouldering his rifle.

"What do you have?" Zeus hissed behind Mason.

"A couple of VBIEDs. I think they are going to try and blow the dam."

"Fuck," the Libyan cursed.

Both men knew that if that happened, a tidal wave of water would be set free to crash over Mosul and drown everyone from here to Baghdad.

"Do you have a shot?"

Mason stepped forward, raising his rifle, and when he did his foot clipped a piece of metal. The object clanged off the ground, reverberating in the tight space. Instantly, the man with the AK leveled his rifle and sent a burst toward Mason.

"Emir, hurry," the driver yelled.

Mason rushed the shot, having to duck for cover as he pulled the trigger.

Out of the darkness a man appeared—heading for the lead truck.

"It's him," Zeus yelled as Mason sent two rounds into the man's chest.

He tried sweeping his rifle toward al Qatar but was engaged by another fighter. Zeus grabbed him by the back of his kit, yanking him behind a stack of crates.

Al Qatar yelled to the driver, "Go."

"Get off me," Mason growled, ripping free from the Libyan's grip. As he pressed the HK against his shoulder, the first truck lurched away, temporarily obscuring al Qatar, who ran around the second vehicle and disappeared from sight. Mason flashed the laser over the cab of the truck and was about to fire through the cab when a muzzle blast erupted from his left.

The round slammed into his NODs, blasting them off his helmet and wrenching his head violently to the side. By instinct, he threw himself backward just as he heard the *crack* of a high-powered rifle.

A second round slammed into the crate next to his head, a millisecond after he'd dropped behind cover. Mason felt a burning sensation tear into the side of his face and blood pouring down his cheek.

He had been a sniper long enough to recognize the sound of an American rifle, and Mason swore as the driver slammed the second truck into gear.

"Cover me," he yelled.

"Mason, wait," Zeus screamed.

Kane shot from cover, his vision obscured by the blood in his eyes. He held down the trigger as he ran, swinging up the HK despite the pain shooting down his left arm. The rifle bucked violently as it hammered through the full magazine. Even though it could have been friendly fire, in his mind there wasn't a shadow of a doubt about who was trying to kill him.

It had to be Warchild.

He felt the bolt lock to the rear as the mag ran dry. He released his grip on the rifle and leapt up for the metal handhold welded to the bed of the truck.

The driver slammed his foot on the gas just as Mason grabbed on. His arm was jarred as the truck jolted forward. He scrambled to get a better grip. His feet bounced off the ground, torquing his back while he held on for dear life.

The HK beat against the small of his back, and he could feel his grip slipping. To compensate, his right hand shot out for the bumper. Mason grabbed on with his left hand, and the pain from his shoulder crashed over him with a vengeance.

He gritted his teeth, forcing the pain away. To add to his difficulties, he was choking on the hot exhaust spraying over his face.

Suddenly the comms came alive, and he heard a pilot check on station.

"Variable 1 and 2 inbound," the pilot said.

With powerful handholds, Mason inched his way into the back of the cargo truck. Sweat and blood poured down his face. He grabbed onto a cargo strap, stretched tight over a row of artillery shells, and hauled himself all the way into the bed.

He lay panting on the wooden floor, fighting to catch his breath.

"Fuck, I'm getting too old for this," he moaned

He ripped the empty mag from the HK and pounded a fresh one into the rifle. Mason was just dropping the bolt when something hit him hard on the top of the helmet.

CHAPTER 59

- - - - - - - - - - - - - -

Renee, running across the tarmac with the rest of the paratroopers, took a knee behind a burned-out hulk that had once been a Humvee. Muzzle flashes were winking off to her right, and she brought up her rifle, searching for a target.

A man ran out into the open with an RPG, and she centered the reticle on his head and pulled the trigger. The round broke clean and blasted through his skull, sending him sprawling on the ground. Another jihadist was maneuvering to her left, and she transitioned smoothly onto his chest and dropped him with a double tap.

Beside her, the 240 gunner slapped a fresh belt into the machine gun. He followed Renee as she crept around what was left of the Humvee. One of the paratroopers nearby dropped to a knee and shouldered an AT-4.

"Back blast area clear," he yelled before firing

the rocket into a sandbagged position fifteen feet in front of him.

The rocket shot from the launcher and detonated before he even had time to throw the empty AT-4 to the ground.

"Fuck yeah," someone yelled as another 240 opened up on the flank.

"On line. On line," the team leader commanded as more paratroopers flooded onto the tarmac, looking for cover while a squad laid down a base of fire.

"What's your name, kid?" she asked the gunner who was stuck to her hip.

"Darren," he replied.

"Okay, Darren, you need to get that gun up."

"Just looking for a spot," he said with a grin.

Renee dropped the mag from her rifle, quickly slammed a fresh one into the mag well, and scanned the area for any threats. She saw a low concrete wall next to a group of cars, a few meters to their right, and motioned for Darren to follow.

A fighter suddenly emerged from a spider hole dug in the dirt ahead of her, but Renee was on the trigger without ever breaking stride. She could see similar positions in a neat row just ahead, and she swung out wide to cover them as they moved.

She held up her hand, telling Darren to stop. Ripping a frag off her kit, she lobbed it into the next hole. The jihadist hiding inside yelped in surprise, but the grenade drowned it out with a deafening explosion.

They reached the wall without further incident. Darren laid his gun across the top and unleashed a long burst into the enemy's flank.

Renee saw a hint of movement to her right and whirled to engage. Her finger was on the trigger when she recognized Zeus running for one of the sedans.

"What the hell are you doing here?" she asked, a feeling of relief washing over her.

"Mason went after al Qatar," he huffed, throwing his rifle into the first car he came to.

"Why didn't you go with him?"

"There's a fucking sniper up there," he said, pointing to the building from which he had just taken fire.

"That's Warchild's position," she said in disbelief.

"Yeah, I fucking figured that out. Are you coming or not?"

Warchild's voice came over Zeus's radio. "Variable 1, this is Savage 7. I have two vehicles moving north and request immediate intercept."

"What channel is that?" she demanded.

"Air to ground, why?"

"Because I think Warchild is about to call an airstrike on Mason."

"Oh, shit."

"Just go. I've got this," she ordered before sprinting off toward the building.

She quickly found the door and yanked it open. In short order, Renee located a flight of metal stairs leading up to the second floor. She placed her foot on the first step carefully and made her way slowly to the top.

"Roger that, Variable, they are headed north." Warchild's voice echoed above her.

"Stand the fuck down," Renee yelled, coming up on the landing where the two men stood, staring out the opening.

"Well, look who it is," Warchild sneered, ignoring the rifle pointed at him.

"Roger that, Savage 7, stand by while we locate," the radio blared.

"Get out of the way, Parker," she said, raising her rifle.

"I can't do that," he said. "If they blow the dam, we're all dead."

"Parker, get out of the way," she repeated, edging forward to get a better angle on Warchild.

"Shoot the bitch," Warchild said, checking the GPS unit strapped to his wrist.

"Renee, this is way above your pay grade. Just turn around and go," Parker said, moving in front of Warchild to block her shot.

"Why are you protecting him?" she asked, lowering the rifle as Parker's hand slid slowly to his pistol.

"We have orders, Renee, and I can't let you get in the way. Not this time."

"For chrissake," Warchild said irritably, "can you just kill her so we can get on with this?"

"Dude, chill the fuck out," Parker said, his pistol creeping out of its holster, while Renee kept her rifle trained on Warchild.

"No, *you* chill out. I don't know why you are so hung up on this bitch, but it's time for you to choose," he said, shoving Parker forward.

Renee reacted without thinking, and as Parker's pistol flashed up, she fired two quick shots into the center of his chest.

"Damn, you shot him," Warchild exclaimed. "I didn't think you had it in you."

"Oh, no," Renee said, Parker's eyes opening wide with surprise. His mouth formed a small O as he fell to his knees. She dropped her rifle, reaching out for him. At the same time, Warchild raised his pistol and pointed it at her face.

"Guess you chose for him."

CHAPTER 60

Mason heard Warchild scramble the jets to his location at the same moment an unknown assailant grabbed his helmet and began twisting. He aimed the HK over his head and managed to pull the trigger before it was kicked out of his hand.

The rifle went off with a *tsk*, and he heard glass shatter. Without warning, the truck lurched suddenly to the right. He felt the sling slip over his head and the rifle clatter away. Luckily, the grip on his helmet relaxed for a brief second.

Mason scrambled onto his stomach and the fighter kicked at his face, forcing him to roll out of the way. His shoulder slammed hard into the shells stacked along the middle of the cargo bed. The man stepped forward, trying to stomp on his face.

The American jerked his head away as the man's boots slammed into his shoulder. Lashing out, Mason kicked the man in the back of the knee, knocking him flat on his back.

As Mason dove for him, a shot rang out from the cab of the truck. He slammed his forearm into the fighter's throat before bringing the rim of his helmet down on the man's nose with a sickening crunch. A spray of blood hit him in the chin, and the man tried to buck him off with his hips.

Al Qatar yelled at the driver, and the truck swayed violently back and forth on the road. The shells rattled against one another as they shifted beneath the ratchet straps. It was obvious that he was trying to throw Mason out of the truck and, to make it worse, he heard his rifle clatter toward the edge of the bed.

An AK punched the remaining glass out of the rear window and a burst of fire swept across the bed of the cargo truck. Mason had his back to the cab when a round crashed into the back of his kit, knocking the breath out of his lungs.

Trying to take advantage, the fighter began scratching at his eyes. Mason slammed his elbow down on the man's already bloody face, as splinters showered over him. One of the rounds from al Qatar snapped the fighter's head to the side, sending a rush of gore over the front of Mason's battle shirt. He knew the man was dead, and he lifted himself off the body as al Qatar inched into the back of the truck.

"Hold it steady," the terrorist yelled at the driver while firing toward the shells that Mason was hiding behind.

Mason ducked down as one of the rounds sparked off the body of the massive shells.

"You're going kill us both," the driver yelled, looking frantically over his shoulder.

"Be quiet," al Qatar snapped. Raising the Kalashnikov, he lined up the shot and pulled the trigger.

The sturdy AK clicked on the empty chamber, and the terrorist threw it away before yanking a large knife from his belt.

"Savage 7, be advised we are going in hot," Mason heard the pilot say while getting to his feet.

He tried to key the radio, but suddenly al Qatar was lunging at him with a wicked-looking knife.

Mason's foot got caught on the ratchet strap right when the terrorist swung the blade at his neck. He saw the blade sweeping toward his neck, and when he tried to move back, he fell. The blade cut through the commo wire, and Mason found himself flat on his back.

Mason could see the hate in the man's eyes as al Qatar brought the blade back down in a wide arc. Mason barely rolled free of the razor-sharp blade, which whizzed past him before cutting into the ratchet strap.

The artillery shells shifted and the tension holding them securely to the floor was released slightly, and the strap began to snap from the pressure.

Yanking his own knife from its scabbard, Mason got to his feet and stepped forward, his left arm moving to block al Qatar's next blow. The outside of his forearm slammed into the man's wrist, and when he tried to bring the blade down for a backhanded strike, Mason stepped inside his guard and sliced his blade across the man's stomach.

Al Qatar yelped in pain, and Mason jabbed the blade toward his ribs, feeling the point hit bone before bouncing off.

The terrorist bellowed in agony, and Mason pressed the attack. He used his elbow to smash al Qatar in the face. The jihadist stumbled backward before Mason's violent onslaught, and the American was just about to drive the blade into al Qatar's skull when the ratchet strap behind him snapped, sending the heavy shells spilling across the floor.

CHAPTER 61

"Oh, no," Renee yelled, dropping her rifle as Parker fell face-first onto the ground.

"All he had to do was put a bullet in you, but he couldn't do it," Warchild said, pointing the gun at her face. "Since you've been at the task force, all you've done is string him along, fuck with his mind until he can't think straight, and now look what happened," he snarled.

Renee sank to her knees, cradling Parker's head.

Warchild mashed the pistol's barrel into her forehead and shook his head. "Real easy like, I want you to unsling that weapon and put it on the ground."

She didn't have much of a choice, so she slowly followed his instructions, placing the rifle on the ground.

Renee's mind scrambled to figure out what had just happened. Why had Parker been protecting Warchild? None of it made any sense. She did know one thing, though: she had to keep the man talking.

"Thought you had it all figured out, didn't you?" Warchild taunted.

"How 'bout you let me up, and we can figure it out together?" she asked, looking up at him.

"It's real simple. We needed your boy Mason to find al Qatar for us, so I told Parker to get all cozy with you and pump you for intel."

"Bullshit, you had plenty of time to find him yourself."

"That's not the way we do it in Anvil. You should know that," he said.

"Savage 7, Variable 1," the radio on his shoulder went off, drawing his attention from the task at hand.

Knowing this could be the only opportunity she had, Renee snapped her right arm up toward the pistol, rolling to her left simultaneously. Warchild's hand was just on the mike when the outside of her palm knocked the pistol off target and he reflexively jerked the trigger to the rear.

The gun went off, scorching the side of her face and causing an immediate ringing in her ear. She could taste the cordite, feel the burning near her eye, as she rolled into Warchild, who slammed the butt of the pistol down onto her back. Renee felt the blow land just off the center of her spine. Trying to stay as close to Warchild as possible, she drove her shoulder up into his stomach and came awkwardly to her feet.

Warchild tried to backhand her across the face,

but she slammed her fist into his groin, causing him to double over. Renee snapped her head up toward his chin and felt his mouth slam shut with a crunch of shattered teeth.

Bellowing in anger, he kicked her in the side of the leg. The blow landed like a swing of an ax, hitting the peroneal nerve with enough force that her lower leg immediately went numb. Renee staggered from the blow, and her leg buckled, allowing Warchild to deliver a kick to the side of her head. She managed to raise her arms in time to block the strike, but the impact knocked her across the room. Grinning, Warchild threw the pistol to the ground and brought his fists up in front of his face.

"I've been dreaming about this," he said, closing the distance between them.

Renee scrambled to her feet. He struck her with a jab and danced around to her left before hitting her with a looping cross. Renee was having trouble standing as Warchild snapped a front kick to her face, forcing her to block low before he pivoted to hit her with a spinning back fist.

Ducking beneath the blow, she slammed her palm into his solar plexus and tried to sweep his leg, but Warchild was able to power out of the move and slapped her disdainfully across the top of the head with an open palm.

"C'mon, bitch, I thought you had more than that," he jeered.

"Come get it, motherfucker," she panted, rapidly running out of gas.

Warchild came toward her, bobbing side to side like a boxer looking for an opening. Knowing he had the size and strength advantage, Renee carefully stayed out of range, making him come to her. She knew that he wanted her to commit, and when he feinted another leg strike, she kept moving, refusing to give him a target.

"I'm over this," he said finally, planting his feet and squared his shoulders in preparation to rush her.

Renee was out of room, caught between her attacker and the wall of the hangar. She jumped forward, snapping a kick to his head, but Warchild was already launching himself at her, his head tucked low between his shoulder blades. She braced for impact, when he suddenly tripped, his hands smacking the floor.

Emerging from the dead, Parker had grabbed Warchild's back leg.

She wasted no time diving out of the way, and as she hit the deck, Warchild cursed and scrambled to his feet. Renee tucked her body, rolled onto her shoulder, and came up with the pistol he had thrown to the ground a second before. The man stopped dead in his tracks, fear replacing the cocky look he had worn a second before.

"What the fuck are you going to do with—?"

Renee brought the front sight up and pulled the trigger before he could finish the sentence. The Glock 23 bucked in her hand, sending two rounds smashing through his chest.

Warchild dropped where he was standing, his

face slamming into the ground, and his lifeless eyes staring up at her as she rushed over to Parker.

"I'm done," he said. "Get on the net and stop the strike on Mason."

"Was he telling the truth?" she asked, grabbing for her radio, hoping it wasn't too late to save Mason.

Parker's eyes were glassy, and his skin looked pale as he struggled to take a breath. A solitary tear ran down the side of his face as he looked up at Renee, and then, ever so slowly, he nodded his head.

CHAPTER 62

The shells bounced heavily across the back of the truck, and one of them caught Mason's leg, knocking him onto his back. He rolled out of the way as the neat stack of high-explosive rounds rolled toward the cab of the truck in a clanging jumble.

Al Qatar grabbed onto the wooden slats of the cargo bed, clawing free of the rolling projectiles as a deep rumble erupted above the speeding truck.

Mason saw a spit of flame flash across the sky as the F-18 opened up with its 20 mm cannons, shredding the back of the truck and punching through the cab. The driver's torso exploded in a pink mist and the truck jerked hard, tumbling Mason toward the open tailgate.

His arms flailed out, trying to grab anything that would check his fall. At the last moment his fingers closed around a jagged piece of wood sticking up from the floor. Above him, the F-18's engines roared as the pilot shot overhead and climbed into the night sky. Mason knew that its next attack would be much more deadly, and while he clung on for dear life, he managed to activate the infrared beacon attached to the left shoulder of his chest rig.

He could feel his grip slipping as the wooden shard began tearing away from the floor. Desperately, Mason began searching for another handhold in the dark. As the truck sped blindly down the rutted road, he could hear the shells banging around near the cab. Without a doubt, he was living on borrowed time.

Suddenly he heard the beeping of a horn. Looking behind him, he saw the wan, yellowish glow of headlights appearing out of the cloud of dust the truck was kicking up.

A small sedan broke through the thick haze, and he could hear someone yelling at him to jump. He knew that if he couldn't get to his feet, he was going to be run over, but he didn't have a choice. Mason was just about to let go when he felt someone grab his wrist.

Looking up, he saw al Qatar with the huge knife hanging above his head.

"Now you die," the terrorist said, bringing the blade down.

Mason let go of his handhold. He skidded toward the bumper as the knife came down, slicing into his already wounded shoulder.

The pain was blinding, and the knife passed through his flesh before hammering into the wooden floor with a thunk. The blade ground against his clavicle, pinning him to the floor like an insect on a corkboard. Al Qatar moved forward to stomp him in the face, while blood cascaded from the wound.

"Shiiit," Mason screamed, grabbing for the knife's handle, unable to ward off the blow he knew was coming.

Five quick shots rang out from the sedan and four of them slammed into the bumper of the truck. Al Qatar grunted, staggering backward as one of the bullets smacked him in the chest.

Mason wrenched on the blade and forced himself up. He could feel his flesh tearing and the blade grinding against bone before he tore it free. Blood cascaded from the ragged hole in a torrent of crimson. He could see the F-18 coming back around, lining itself up for a bombing run.

"Jump," Zeus yelled, his head hanging out of the window as he slowed the sedan.

In an instant, everything slowed down. Mason could clearly see the bomb leave the pylon. He reeled drunkenly forward, hearing the bomb cutting through the air. As he threw himself into the night, the last thing that crossed his mind was, "I kept my promise," and then he was knocked out by the massive explosion.

CHAPTER 63

The sun crept over the horizon, illuminating the battlefield in shimmering grays and reds as it cut through the pall of black smoke rising toward the heavens. Bodies lay intermingled with the charred debris left behind by the night's bombardment.

Renee watched them carry Parker's body bag out on a stretcher. She was jonesing for a cigarette and found she couldn't take her eyes off the man who'd almost gotten her killed. What Warchild had said about Anvil stuck in her brain, and she was exhausted, but she knew she couldn't leave until she found Mason and Zeus.

The medics carried Parker into the back of the Chinook and placed him among the dead. Soon the helo leapt into the sky, blowing a cloud of grit across the tarmac.

"I knew you'd make it," Darren said, his grime-covered face twisting into a huge smile.

"You got a smoke?" she asked, looking at the barrel of his 240 Bravo, which was stained a grayish white from all the ammo he'd fired.

"Why, hell yes," he said.

He pulled a pack of Camel Lights out of the pocket sewn into his sleeve and shook out two cigarettes before dragging a match across a green matchbook.

Renee leaned in as he lit her cigarette and took a deep drag, savoring the nicotine that rushed into her system.

A group of engineers was already working to clear the runway, while helos loaded with ammo and food looked for places to land. Scattered small-arms fire crackled in the distance, as if to tell the paratroopers that there was still a fight ahead of them.

Renee knew that once the runway was clear, more troops would arrive, and then they would move out to retake Mosul.

"You going out with us?" Darren asked.

"No, I have to find someone."

"Well, I've gotta go. Glad you didn't die," he said with a smirk.

"Yeah, you too."

It took ten minutes to walk to the edge of the massive crater blown in the middle of the road that al Qatar had taken. Not much was left of the two trucks, and the pieces that hadn't been vaporized were still smoldering. The concrete was scorched black near the center of the crater, while the edges had been turned a chalky gray by the heat.

Renee knew that no one, not even Mason Kane, could have survived the blast. She felt the tears burning as they welled up. Wiping her eyes, she was about to turn away when she noticed a bloody bandage blowing across a fresh set of tire tracks.

She used her boot to pin the gauze to the ground and kneeled down to pick it up. As Renee held the bandage in her gloved hands, she followed a set of tire tracks with her eyes until they disappeared to the north. She had no way of knowing if it was Mason's blood on the gauze, but she willed herself to believe that he was still alive. Suddenly she felt an ember of hope catch inside her.

Renee heard a vehicle approaching from her rear and turned to see a Toyota Hilux bouncing toward her. The driver slammed on the brakes, and once he ground to a halt, he stuck his head out the window.

"Hey, are you Renee?"

"Yeah," she said, making her way over to the Hilux.

"Sergeant Major Mitchell sent me to find you. Get in."

Renee took one more look at the massive crater and walked around to the passenger side of the pickup. She was exhausted, and a groan escaped her lips as she got in, placing the barrel of her rifle between her feet.

"What's up now?" she asked.

"Sergeant Major just said that they didn't find the body you were talking about."

"Wait, what?" Renee demanded as he put the Hilux in gear.

"He said they checked the building, but there's no body."

CHAPTER 64

- - - - - - - - - - - - - - -

Mr. David checked his ticket as the boarding agent came over the public announcement system inviting all first-class passengers to board. Lifting his leather satchel off the ground, he was about to move toward the ticket counter when his phone vibrated in his pocket.

Taking it out, he looked at the screen. A smile crept across his face.

"I've been waiting for you to call," he said.

"Been a long week, and the cell service in Mosul was shit," Mason replied with a laugh.

"I'm just getting on a flight. Where are you?"

"Probably better if you don't know. Things are about to get bloody."

"Mason, there is still a lot of work left to do."

"I'll see you around," Mason replied.

The desk agent announced a second call for all

first-class passengers, and David handed the man at the gate his ticket.

He walked down the jet bridge, still holding the phone.

"You still there?"

CHAPTER 65

- - - - - - - - - - - - - - - -

Mason hung up the phone and looked down at the sling securing his arm to his chest.

He was due for another pain pill, but instead of taking one, he walked over to the window.

Outside the shitty one-room apartment the emerald water of the Mediterranean Sea flickered in flashes of silver and gold while sea gulls whirled and shrieked overhead. The salty air breathed through the open window, gently caressing his face.

"You're right, Cyprus does have nice beaches," he said into the microphone attached to his collar.

"I don't think this counts," Zeus's voice replied through the tiny earpiece.

"Relax man, we're almost done," Mason said, his hand moving unconsciously to the bandages that itched beneath his white button-up shirt.

"Uh-huh. You better not be scratching at the stitches," the Libyan scolded.

Mason snatched his hand away with a wry grin,

and scanned the surrounding rooftops for any sign of Zeus.

It had been two weeks since Mosul, and his arm was still stiff and heavy. The doctor told him that he was lucky al Qatar's blade hadn't done more damage. An inch higher, and Mason could have suffered permanent nerve damage, but as it was, he should heal nicely.

"He's coming up," Zeus said a second later.

Mason moved away from the window, slipping the silenced .22 from his waistband before positioning himself behind the door. He desperately wanted a cigarette, but knew the smell would alert his target. It seemed like an eternity, but finally he heard movement in the hall followed by a key slipping into the lock.

Warchild checked the apartment from the threshold, like a rat searching for predators before coming out of its hole. The first thing Mason saw was the Glock clutched in the man's hand and the backpack strap hanging off his right shoulder as he stepped inside and moved to clear the bathroom.

Mason bumped the door shut with the outside of his left foot, and chopped the butt of his pistol across the base of Warchild's neck.

Warchild dropped to his knees, the backpack flying off his shoulder, and the pistol clattering across the floor. Mason moved to his right and snapped a wicked kick across the man's face, knocking him flat on his back.

"Rule number one, always check behind the door," Mason said, centering the .22 on the man's forehead.

"You . . . you're fucking dead," Warchild sputtered, before spitting two of his teeth onto the concrete floor. He had shaved his mohawk, and in its place dark stubble was beginning to grow in.

"Not yet. I have no idea how you made it this far, you have no fucking field craft."

"Go fuck yourself."

"Don't be mad at me, you're the one too lazy to cover his own tracks."

Warchild glanced at the pistol lying three feet to his left, and Mason smiled.

"Really? You think you can make it?"

Warchild shifted, and the .22 coughed, sending a bullet ice-picking through Warchild's shin.

The man howled before gritting his teeth and taking the pain.

"You going to beg?" Mason asked, lining up the kill shot.

"Would you?" Warchild grunted.

"Nope," he replied before firing a round through the man's eye.

Warchild's head snapped back, and his skull bounced off the floor with a meaty thud. Mason took a step forward and fired again—ensuring that the man was dead. He stooped to collect his expended brass, and after placing them in his pocket, set the pistol on the table.

Using his good arm, he rifled through Warchild's pockets, before picking his pistol off the ground and stuffing it in the man's backpack.

"I'm coming out," he said, grabbing the .22 off the table and heading for the door.

ACKNOWLEDGMENTS

- -

First and foremost I'd like to thank the Lord for his faithfulness and grace.

Writing a book is the easy part. It's the professionals behind the scenes who do the real work. Once again, my agent Bob Diforio, along with Matthew Benjamin and his team at Touchstone, have taken dreams and turned them into reality.

Without all of your tireless shaping and polishing, *Warning Order* would just be a stack of paper. I cannot express how grateful I am to have you guys on my team. I honestly can't imagine working with anyone else.

ABOUT THE AUTHOR

Joshua Hood graduated from the University of Memphis before joining the military and spending five years in the 82nd Airborne Division, where he was team leader in the 3-504 Parachute Infantry Regiment. In 2005, he was sent to Iraq and conducted combat operations in support of Operation Iraqi Freedom from 2005 to 2006, and from 2007 to 2008 he served as a squad leader in the 1-508th Parachute Infantry Regiment and was deployed to Afghanistan for Operation Enduring Freedom. Hood was decorated for valor in Operation Furious Pursuit. He is currently a member of a full-time SWAT team in Memphis, Tennessee, and has conducted countless stateside operations with the FBI, ATF, DEA, Secret Service, and US Marshals.